D1269796

# DIVE
# TRILOGY

**SPECIAL EDITION**

# DIVE
# TRILOGY

**SPECIAL EDITION**

# GORDON KORMAN

## SCHOLASTIC INC.

New York    Toronto    London    Auckland    Sydney
Mexico City    New Delhi    Hong Kong    Buenos Aires

*The Discovery*, ISBN-13: 978-0-439-50722-6, ISBN-10: 0-439-50722-7.
Copyright © 2003 by Gordon Korman.

*The Deep*, ISBN-13: 978-0-439-50723-3, ISBN-10: 0-439-50723-5.
Copyright © 2003 by Gordon Korman.

*The Danger*, ISBN-13: 978-0-439-50724-0, ISBN-10: 0-439-50724-3.
Copyright © 2003 by Gordon Korman.

12 11 10 9 8 7 6 5 4 3 2 1          8 9 10 11 12 13/0

Printed in the U.S.A.                    23

ISBN-13: 978-0-545-09307-1
ISBN-10: 0-545-09307-4

First compilation printing, June 2008

# Contents

## BOOK ONE: THE DISCOVERY

# DIVE

*For Ron Kurtz,*
*Bubble Blower Extraordinaire*

*08 September 1665*

*When the explosion rocked the* Griffin, *young Samuel Higgins knew instantly that the boat was doomed.*

Thirteen years old, and dead already, *the ship's boy thought to himself as the towering mainmast splintered in a shower of sparks.*

*The sail, now a billowing sheet of flame, settled down over the treasure that lay stacked about on the deck of the barque. Chests piled high with coins and jewels, silver bars by the hundredweight, ropes of pearls, chains of gold. Samuel watched it disappear beneath the burning canvas. He could feel the deck heaving under his feet as the* Griffin *began to break apart. A flood of gleaming pieces of eight poured through the gaping holes between the deck planks. It was more money than Samuel had ever seen, worth more, probably, than his entire village in the north of England, and perhaps the surrounding shire as well. It was a fortune that would have turned the head of the king himself.*

THE DISCOVERY

*And yet it could not buy five more minutes of life for the* Griffin *and her doomed captain and crew.*

*The voyage back to England would have taken at least three months. The descent to the bottom of the Caribbean took less than three minutes.*

*There lay the treasure, the spoils of a new world, silent, waiting. . . .*

# CHAPTER ONE

The catamaran bobbed like a cork, even in the sheltered waters of the harbor on the Caribbean island of Martinique.

Kaz looked dubiously from the flimsy double-hulled boat to the young man who stood balanced on deck, holding out his hand to help the newcomer aboard. "If you want to kill me, why don't you just shoot?"

It got a big laugh. "Come on, Kaczinski. Safest thing afloat."

Swallowing hard, Kaz stepped onto the swaying craft. Putting aside unease was second nature to hockey players, especially in Canada, home of the best of the best. Some of the kids he skated against would go on to NHL careers. They said he'd be one of them — Bobby Kaczinski, the best young defenseman to come out of the Toronto area in the past twenty years.

All that was over now. He stumbled, his knees weak for a moment. It had nothing to do with the motion of the catamaran.

He had come to call it "the dream," although it plagued him as often waking as sleeping.

THE DISCOVERY

Game six of the Ontario Minor Hockey Association finals. Drew Christiansen — Kaz had not known the boy's name then. Now he would never forget it.

Drew Christiansen, whose life he had ruined.

Drew had taken a pass in front of the Red Wings' net. He was Kaz's man, his responsibility. The check was completely legal, clean as a whistle. Everyone agreed on that — the refs, the league officials, even Drew himself. A freak accident, the doctors called it. A one in a million shot.

Kaz remembered the split-second play down to the slightest detail — the urgency to defend his goalie, the satisfaction of a heavy hit. And then a discordant note: *He's not getting up.* And then, *Why is his neck at that funny angle?*

Followed by the nightmare truth: Drew Christiansen would never walk again.

The handshake of greeting came just in time to steady Kaz.

"Tad Cutter, Poseidon Oceanographic Institute," the young man introduced himself. "I'm leading your dive team."

"People call me Kaz." He tried to size up the institute man. Mostly, he was searching for some hint as to why a world-famous oceanographic group had selected a beginning diver for a summer internship. A month ago, Kaz had never stepped into flippers in his life. It had been a mad scramble to get scuba-certified for this program.

But there were no clues in Cutter's blond, blue-eyed features. He flashed white teeth. "Sit tight and start on your tan, okay? I've got one more to pick up." He leaped onto the dock and jogged off.

*Who am I kidding?* Kaz thought. *Poseidon didn't pick me for my diving. Allagash got me this gig.*

Steven P. Allagash was the sports agent Mr. Kaczinski had hired to guide his son's career all the way to the pros. *Ex-agent,* Kaz reminded himself, since Bobby Kaczinski would not be strapping on skates again.

Allagash had been clearly alarmed at the possibility of such a hot prospect getting away. "Don't make any rash decisions," he had urged. "Forget about hockey for a while. Take some time off this summer. Do something you always wanted to do. I'll set the whole thing up. Just name it."

Kaz had drawn a blank. As long as he could remember, his entire life had been hockey. Camps all summer, games and practices all winter. He had never played any other sport. Why risk an injury that could take him out of hockey? He'd never even had a hobby.

"Come on," Allagash had prodded. "What are your interests?"

The entire back wall of the agent's office was an enormous Plexiglas fish tank. Kaz had always been fascinated by the dozens of brightly colored tropical species that moved through the artificial habitat.

"Fish," Kaz had replied finally. "I like fish."

Fish would do. Diving would do. Anything but hockey.

As he dropped his gear and seated himself on the boat, he realized for the first time that he was not alone. Fast asleep amid a mountain of luggage lay another boy, smaller than Kaz, but probably the same age.

The catamaran bumped up against the tires that lined the dock, and the sleeper shook awake.

He rubbed his eyes behind thick glasses and yawned. "You don't look like Adriana, so I guess you must be Bobby."

"Call me Kaz." He indicated the many bags and cases that littered the deck around the other boy. "Diving equipment?"

"Camera equipment. Dante Lewis. I'm a photographer."

"An underwater photographer, right?" Kaz prompted.

Dante shrugged. "That's what we're here to find out."

Kaz was amazed. "Are you telling me that you're new at this too?"

Dante stared at him. "Are *you*?"

"I got certified, like, ten minutes ago!"

Dante was wide-eyed. "I figured they only took me because they needed a photographer. What about you? Any special skills?"

Kaz searched his mind and came up empty. "I used to be a hockey player."

Dante took in the heat shimmer over the endless turquoise Caribbean. "I don't think the rink freezes hard enough down here."

"That's okay," Kaz deadpanned. "I didn't bring my skates." He frowned into the colorful sails in the harbor around them. Poseidon was one of the top ocean research outfits in the world. Renowned scientists begged to get hired on. Fellowships went to graduate students who were proven geniuses. When they threw open four summer internships for kids under sixteen, they must have gotten thousands of applications. Maybe tens of thousands. They had their pick of the universe.

*Why choose us?* It didn't make any sense.

They'd been waiting for half an hour when Cutter returned with the third team member. Adriana Ballantyne was a tall, slender thirteen-year-old girl who was dressed more for the deck of a luxury liner than a weathered island-hopping catamaran that smelled of diesel and fish.

Kaz had never seen anyone so color-coordinated. Her deck shoes matched her belt, the temples of her designer sunglasses, and the leather handles of her luggage.

"Diver, right?" he asked as she stepped aboard.

"Right," she confirmed. "I guess." And even less certainly, "Sort of. I did some scuba in the south of France this past Easter."

What was going on here?

The catamaran may not have been the most elegant craft in the seven seas, but it got the job done. They covered the distance from Martinique to Saint-Luc in two hours. As they rounded the curve of the shoreline, Cutter damped down the engine to slow their speed.

"Hey," he called in the comparative quiet that followed. "There's Star. She's on our team too. Look at her go!"

Three pairs of eyes focused on the clear blue water a couple of hundred yards out from an isolated cove. Star Ling was diving in just mask and snorkel, moving with a strength and expertise that was obvious to any observer. She cruised just below the surface with the pointed, unerring trajectory of a torpedo. When she dove, her descent was crisp and quick, easily conquering her body's natural buoyancy. She sounded deep, unhurried by the need for her next breath — a sign of superior lung capacity.

"She's awesome!" breathed Adriana.

As the catamaran angled in toward the harbor half a mile up the coast, Star took to the surface and swam in to the beach. They watched her rise and step out of the water and onto the sand.

At first, Kaz thought she'd stumbled. But then it happened again. And again.

"She's limping!" he exclaimed out loud. "She's a — " He was about to say "cripple" when the image of Drew Christiansen cut into his mind like a jagged fork of lightning. *You can't use that word,* Kaz thought to himself. *You've forfeited the right.*

"She's handicapped!" Dante exclaimed in wonder.

Cutter laughed. "Don't let her hear you say that! She's the toughest kid I've ever met."

*Three beginners and now this,* Kaz reflected.

Who was making the decisions at Poseidon Oceanographic?

THE DISCOVERY

# CHAPTER TWO

Dr. Geoffrey Gallagher raised his pointer to the bleached skeleton mounted on the wall beside his desk — the gaping jaws of a great white shark, measuring three feet across.

"We see that the teeth are serrated," Poseidon's director lectured to the red light of the video camera that was trained on him, "and angled distinctly inward so that each bite directs the prey down the gullet. *Carcharodon carcharias* has been called nature's perfect predator, the apex of the ocean's food chain. And from personal experience, I can attest to that fact." He tapped a razor-sharp tooth.

With a crack like a rifle shot, the upper jaw fell shut to the lower, snapping the pointer cleanly in two.

Dr. Gallagher jumped back with a very unmacho shriek.

"Cut!" roared the cameraman, doubled over with laughter.

There was a knock at the door.

"Later," called Gallagher, fumbling around for another pointer.

DIVE

The knock came again, this time louder and more insistent.

"Not now!"

The door opened, and in marched Bobby Kaczinski, Dante Lewis, Adriana Ballantyne, and Star Ling.

At first, Gallagher had absolutely no idea who the four teenagers were. Saint-Luc was not a major tourist island like Martinique or Aruba, so the only kids around were locals. Then he remembered the summer internships.

Oh. *Those* kids. He had begged the head office in San Diego to place them somewhere else. But no. It had to be here. Poseidon had even sent a team from California to run the program — Tad Cutter and his crew.

"Welcome!" he beamed, hiding the broken pointer pieces under some papers on his desk. "This is going to be a very exciting summer for you young people. I'm sure you'll be participating in a lot of important research."

They waited, as if for more detail. He stared at them, willing them to go away.

Finally, Star stepped forward. "But Dr. Gallagher, what do we do?"

"Poseidon Saint-Luc is a tremendously busy place," Gallagher explained, "with dozens of different projects all going on at the same time — "

"I mean *now*," she persisted. "What do we do today?"

Gallagher was taken aback. "Well, what does Mr. Cutter say?"

"We haven't seen him since yesterday," supplied Kaz.

"Since *yesterday*?" The director was completely mystified.

The silent man in the room, gray haired and stocky, had been lounging on the couch, observing the videotaping with some amusement. Braden Vanover was one of several ship's captains who worked for Poseidon. He spoke up now. "Cutter and his crew went out at first light on Bill Hamilton's boat."

The director's voice was shrill with frustration. "Why didn't they take these kids? That's the whole reason Cutter's people are here! Without the kids, what are they doing — sunbathing . . . ?" He spied the videographer watching with interest, and fell silent. Jacques Cousteau never had a tantrum when the camera was on him.

Captain Vanover stood up. He had no official connection with the internship program, but he felt bad for the four teens. It was fairly obvious Cutter was ignoring them. "Tell you what. I'll grab English and take them out to get their feet wet."

Gallagher looked pathetically grateful. "Great, great! Did you kids hear that? You're diving today." He put his arm around the shoulders of the girl with the limp. "And I'm sure you'll make an excellent tender while the others are in the water."

Star's eyes flashed. It was obvious to everyone in the room except the director that he had said very much the wrong thing. She was about to speak, was already opening her mouth, when Kaz jumped into the fray.

"Star's a diver like us, Dr. Gallagher," he said quickly. "In fact, she's the best we've got."

"Yes, of course," Gallagher mumbled, and busied himself with resetting the upper portion of the great white's jaw. He very nearly sacrificed a finger as the thing slammed shut again.

It was on the gravel path that led to the guest cabins that Star turned on the big hockey player.

"Where do you get off fighting my battles for me?" she demanded. "When I've got something to say, I say it myself!"

"Yeah, well, maybe that's the problem," Kaz retorted. "If you called Gallagher an idiot — which he is, by the way, so you would have been A-one right — you could have gotten the head of the whole institute mad at us. I wasn't protecting you; I was protecting *me*."

THE DISCOVERY

"Even so," she muttered, "mind your own business."

"Count on it," he assured her.

"Hey," said Dante. "We're getting a chance to do something. Let's not blow it."

# CHAPTER THREE

Star sat on the deck of the R/V *Hernando Cortés*, watching the harbor at Côte Saint-Luc disappear in the glare of an overpowering Caribbean sun.

"The reefs northeast of the island are pretty spectacular," called Captain Vanover from the cockpit. "They're part of the Hidden Shoals of the French West Indies. Best diving in the world."

Star felt a shiver of excitement. "I know!" she exclaimed. Not from personal experience. But before this trip, she had read everything she could get her hands on about the coral formations around Saint-Luc. This was a great opportunity and she was going to make the most of it.

Kaz, Dante, and Adriana were already struggling into lightweight tropical wet suits. And struggling was the word for it. They looked like three fat ladies trying to squeeze themselves into undersized girdles. Were these guys divers or circus clowns?

Star could slip into a wet suit as easily as putting on a glove. It was a three-second job for her, bad leg and all. Her secret: liquid dish detergent to lubricate her skin. The thin rubber material slid right on.

She made a face, still smarting over Dr. Gallagher's assumption that she couldn't possibly be a diver. People were such idiots about handicaps. They stared at you, pitied you, tried to smooth the way for you. For Star Ling, that limp was normalcy. A mild case of cerebral palsy, that was all — a certain amount of weakness on the left side. She couldn't remember, of course, but her very first step had demonstrated that limp. It was a part of her and always had been.

It wasn't nothing. She didn't delude herself about that. She wouldn't win any footraces or dance with the Bolshoi. But in the water, everything changed. There was no weakness, no asymmetry. She had felt that on her first trip to the county pool, age four. And she still felt it every time she slipped off the dive platform of a boat. The laws of physics that held her back on dry land melted away in a rush of familiarity and comfort that seemed to say, "You're home."

Her eyes wandered aft, where Captain Vanover's lone crew member was hefting heavy scuba tanks as if they weighed nothing. Menasce Gérard was a hulking six-foot-five-inch native dive guide who went by the puzzling nickname "English." No one seemed less English than English, a young West Indian man whose first language was French. Secretly, Star had assigned him a different moniker — Mr. Personality. The guy was just about the most humorless human being she'd ever encountered.

They'd been on the boat for nearly half an hour, and he had yet to crack a smile. In fact, she wasn't sure she could confirm that he had teeth, since he rarely opened his mouth at all. He answered most questions with a series of gestures, shrugs, and grunts.

That didn't stop Adriana from spewing a line of chitchat at him. Maybe that was how things worked at whatever snooty country club her family belonged to. You kept talking without bothering to notice that you weren't getting any answers.

"But why do they call you English?" Adriana burbled on. "You're French, right? I mean, people from Saint-Luc are French citizens."

English barely shrugged as he checked the pressure gauges on the cylinders of compressed air.

"Your name isn't English," she continued. "I just don't understand why anyone would want to call you that."

"Will you give it a rest?" Star groaned. "I once knew a guy named Four Eyes who didn't wear glasses. So they call him English. What's it to you?"

Adriana wasn't ready to drop the subject yet. "Well, were the English ever on Saint-Luc?"

At that moment, the enormous guide chose to break his silence. "Yes — and no."

"Yes and no?" Dante queried.

"Saint-Luc, this is always French. But, *alors*, in the old times — " He shrugged again. "Yes and no."

"He means everybody was everywhere in the Caribbean, way back," Vanover supplied. "Pirate crews came from all nationalities. Merchants too. There were raids, shipwrecks. You could never be sure where an Englishman or anybody else might end up."

"But in those days a shipwreck was pretty much a death sentence," Adriana pointed out. "None of the sailors even learned how to swim. That was on purpose. They preferred to drown immediately rather than prolong the agony."

"Thank you, Miss Goodnews," put in Kaz, stashing his dive knife in a scabbard on his thigh.

The captain was genuinely impressed. Like the others, he had pegged Adriana as a rich kid who happened to dive because she collected hobbies the same way she collected designer clothes.

"Not a lot of people know that," he said to her. "Been reading up on the Caribbean?"

Adriana flushed. "My uncle is a curator at the British Museum in London. I've spent a couple of summers working for him. You pick stuff up."

Her brow clouded. This year the job had fallen through because Uncle Alfie was in Syria on an archaeological dig. Worse, he had been allowed one assistant, and had chosen Adriana's older brother, Payton. That had left the girl at loose ends, which was a condition never tolerated by the Ballantynes. Adriana's parents spent their summers traveling to hot and trendy places to rub elbows with supermodels, dukes, rock stars, and dot.com tycoons. In all the years she could remember, there had been no summer vacation that she or Payton had spent with the family.

Adriana had a mental picture of her parents shopping their daughter to every museum and research outfit that was prestigious enough to deserve a Ballantyne. Good thing her scuba certification was still current, because Poseidon was about as prestigious as it got. She'd naturally assumed that her family's connections had cinched the job for her, but now she wasn't so sure. None of the others seemed any more qualified than she was, except maybe Star.

THE DISCOVERY

As they approached the boundary of the Hidden Shoals, Vanover cut power, and English climbed up to the crow's nest to scan for coral heads that might present a danger to the boat. Here on the reefs, it was not uncommon for towers of coral, reaching toward the sun's nourishing light, to grow until they lurked just below the surface. Over the centuries, many a ship had been fatally holed by such a formation.

At last, they anchored, and preparations for the dive began in earnest. Kaz thought the equipment checks would never end. Tanks charged? Weight belts on? Compressed air coming out of the regulators? Buoyancy compensator vests inflating and deflating properly? It was just like certification class, where they treated you like kindergartners. Did divers ever dive? Or did they spend all their time getting ready?

Dante broke rule number one by trying to walk with his flippers on. He fell flat on his face, nearly smashing his Nikonos underwater camera, which was tethered to his wrist. English helped him up, looking at him pityingly.

Finally, they took to the water, gathering on the surface to pair off.

Kaz spit into his mask to prevent it from fogging. He placed it over his eyes and nose and inhaled to create the watertight suction. He bit down on the regulator and deflated the buoyancy compensator around his neck until he slipped beneath the waves, squeezing the nosepiece of his mask and blowing out to equalize the pressure in his ears.

Underwater. This was only his third dive, and each time he was amazed all over again by this silent alien world, so close at hand, and yet so hidden. People talked about "escaping" into a book or movie. But this was real escape. Down here, hockey was a million miles away, an obscure pastime attached to another life.

His two certification dives had been in cold, murky Lake Simcoe, north of Toronto. So the clear sunlit seascape beneath the surface of the Caribbean was dazzling. The visibility seemed almost infinite, but that wasn't the astonishing part. It was just so *busy* down here, so alive! Steven Allagash's wall-size fish tank was a foggy wasteland by comparison. Thousands of fish of every shape, size, and color darted in all directions.

A tiny, brilliantly striped angelfish ventured up to investigate him. Kaz was fascinated. The curious little creature seemed completely unafraid of the much larger animal that had invaded its ocean. It continued to nose around the bubble stream that rose from his breathing apparatus.

All at once, a shadow passed overhead. In a flash of sudden violence, a round, fat grouper swooped down like a dive-bombing eagle and snapped up the hapless prey.

*Whoa. Sorry, guy. Got to keep on your fins. It's a jungle out here.*

Almost as an afterthought, he looked around for Dante, his dive partner. To avoid wearing his glasses underwater, the photographer sported a prescription dive mask that distorted his features into a mountainous nose under saucer-wide, staring eyes. It was a shocked, almost crazed appearance. Kaz chuckled — and swallowed water in the process. *Concentrate,* he reminded himself with a cough.

Dante was obviously very impressed by his surroundings, because he was firing off pictures of every shrimp and minnow. Six minutes into the dive, the photographer was officially out of film.

Even through his mask and a cloud of bubbles, English's disgust was plain. Impatiently, he grabbed the two novices each by a wrist and began to swim them toward the reef. Off to the side, they could see the girls moving in the same direction.

As the reef loomed up, the detail of the coral formations began to come into spectacular focus. The colors were unbelievable, almost unreal, like the product of some Hollywood special effects department. The shapes were positively extra-terrestrial: huge plumes of lettuce coral; branched spikes of staghorn; mounds of brain coral the size of dump trucks, all stacked upon each other in a mountain that rose to a summit that was perhaps ten feet below the glittering surface.

Kaz checked the gauge on his diver's watch and realized with some surprise that they had descended to forty feet, which was twice as deep as he'd ever ventured before.

Adriana reached out to touch the coral. In a flash, Star's hand shot forward and grabbed her wrist. The experienced diver gestured with a scolding finger.

*I knew that,* Kaz thought to himself. The reef was a living organism, composed of uncounted millions of tiny animals called polyps. Even the slightest touch would kill the outermost layer of creatures, damaging the reef. Not to mention that the polyps would sting you.

English flashed the hand signal for descent and led them down to sixty feet, to the base of the coral edifice. Kaz adjusted his B.C. to neutral buoyancy to stop the descent. *I could get good at this,* he reflected, pleased to be developing a talent that had nothing to do with skating, shooting, and attempted murder.

THE DISCOVERY

Here the coral formations gave way to a variety of sea flora growing out of a firm sandy bottom — the Hidden Shoals proper. Life was everywhere, although not quite as colorful as higher up on the reef. At this depth, the sun's rays could not fully penetrate the water. It was a land of twilight.

Kaz's attention was drawn to a small hurried movement below. At first, it seemed as if the sand itself was boiling up into little aquatic dust devils. He angled his body so that his face mask was positioned just above the disturbance and took a closer look.

All at once, the swirling sand was gone, and a large eye was looking back at him.

"Hey!" His cry of shock spit the regulator clear out of his mouth.

It was amazing how loud his voice sounded underwater. And not just to himself, either, because Dante headed straight for him.

A dark slithering blob exploded out of the seabed, leaving a thick cloud of black ink in its wake.

"Octopus!" cried Dante, losing his own regulator in the process.

The identification was unnecessary. Kaz could see the eight undulating arms trailing behind the fleeing body. It was so fluid that the size was hard to guess — maybe a baby pumpkin at the center of a two-foot wingspan.

English flashed out of nowhere, placed himself in the creature's escape path, and allowed it to come to him. He grabbed it by two flailing tentacles. Instantly, the thing turned an angry orange before cloaking itself and the dive guide in a second, much larger emission of ink.

Fumbling for his mouthpiece, Kaz lost sight of them, but caught a glimpse of English, much higher up, carrying his prize to the surface.

Dante pulled a five-by-seven underwater slate out of his B.C. pocket. With the tethered pencil, he scribbled a quick message on the rigid plastic, and showed it to Kaz. It read: DINNER?

Kaz just shrugged.

The dive guide was back almost immediately, but the dark face inside his mask yielded no clue as to the octopus's fate.

At that point, the team had been down for half an hour. English directed them to another section of reef — a gradual upward slope where they could be closer to the surface when their air began to run low. It was important to ascend slowly to avoid decompression sickness. If a diver went up too quickly, the sudden lowering of water pressure was like popping the top on a soda can. Nitrogen gas in the bloodstream could fizz up like a Pepsi. It was no joke — the bends could cripple you for life or kill you.

As he watched the sunlit surface draw closer and closer, Kaz was growing increasingly comfortable. With every passing minute, technique and mechanics became more automatic, allowing him to enjoy the reef and its many inhabitants. *If this keeps up,* he thought, semi-amused, *I could get to like scuba.*

The thought had barely crossed his mind when he saw the silhouette. Alien, yet at the same time familiar, it was approaching from dead ahead — the triangular dorsal fin, the black emotionless eyes, the pointed snout.

*Shark.*

# CHAPTER FOUR

In a split second, his mind sifted through thousands of pictures and diagrams, the nightmare images of a personal library of shark books. A nurse shark, probably. Maybe a reef shark. About four feet long — puny by *Jaws* standards.

*But when you come across one, the real thing, with all the fearsome features, all the weapons in the right places —*

It never occurred to him to try to swim away or to scramble for the surface. He just hung there, turned to stone, watching the big fish's unhurried approach.

Go away, he pleaded silently. *Don't come near me.*

He could see the teeth now. And he knew, in the absolute core of his being, that this predator was coming for him and him alone.

He would never have believed himself capable of such panic. Before he knew what he was doing, the dive knife was in his hand, and he leaped at the shark, plunging the blade into the soft underside. Strong arms grabbed him from behind, but nothing could stop him now. With a vi-

THE DISCOVERY

cious slash, he slit the shark's belly open from stem to stern.

The creature convulsed once, jaws snapping. Then it began to sink, leaving a cloudy trail of blood.

Kaz was spun around, and found himself staring into the furious eyes of Menasce Gérard. The guide gestured emphatically for the surface.

Kaz shook his head. Couldn't he see? The danger was over; the shark was dead.

English did not waste a second command. He placed an iron grip on Kaz's arm, inflated his B.C., and dragged the boy to the surface. They broke to the air thirty yards astern of the *Cortés*.

"Get on the boat!"

Kaz was bewildered. "But it's okay! I got him!"

The guide was in a towering rage. "The boat! *Vite!*"

The five divers moved toward the ship, swimming through the light chop.

As he stroked along, Kaz was still shaking from the excitement of his shark encounter. He felt terrified and pumped up at the same time. He had spent years playing a sport at the very highest level, and yet nothing could have prepared him for the raw exhilaration of a life-and-death struggle. The world had never seemed so vividly alive.

English pulled ahead, his flippers kicking up foam like a paddlewheel. He scrambled onto the dive platform, shed his gear with a single motion, and began hauling his charges out of the water, bellowing like a madman.

Captain Vanover appeared on the deck above them. "What happened?"

English turned blazing eyes on Kaz. "Why do you do this idiot thing? You are maybe crazy? *Fou?*"

Kaz gawked at him. "I was protecting myself!"

"That *petit* guppy wouldn't attack you!"

"How could you know that? He was coming right at me!"

"You move out of the way, *alors!*" English roared. "This is not the rocket science!"

"I'm sorry, okay?" Kaz said defensively. "I'm sorry I interrupted everybody. Let's go back and finish the dive."

"*Oui, bien sûr!*" the guide agreed. "A wonderful idea! After you, monsieur."

Kaz frowned. "What's the problem?" But then he saw it, boiling up from the ocean where they had been diving only minutes before — churning white water around a mass of flailing fins, tails, and sleek bodies. A feeding frenzy — dozens of sharks going after the carcass of the dead one, creating even more carnage with a barrage of snapping jaws.

"Blood in the water, kid," the captain said mildly. "It's like ringing the dinner bell."

All of Kaz's heroic exhilaration morphed into a wave of queasiness. If it hadn't been for English, they would all be in the middle of that, being torn to pieces, thanks to Kaz's mistake.

Now the guide turned on Vanover. "I have not nine lives, me! Why do you send me down with babies? Except the girl." He indicated Star. "She is good. But these three — pah!" And he picked up his equipment, hopped onto the deck, and stormed below.

The four teens remained rooted to the dive platform, unsure of what their next move should be.

The captain couldn't help but notice their intimidation. "Would it make you feel better if I told you he has a heart of gold?"

"He's okay," Star conceded.

"That's because he said you're good," Dante accused.

"I *am* good," she retorted.

The stocky man reached over and began

helping them up to the deck. "I could throttle those pinheads in Hollywood for getting the whole world so hung up on sharks. There's nothing on that reef for a diver to be afraid of. You run into a shark down there, rest assured he's more scared of you than you are of him. Except maybe old Clarence."

Four pairs of ears perked up.

"Clarence?" Kaz echoed, pulling off his dripping flippers.

"Five or six years back," Vanover related, "we had a rush of marlin. You couldn't put a foot in the water without stepping on a fin. The sharks came a few days later. Tiger sharks. Big. They shut this place down for two weeks. Nobody dove, nobody swam, nobody even fished. One pigheaded scientist took a sonar tow out. It came back chicken wire. When the marlin moved on, the sharks followed. No one knows why Clarence didn't go with them. Maybe he was too old to keep up."

"You mean he's still here?" Adriana asked timidly.

"Every few months or so somebody spots him," the captain replied. "He never hurts anyone. Still, you don't fool around with an eighteen-foot tiger shark. But these other reef rats around here — they're harmless."

THE DISCOVERY

The teen divers gazed out over the water to where the feeding frenzy was in full swing.

"Oh, well," Vanover conceded, "if you're going to put blood in the water, all bets are off. Sharks are only human, you know. Your dive knife isn't supposed to be a weapon. It's for cutting your way out of fouled lines and hoses in an emergency. You use it as a last resort. And don't ever pull it on a barracuda. All he'll see is a flash of silver, just like half the fish he eats. He'll take a bite — don't think he won't." Vanover smiled at them benignly. "Now, get out of those wet suits before you roast."

It was a very chastened dive team that sat in a row along the starboard gunwale as the *Hernando Cortés* carried them back to Côte Saint-Luc harbor.

"I knew all that stuff about sharks and barracudas," Star commented. "I just didn't want to be a brownnose."

"Me neither," put in Kaz. "That's why I got the Furious Frenchman mad at me."

"He's scary," Adriana agreed fervently. "Given a choice between him and the sharks, I'll take my chances with the sharks."

"Not me," Dante said feelingly. "Did you catch that story about the tiger shark? They attack humans, don't they?"

Star snorted. "There's a lot of nasty stuff in the ocean. But if you let it spook you, it's like never leaving the house because you never know when a bear is going to wander out of the woods. People dive their whole lives with no problem. So there's a tiger shark somewhere. Big deal. The ocean's full of animals. That's why we take the plunge."

Kaz's eyes fell on an odd piece of equipment mounted on the bulkhead at the base of the Cortés's flying bridge, behind a stack of orange life vests. It looked like a baby's crib that had been taken apart, only the slatted panels were larger, and made of titanium. He had noticed it before, and reflected that the thing was kind of familiar. Now he recognized it — an antishark cage, complete with ballast tanks and control panel.

*If sharks are so harmless, why do they need an antishark cage?*

Dante interrupted his reverie. "Speaking of animals . . ."

Kaz followed his pointing finger to a large metal bucket sitting just astern of the cockpit. It was filled to the brim with water that kept spilling out with the movement of the boat. They watched, fascinated, as a slate-gray tentacle that matched the galvanized metal of the pail probed tentatively over the rim. A moment later, the octopus hoisted itself up to the edge of the bucket and dropped to the deck. Immediately, it began a quick, amoebalike oozing motion toward the nearest exit. When it spied the four teenagers, it froze for a moment, eyes fixed on them as its body assumed the olive-drab color of the planks.

"Go for it, dude," whispered Dante. "He's going to cook you."

The octopus apparently took that advice to heart. It slithered to the gunwale and promptly disappeared over the side.

As they were unloading equipment on the dock at Côte Saint-Luc harbor, Menasce Gérard had his first look into the empty bucket that had once held his dinner. His frown was a thunderhead.

Adriana read his mind and saw accusation in it. "I swear we didn't do it, Mr. English! He climbed out, ran across the deck, and jumped in the ocean. Honest!"

But once again, the dive guide had retreated into a series of grunts — grunts of suspicion.

*17 April 1665*

At thirteen years old, Samuel Higgins remembered his mother, but the mental image was fading.

He'd been only six, after all, when Sewell's men had come for him — small enough to be carried off, kicking and howling, in a burlap sack. It was a kidnapping, to be sure, but no constable or sheriff ever came to far-off Liverpool to search for him. What reward might there have been? Samuel's family had nothing. And now six-year-old Samuel had no family.

He would not have been hard to find, if anyone had been looking. Sewell, the chimney sweep, had many climbing boys working for him — all undersized and underfed, abandoned or kidnapped. Samuel, it turned out, excelled at the dirty work. He could scamper up a chimney as easily as walking down the cobblestone alleyways of the port city. And, unlike the boys who worked alongside him, he did not grow long of limb or broad of shoulder as he reached his adolescence.

"Don't worry, lad," laughed old Mr. Sewell over and over, "I've seen a hundred like you. You'll be *dead of a fall long before you're too big to climb one of those chimneys."*

*The man was as sharp as he was heartless, but he turned out to be wrong about that. Samuel never succumbed to the terrible accidents that extinguished the short, unhappy lives of the other boys. And the day did finally come when young Samuel Higgins could no longer fit into the narrow sooty tunnels where he'd earned his keep since he was only six.*

*"Sorry, lad," Mr. Sewell had told him. "If you do no work, I can't be keeping and feeding you."*

*It had not been a loving family. But at least he'd belonged. Now he was being driven out. Would the world ever find a place for Samuel Higgins?*

*Sewell had been hard, but hunger, Samuel's new master, was even harder. At first, he considered a return to the countryside and his mother. But he was not certain where he might find her, or if she was even alive. This life — with Sewell — was the only life he remembered. And now that was over.*

*His heart yearned for his lost family, but his empty belly was in charge. There was no future in England for a penniless boy except starvation and death. His only hope, his one chance, lay with the sea.*

*He signed on with the Griffin for a plate of stew and a promise of future wages — not a princely con-*

tract, to be sure. But considering that his former employment had come as the result of a kidnapping, this represented freedom, and he was much satisfied. He had no inkling, at that time, of the true purpose of the Griffin and its fleet, nor what its business was in the vast ocean that stretched westward to a new world. He knew only that there was food in the galley for him to eat, and a small rectangle of deck planking outside the captain's quarters where he could sleep. Home.

As the captain's boy, Samuel was the personal manservant to Captain James Blade. His duties included everything from delivering the captain's meals to cleaning and brushing his uniform and wigs, delivering messages to crew members, and emptying the man's chamber pot.

To Captain Blade, Samuel was less than human, a utensil, like a spoon or a shaving razor. "Boy!" he would bark when he needed something. Or often he'd shout, "You!"

The one time that Samuel had the audacity to venture, "My name is Samuel, sir," the captain pulled out a furled snake whip from his belt and smacked him across the side of the head with the bone handle.

"You can ride on this ship or in the waves below — take your choice, boy. But you'll not open your lip to me!"

THE DISCOVERY

*The blow knocked Samuel clear through the hatch to the captain's quarters, sending a laden tray of food flying every which way.*

*"And swab this deck!"*

*There was an emerald the size of a musket ball set in the handle. It left a deep, bloody gash in Samuel's cheek. The wound did not stop oozing until they had passed the Canary Islands.*

# CHAPTER FIVE

Tad Cutter and his team had been sent from Poseidon's head office in San Diego, California, to map the reefs of the Hidden Shoals northeast of Saint-Luc. Like many scientific undertakings, the results may have been interesting, but harvesting the data was very boring work indeed.

The job consisted of dragging a sonar tow that would measure the depth of the seabed below. To do this over 274 square miles of ocean would take every minute of the eight weeks budgeted for the project. To help them, Cutter and company had been assigned the four teenage interns. But as the early days of summer passed, Kaz, Dante, Adriana, and Star found themselves completely ignored by the Cutter team.

Day after day, the four would awaken in their cabins in the Poseidon compound to find that Captain Bill Hamilton and his *Ponce de León*, the boat assigned to Cutter, were already out there mapping, and had left them behind.

Cutter always had an excuse. "Sorry, guys, but we're just so *busy*. To gather this much data in just a couple of months leaves us no wiggle room. If you're not on board at five A.M., we've got to take off without you."

The next day, they were there at five only to find that the *Ponce de León* had slipped its moorings at four-thirty. The day after that, they arrived at four. There they waited by the boat for three hours before realizing that Cutter and his crew had taken the catamaran to Martinique for supplies.

"We have to complain," argued Dante. "This is our internship, and they're not letting us do it. It's a rip-off."

But there was no one to complain to. Dr. Gallagher was far too busy to see them. And when they ran into him around the institute, he was always lecturing to the video camera that seemed to follow him like a tail. In addition, the director now wore a thick bandage on his forearm, which he carried in a sling. They were all pretty sure it had something to do with his great white shark jaw.

"If he doesn't get away from here fast," Kaz observed, "one of these days that thing is going to come down off the wall and eat him."

Captain Vanover was sympathetic, but not a lot of help. "I know it's lousy, but Tad's probably not doing it on purpose. These research guys — when they get their teeth into a project, they're like zombies. They eat, sleep, and breathe work.

They just can't focus on anything else. Don't let it bum you out. I'm sure your time will come."

"Maybe," grumbled Dante, "but what year?"

Vanover promised to take them out for another dive. But the *Hernando Cortés* was booked almost every day by other scientists, so they would have to wait until the ship was free. In the meantime, the captain agreed to have a word with Bill Hamilton.

The only other person they knew around the institute was English, and no one was in the mood to ask him for favors. Whenever they passed the hulking dive guide in the halls or on the gravel paths of the grounds, they would slink by, and he would look right through them.

"You should talk to him," Dante urged Star. "He likes you."

"He doesn't like anybody," she growled. "He just hates me the least. Besides, he doesn't have any clout around this place."

Poseidon was only a part-time job for English, whose main employment was as a hard-hat diver for the oil rigs off the west side of the island. There his skill and toughness were legendary. He would work at incredible depths of one thousand feet or more, welding underwater pipe and repairing drills and equipment that weighed hundreds of tons.

The more they learned about Menasce Gérard, the more cowed they became.

Their situation did not make for a happy group. Staff members who took pity on them gave them odd jobs to do around the institute. But photocopying, pencil sharpening, and stirring iced tea were not what they had traveled to the Caribbean for.

The others were jealous of Dante, who at least had some meaningful work to do. He got permission to spend a couple of hours in the Poseidon darkroom, developing his underwater photographs. The pictures, though, were a big disappointment. They were excellent wildlife studies, beautifully framed and composed. But the color processing had been so overdone that the pale turquoise Caribbean appeared a deep purple.

"This is the reef?" Star said dubiously, examining the prints. "It looks like outer space."

"It needs to be lighter," Dante agreed.

"It needs to be *blue*," Star amended. "A coral reef is the most beautiful scenery on Earth, not that you can tell from what you shot. You don't have to be a genius to make it look good. Just so long as the water isn't purple."

"I specialize in black and white," Dante admitted sheepishly. "I'm just getting the hang of working with color in the lab."

They were all unhappy, but Adriana was downright miserable. After three summers with her uncle at one of the top museums in the world, this felt a lot like exile.

It was exile, she reminded herself, thinking bitterly of Payton with Uncle Alfie in Syria.

And for what? To run errands for a bunch of oceanography nerds. With the British Museum, she had dug on Roman ruins, translated hieroglyphics, and helped to present a paper at Buckingham Palace. This place was a joke by comparison, and a bad joke at that.

Eventually, though, the gofer jobs would run out, and the four would end up in the tiny village of Côte Saint-Luc, looking to keep busy. It wasn't easy. Since Saint-Luc had no tourism, there was virtually nothing to the town itself. There was a small church with a bell tower, a butcher shop with emaciated chickens hanging upside down in the front, and a dark store with flyspecked windows that sold such strange and random items that Dante had taken to calling it Voodoo "R" Us.

There were two restaurants — a bar and grill that was much more bar than grill, and a European-style café that could have been on any street in Paris.

They preferred the bar and grill because the conch burgers were cheap, and Dante liked to sit at the outdoor tables, snapping pictures of the locals with his underwater Nikonos. When there were no passersby, he photographed his three dive mates.

Kaz, who was camera shy, commented, "One more click out of that thing, and it's your nose ring."

"Take me," put in Star. "I've always wanted to be purple."

Dante put down the camera with an exaggerated crash. The boredom and frustration were beginning to set them at one another's throats.

"We've been here a week," said Star, turning her attention to Adriana, "and you have never worn the same pair of shoes twice. How many shoes did you bring? How many shoes do you own?"

"Enough to wedge one where the sun doesn't shine," Adriana snapped back readily.

"Nice shot," chuckled Kaz, his mouth full of fries.

"Mind your own business, rink rat," Star warned. "What do hockey players know, besides how to put each other in the hospital?"

She wasn't sure how, but it was clear that she'd struck a nerve with that comment, because of the deathly quiet of Kaz's reply:

"Don't you ever, ever say that again."

Tempers flared like that regularly. But nothing came to punches; nobody stormed off down Rue de la Chapelle. All four knew that there was nowhere to go.

*We're stuck here,* Adriana reflected, *out in the back of beyond. We're in this together.*

And suddenly, she was looking straight at it. Across the narrow alley was a tiny neat cottage. The windows were open for ventilation, and in the largest one hung some kind of large wooden sculpture. She couldn't make out exactly what it was, but she had worked at the museum long enough to recognize its age. Time had dulled the sharpness of the carving, the paint was present only in small faded chips, and the wood was weathered and bleached. She had seen pieces like this before — ornate newel posts from mansions and cathedrals that dated back hundreds of years.

She jumped up, almost knocking over her chair. "Guys, you've got to see this!"

They followed her across the dirt lane to the little house.

"It's an eagle," she explained, now that she could see the piece close up.

"What?" asked Star. "That lump hanging in the fishnet? I thought it was a big piece of driftwood."

**THE DISCOVERY**

"See? Here's the beak and the wings, and the talons are carved in relief against the body," Adriana went on excitedly. "I make it at least three hundred years old, maybe more."

"It's busted," commented Kaz, indicating the jagged break along the eagle's body. "It looks like a giant snapped it off the top of a totem pole."

"Totem poles are North American," Adriana lectured. "I think this came from Europe."

Star looked disgusted. "I know you're, like, wondergirl from some snooty museum, but how could you possibly know something like that?"

"It's oak!" Adriana exclaimed. "There's no oak on Saint-Luc. It's all tropical stuff here. It had to have been brought in by ship. Dante, take a picture. I can scan it at the institute and e-mail it to my uncle."

Dante hefted the camera, grumbling, "You don't need a Ph.D. to tell you what that is. I'll tell you right now." He clicked the shutter. "That's the ugliest thing I've ever seen in my life!"

As Dante spoke, the occupant of the little house appeared in the window. Kaz tried desperately to clamp his hand over the photographer's mouth, but it was too late. The man had heard everything.

It was English.

The enormous guide scowled at them, reached out his long muscular arms, and closed his hurricane shutters with a loud slam.

"Nice timing," snickered Star.

"Oh, why did it have to be *him*?" Dante lamented. "Hey, what are you doing?"

Adriana was marching purposefully to the front door. She rapped smartly and called, "Mr. English, it's us again. Could you please tell us the history of that piece in your window?"

At first, it seemed as if English intended to ignore them. But finally, he thrust open the door, glowering at Adriana.

"You Americans, you have the nerve! You call every shark in the ocean with your macho *stupidité*! Then you steal my octopus! Now you come and insult me in my own home! *Vas-t'en!* This means go away!" And he shut the door in her face.

"I'm from Canada," called Kaz, but he kept his voice low.

Adriana reached out to knock again, but Star grabbed for her wrist. "Forget it. Who cares what he hangs in his window?"

"So long as it isn't us," added Dante feelingly.

But that night, over dinner at the Poseidon commissary, Adriana asked Captain Vanover about the diver's strange window decoration.

THE DISCOVERY

The captain chuckled. "No wonder you couldn't get an answer. I think he's embarrassed about that thing."

"How come?" asked Star.

"It's an old family legend," Vanover explained. "Probably a load of hooey. He'll tell you when he's good and ready." He added, "Or he won't."

"He definitely won't," predicated Dante. "Not after I called it ugly."

Adriana shook her head in amazement. "That piece must be hundreds of years old, and he just hangs it in an open window. I hope he has insurance."

The captain brayed a laugh. "That's a good one — stealing from English!" He noticed Tad Cutter walking to a nearby table. "Hey, Tad — over here."

The blond, blue-eyed man set his tray down at an empty place. "Hey, Braden — guys — "

"Your sonar's been in the water for almost a week now," the captain said amiably. "Why don't you have the kids give it a scrub when they're diving with you tomorrow?"

If Cutter was caught off guard, he didn't show it. "Yeah, it must be pretty crusty with salt by now. Thanks, guys. See you in the morning." He walked off to join his crew.

"He's going to blow us off," Star predicted resentfully. "He says that every night, and he hasn't
taken us out once."

"Oh, I know that," the captain agreed. "But if
you're going to teach a horse tricks, it helps to be
smarter than the horse. Wait till midnight and
then go sleep in the boat."

# CHAPTER SIX

The R/V *Ponce de León* had four tiny crew cabins belowdecks. Just after midnight, the young divers split up, one to a berth, to wait for dawn and Tad Cutter.

Dante spread his bedroll over the hard bunk and went to sleep — if you could call it that. The waves lapping against the metal hull, while not loud, seemed to echo through the boat with a teeth-jarring quality. Every time he did manage a light doze, his head was pushed against the bulkhead by the motion of the boat in the water.

The *blue* water, Dante reminded himself. *Think in color.*

That was easier said than done. His little "problem" —

*That's a private matter! Nobody's business!*

The headlines in the clippings in his mother's scrapbook appeared in a collage before his eyes. *13-year-old Wins Adult Photography Prize; Prodigy Behind the Lens; Move Over, Ansel Adams . . .* The critic from the *New York Times* wrote that his use of light and shading was representative of an artist four times his age.

And that should have been enough for them, right?

But the next line was always the same: Can you imagine what he'll do with color?

Well, that mystery was over. He knew exactly what he was going to do with color. He was going to butcher it. He was going to make the sea purple.

That's why he had jumped through hoops to learn to dive — a talent he could have been very happy without. A coral reef was the most colorful item on a planet full of color. If the rich hues and tones couldn't reach out to imprint themselves on his artistic sense in this place, then it was never going to happen. And coral reefs didn't exactly turn up on every street corner. You had to go where they were — and that meant underwater.

*Quit complaining. You're here. You're diving. You haven't drowned yet . . .*

But would they ever get to dive again? Who knew how Cutter would react when he found the four of them lying in wait on the *Ponce de León*?

At long last, sleep claimed him. But it was uneasy sleep, marred by dreams of everything that could go wrong on a dive.

*Descend too fast without equalizing pressure . . . bust an eardrum . . . excruciating pain . . .*

THE DISCOVERY

He tossed in the narrow berth. Amazingly, that was one of the *milder* diving hazards.

*Nitrogen narcosis — the rapture of the deep . . . dissolved nitrogen gas causes a state almost like drunkenness . . .*

Dante had never been drunk. But he was pretty sure a hundred feet below the waves wasn't the place to do it. There were horror stories of "narced" divers who actually forgot which way was up until they ran out of air and drowned. But that still wasn't the ultimate scuba nightmare.

*The bends . . . bubbles in the bloodstream . . . tiny time bombs in the body . . . all you can do is wait to see if you're crippled for life or even . . .*

"Killed!" He sat bolt upright in his bunk. The *Ponce de León* was moving. He could feel and hear the thrum of the engine.

He opened dry crusty eyes and found himself gawking at the most beautiful woman he'd ever seen — tall and tan, with long dark — brown? — hair.

She seemed just as surprised to see him. Then she smiled. "Look, Chris," she called through the low hatch. "Stowaways."

A bearded man appeared beside her, his arms laden with gear. He looked at Dante in dismay. "The kids!"

"We're all here," Dante managed, trying to keep from staring at her. "Tad said you wanted our — help."

She grinned even wider — a magazine cover smile. "I'm Marina Kappas, Poseidon, San Diego. The sourpuss here is Chris Reardon." She held out her hand. "We could really use you today."

Dante scrambled from his bedroll and shook it. It was electric just touching her. "Dante. Dante Lewis."

"The photographer!" she beamed. "I'm really excited to take a look at some of your work."

Reardon seemed bewildered by the friendly exchange. "Marina — can I talk to you?"

"Not now."

"But — "

A cloud passed briefly over her perfect features. "I said not now. Why don't you go on deck and tell Tad the good news."

Dante set about rousing his teammates with the information that they had been discovered.

"You mean Cutter walked right in on you?" asked Kaz, scrambling out of his bunk.

"Not Cutter — Marina." Dante couldn't resist adding, "Wait till you see her!"

"Was she mad?" Adriana probed.

"Actually, she seemed kind of happy to see

me," he replied honestly. "Her friend wasn't all that thrilled, though."

Topside, they introduced themselves to Bill Hamilton, captain of the *Ponce de León*. Cutter was half buried in the motor of a Brownie floating air compressor, tinkering with a wrench.

Noticing them, the team leader grunted, "Good. You're up. You'll be logging a lot of dive time today — too much for scuba. But this big baby can keep you down there for hours."

Their uneasiness quickly turned to confusion. Cutter was acting as if their presence today was not only expected, but vital. As if he *hadn't* been dodging them for close to a week!

Kaz spoke up. "It takes so long to clean a sonar tow?"

"Oh, I checked that; it's fine," Cutter assured them. "We need you for something much more important. There are a lot of caves down there that the sonar won't pick up. We need you to find them for us."

"And explore them?" Star asked eagerly.

Cutter shook his head. "Too dangerous. Just tag the mouth with one of these marker buoys. That'll fire off a float to the surface. Then we'll catalog the location from topside. Got it?"

There was genuine excitement as the four divers suited up.

"Maybe we were wrong about Cutter and his people," Adriana suggested, pulling the thin wet-suit material until it fit snugly at her wrists. "It looks like they're really going to let us do some work this summer."

Star was skeptical. "I've seen a lot of reef maps. They don't have caves marked on them."

"This one will," put in Dante, detaching his regulator from its tank. On this dive, they would be breathing air directly from the Brownie, via long flexible hoses. "Remember, Poseidon's number one. They do everything to the max."

Seeing Star limp as she stepped into the light-weight suit, Marina rushed over to steady her.

Star wheeled away. "What do you think you're doing?"

Her outrage was so genuine, so harsh, that the researcher was struck momentarily dumb.

"Leave her alone, Star — " Dante began.

"Do you think I'm a beginner at this?" Star persisted.

Marina found her voice at last. "I saw you stumble. It happens to everyone in rolling seas — even top divers."

"Thou shalt not help Star," Kaz intoned apologetically. "That's kind of the eleventh commandment around here."

The slight girl glared at him as Marina went

back to help Cutter with the compressor. "You're *hot* for her! You too, Dante!"

"So what if we are?" Dante shot back at her. "You're our dive partner, not our mother. What's it to you?"

Star's anger did not fade until she had slipped beneath the choppy surface. It was impossible to stay mad down here, in the crystalline waters, passing through a school of chromis, swimming in tight formation, an orange cloud.

Sure, she was sensitive about her handicap. But she certainly couldn't blame Marina Kappas for being beautiful — or Dante and Kaz for noticing.

Anyway, underwater, Star Ling had no handicap. This was her medium, the world her body had been designed for. She slowly fan-kicked her flippers on the descent. If, at that moment, she had suddenly woken up with amnesia, she would have noticed no weakness at all on her left side. And that was exactly the way she liked it.

The reef here was fairly shallow — only about forty feet at its deepest — and flatter than the dive site they had visited with Vanover and English. But life and color were everywhere. Decorating the coral were fire-engine-red sponges, towering sea fans, and starfish the size of throw rugs. Snakelike trumpet fish, multihued creatures straight out of Dr. Seuss, stabbed down from above, feeding on the polyps. A curious tetra darted around the safety line hooked to her belt. She chased it away with a flurry of bubbles.

"Hey!"

The sound carried so well through the water that she recognized Dante's voice. She spied the young photographer not far away, hovering neutrally buoyant, waving wildly. As she swam closer, she spied the cause of his excitement — a black hole in the limestone seafloor about the circumference of a prizewinning watermelon.

*He calls that a cave?*

Pulling her slate out of the B.C. vest, she scribbled *TOO SMALL*. But Dante shook his head and began fumbling with one of the marker buoys on his belt. He lost his grip on the cartridge, and it floated to the sand at the mouth of the opening.

Dante reached down to recover it.

Now it was Star's turn to shout aloud. "No!"

# CHAPTER SEVEN

Just as Dante's glove closed over the cartridge, the grotesque head of a moray eel exploded out of the hole, revealing an improbably gaping mouth of inch-long needles. Shocked, he snapped back his arm, and the jaws bit down on the metal of the marker buoy, sending broken teeth in all directions.

In a panic, Dante dropped the cartridge and reached for the valve of his B.C. Star grabbed him before he could inflate the vest and shoot upward.

She pushed her mask right up against his, communicating her message with dark eyes: *Calm down. It didn't happen. You're okay.*

Dante nodded, gasping into his regulator. He was a pretty crummy diver, Star reflected, but sometimes luck was more important than skill. The big eel could have taken a substantial chunk of flesh out of his hand.

Not far away, Kaz and Adriana were tagging a cave entrance with another one of the marker buoys. There was a pop followed by a hiss, and the float rocketed to the surface.

DIVE

*One down and five hundred to go,* Star thought to herself. She still couldn't figure out why Tad Cutter needed this. To map every grotto and nook in a reef system the size of Hidden Shoals would take years, not a couple of months. It didn't make sense.

She was enjoying the chance to dive without the bulky scuba tank. It was a feeling of freedom, although she was tethered to the Brownie by her air hose and safety line. Soaring and swooping with the fish, pretending to be one of them — it was a childish game, but Star never got tired of it.

She swam with a school of mackerel until they were scattered by a big loggerhead turtle. The loggerhead's stony shell felt ancient against her gloved hand — a piece of prehistory here in the twenty-first century.

She spotted Kaz hovering over another cave, unclipping a fresh marker buoy from his belt. He wasn't much of a diver either, she reflected. But there was an ease, almost a grace to his movements — something only natural athletes had.

As Star watched him work, a large barracuda loomed up behind the boy.

*Should I signal him?*

She remembered the incident with the shark. Kaz was easily spooked, and might do something stupid. Besides, barracudas never attack humans on purpose.

But the seven-footer was nosy. Star bit her tongue as the protruding lower jaw probed right up behind Kaz, the gleaming teeth mere inches from the back of his neck.

All at once, Kaz turned around, coming face to jaws with the notorious predator. Shocked, he triggered the marker buoy. The pop startled the barracuda, and it turned tail and darted away. Star laughed, sending clouds of bubbles rushing for the surface.

Adriana was nearby, paralleling the bottom, trying to shoo away an aggressive triggerfish. She was a little more comfortable in the water than Kaz — a tourist rather than a beginner. The girl had obviously done some diving on high-priced vacations in the past.

It bugged her. Not that Adriana was rich, but that Poseidon had matched Star with such unqualified teammates.

*Then again, how could they be sure I was any good? They knew about my cerebral palsy. . . .*

It was almost as if Poseidon had gone after weak divers on purpose.

"Look!" came a cry.

Dante again. If the boy didn't stop yelling underwater, he was going to drink enough salt to give himself high blood pressure.

He was pointing and waving — probably at another rabbit hole he considered a cave. But when she swam to his side, he was gazing into the distance, where the reef fell off into deeper water.

She squinted, trying to zoom in on the object of his interest. Light, and therefore visibility, diminished with depth. She shot him an expansive shrug. Because of the need to communicate without words, divers often used exaggerated gestures like stage actors playing to the back row.

Dante deflated his B.C., descending into the twilight. Star followed. A tug at her belt told her that the safety line had become taut, and that they were now pulling the Brownie along with them. She glanced over her shoulder and saw that the others had noticed it too. Kaz and Adriana finned after them.

*What does Dante think he sees?* There was such a thing as an underwater mirage. His magnified eyes behind his mask gave him a deranged appearance. It was easy to believe he was hallucinating.

And then she spotted it.

In the middle of this most natural of settings, it was jarring to see something so artificial, so man-made. The sunken airplane sat in the sand, its fuse-lage partially encrusted with coral and sea life. One wing had broken off on impact with the water. It lay a short distance away, hidden by seaweed.

Star's heart began to pound so hard she was afraid it might burst her wet suit. This was the ultimate diver's prize. A wreck! She had read about this experience in scuba magazines. But the excitement of the real thing went far beyond anything she could have imagined.

She approached slowly, reverently, half expecting the plane to vanish just as she reached out to touch it. Never had she imagined this could happen to her — and certainly not when she was teamed up with a bunch of landlubbers like this bunch! The others hung back, watching her uncertainly.

When she spotted the insignia on the side, a gasp escaped her — a larger bubble among the many smaller ones. The marking was obscured by anemone growth, but it was unmistakable. A swastika. This was a German warplane from World War II!

She swam over to peer into the cockpit, wondering if she'd see a skeleton at the controls. But, no. The big bomber was deserted.

The windshield was shattered, providing a narrow entryway to the downed plane.

Star hesitated. Wreck diving could be dangerous.

*But this is the chance of a lifetime!*

She entered the cockpit and squeezed between the pilot's and copilot's chairs into the body of the plane. The space was tiny — it was hard to believe that an entire crew of grown men had flown in this cigar box. Just a few feet into the fuselage and she was in near-total darkness. The only light was from two turrets of bulletproof glass. Out of each pointed a swiveling machine gun, harmless now, encased in a layer of coral. It was a grim reminder that this silent metal husk was once an instrument of war, a delivery system for death.

She snaked back toward the bomber's tail. Here, there was absolute blackness, and the walls closed in until she was in the narrowest of tunnels.

As she reversed course, her flipper caught on the low ceiling and came off. Alert, she was able to trap it between her legs. Putting it on again in the cramped space was a major operation, and she was surprised at how exhausted it left her. Her bubbles, trapped below the ceiling of the craft, converged to form a small pocket of air.

*I'd better get out of here.*

But not without a souvenir — some kind of

proof that she'd been there. *Artifacts*, the wreck divers called them. Plates and silverware from sunken ships were especially prized. But what to take from a plane? She couldn't exactly snap off a three-hundred-pound propeller.

Once again, her eyes fell on the machine gun. A full strap of ammunition dangled from the carbine, waving lightly in the current.

She crawled rather than swam up to it, grasping holds on the floor of the cabin. Popping the shells out was easier than she expected — the old strapping fell apart on contact, and the bullets dropped into her glove. The thrill of their touch was almost tangible.

*World War II in the palm of your hand,* she reflected. *Hey —*

Fiddling with the gun had disturbed the layer of silt that covered the plane. A storm of swirling brown particles filled the turret. The bullets slipped through her fingers and disappeared.

Going after her prize was instinct. Any diver would have done the same thing. She ducked into the cloud as if bobbing for apples. That was when she felt it — no flow of compressed gas from the demand regulator between her teeth.

She was out of air.

# CHAPTER EIGHT

*No!* Star thought desperately. *Impossible! I'm not breathing out of a tank!*

The truth came to her in an icy shot of fear. A kink in her hose! Her air supply must have caught on something — a knob, a handle. But where? A frantic glance toward the back of the cabin revealed only darkness.

She tugged gently but insistently at the hose, hoping to jar it free. The life-giving gas would not come. *Come on!* She yanked harder, knowing all the while it was a bad idea, that she was likely to foul the supply even further.

Star Ling was such a confident diver that when panic came, the feeling was completely alien to her. Her first inclination was to spit out her mouthpiece and shoot for the surface, but when she tried to crawl out the opening in the gun turret, her tether line held her back. She was trapped in this submerged metal coffin.

She pulled out her knife and began to flail blindly behind her, but she couldn't see anything in the billowing storm of silt.

It was the glint of the steel blade in the gun

turret that told Kaz something was wrong. When Star saw him swimming toward her, she realized he was her only hope. She gestured madly with her finger across her throat — the diver's signal for *no air.*

It seemed to take forever for him to get there. *Water acts as a magnifying glass,* she reminded herself. *He looks closer than he is.*

The thought was little comfort. She was close to unconsciousness, her field of vision darkening at the edges. She struggled to stay alert. Would this hockey player even know what to do when he reached her?

*He's paddling with his hands, for God's sake! A mistake right out of Diving 101!*

And then he was right there. She caught a glimpse of herself reflected in his mask and realized just how far gone she was. Her face was ashen, her eyes bulging in horror. She could not hold on much longer. The blackness was overtaking her.

Kaz sucked hard on his regulator, then spat it out and forced the mouthpiece between Star's blue lips. The delicious blast of air snapped her back from the edge of the void. She breathed deeply, fighting to keep herself from hyperventilating.

Kaz crawled in through the opening in the turret and searched the floor of the plane. He fanned the water to disperse the curtain of silt. When he spied her regulator, he grasped the problem immediately. The hose had wrapped itself around the bombardier's joystick so tightly that the flow of air had been cut off. The snarl was complicated further by Star's safety line, which was tangled up with the air supply and also snagged on a hook above the bailout hatch. Kaz used his knife to cut the line, then freed the hose and breathed from the mouthpiece.

Star watched him in wonder. The boy was an awkward diver, but in this crisis, his actions were swift and decisive. *Must be the hockey training,* she thought grudgingly. She hated to admit it, but Bobby Kaczinski had very probably just saved her life.

She could feel herself trembling in spite of the warm water. The incident had rattled her — but not enough to keep her from grabbing another handful of bullets as they exited the plane.

They surfaced beside the Brownie and held on, rolling with the choppy seas.

Dante was already shouting as he spat out his mouthpiece. "Are you okay?"

"Don't tell anybody what happened!" Star ordered. "Not Cutter — nobody!"

THE DISCOVERY

"What *did* happen?" asked Adriana. "It looked like you got stuck in that plane."

"If they don't trust our diving, they'll ground us in a heartbeat!" Star persisted. *"Promise!"*

Kaz was thunderstruck. "Is that all you've got to say? You could be dead right now!"

"I got in a jam and my partner helped me out of it," Star insisted. "That's how the buddy system's supposed to work."

"This is only my fourth dive!" Kaz sputtered. "My second in the ocean! What if I messed up? They don't teach that in scuba class, Star! What if I didn't know what to do? I'd have to live with that!" The image of Drew Christiansen, lying prostrate on the ice, came to him, and he fell silent. How much guilt could fit on one conscience?

"Don't you realize what we just saw?" cried Star. "People dive their whole lives and never find a wreck!" She turned to Dante. "That's some set of eagle eyes you've got! Maybe we're all crazy and water really *is* purple."

"I just" — he paused, uncomfortable — "got lucky."

"A German plane!" exclaimed Adriana. "Maybe it's from one of the famous bombing runs on Curaçao. It's a real find for the historical community."

"It's a real find for *us*," Star corrected sharply. She unzipped the pouch on her dive belt and came up with the handful of bullets. "And we've got the artifacts to prove it. I can't wait to rub these in Cutter's face. Let's see if he treats us like a bunch of tadpoles now!"

Since the *Ponce de León* was combing the reef with its sonar tow, the four had to wait on the floating Brownie for the research vessel to pass by. Dante spotted it almost immediately, a tiny blip in the heat shimmer on the horizon. Twenty minutes later, the ship was pulling alongside them.

Kaz saw Chris Reardon first, half asleep in the stern, a fishing rod in his hand, trawling for tuna over the gunwale. "Hey, Chris!" he called.

Reardon let out a loud belch, but otherwise gave no indication he'd heard.

"Get that rod out of the water!" a sharp voice ordered him. "You'll skewer one of the kids!"

Marina was rushing down to the dive platform to help them aboard. She frowned at the two marker buoys bobbing in the waves. "I know there are a lot more caves than that."

"Dante found a wreck!" Star panted.

The researcher's eyes were instantly alert. "A wreck?"

"A World War II airplane," Adriana supplied.

THE DISCOVERY

"Look!" Star thrust a fistful of coral-encrusted bullets in Marina's face.

Marina stared for a moment, and then her supermodel's features relaxed into an amused grin. "Star, that's not — "

But Star was already limping toward the main companionway, calling, "Tad!" The others followed her, wet suits dripping.

Tad Cutter was seated at the foldaway table in the galley, poring over an endless data printout on continuous form paper.

"There's a plane down there," Star told him excitedly. "A German bomber." She slammed the machine gun bullets onto the computer.

Cutter looked from the bullets to their earnest faces and laughed — full-throated guffaws that filled the salon.

"Hey!" Star was insulted. "You may think we're a bunch of pests to be ignored, but we know what a plane looks like!"

"No!" the team leader managed, struggling to regain his control. "You guys are right. There's a plane down there. But it's not from World War II."

"Yes, it is," Adriana insisted. "A Messerschmidt bomber, propeller driven, with a swastika and German cross markings. The Nazis used them in the Caribbean against Allied oil-drilling operations."

"And that's exactly what the movie was about — a German bomber that crashed into the sea," Cutter informed them. "The studio folks built an exact model of a Messerschmidt, towed it out here, and sank it on the reef. *That's* what you found. Not a wreck — a Hollywood set."

Star's face fell the distance between an undiscovered wreck and an underwater phony. The others looked on in dismay. A minute ago it seemed as if they had earned the respect of Cutter and his crew. Now they were nobodies again.

The blond man picked up one of the bullets. "This isn't nearly enough coral growth for an artifact from World War II. After sixty years, the whole shell casing would be covered, most likely. This looks about right for three years on the reef — the time since that movie got made."

Marina appeared at the companionway. "Don't take it so hard. You're not the first divers to find that plane and think it was something special. I doubt you'll be the last." She smiled. "There are a lot of caves down there. We'll need you back in the water as soon as possible. Use the oxygen to help you outgas. It's topside — the tanks with the green labels."

Since the body absorbs some of the nitrogen from compressed air at depth, it was important to expel that nitrogen before diving again the same day. Breathing pure oxygen sped up the whole process.

On deck, Dante pulled a tank from the rack, struggling under its weight.

Kaz frowned at the other boy. "She said green labels."

"Yeah?"

"These are red."

"Oh — right." Embarrassed, Dante fumbled with the cylinder and dropped it. Kaz got his foot out of the way a split second before the heavy metal hit the deck.

Dante grimaced. "Sorry." That was becoming a pretty useful word for him. *Sorry for nearly shattering your toe; sorry for handing you a tank of God-knows-what that might have poisoned you; sorry for spotting the plane that almost became Star's tomb.* There was no question about it. He stank at this internship. And not just the diving part. Everything he did around here turned out to be wrong.

Kaz hauled out four of the oxygen cylinders and the divers divided them up. He placed the clear plastic mask over his mouth and nose and turned on the valve. "It isn't so bad, right?" he asked, his voice muffled. "I mean, we look like idiots, but they still want us to tag caves for them. At least we didn't lose our jobs."

"I still say something's fishy about that," put in Star. "We've got two markers in the water. Have any of those guys even bothered to record their positions?"

In answer, a loud snore came from the stern of the boat, as Reardon continued his hunt for a prizewinning tuna.

Adriana placed the mask over her face and then withdrew it, licking her dry lips thoughtfully. "The only thing that bothers me is that they're supposed to be doing a sonar scan, right? Mapping the reef. But the data Cutter's studying isn't sonar data."

Kaz snapped to attention. "It isn't?"

"One summer, the British Museum had a team searching for ancient Roman artifacts in the Thames River — shields, helmets, armor. They used a side-scan magnetometer to pick up signs of metal underwater. Well, the data from that scan is exactly like the data on Cutter's table."

Star snapped her fingers. "They're looking for something in the ocean. Something metal."

Dante was confused. "Then why do they want us down there marking caves?"

All at once, a wide smile of understanding appeared on the slight girl's face. "It's bell work!"

"Bell work?" repeated Adriana.

"When I was in fifth grade," Star explained,

"my teacher always put a few math problems on the board for when we came in after the bell. It wasn't stuff we had to know — not on any test or anything. It was just supposed to keep us busy while she finished her coffee in the faculty room. That's what this cave thing is all about — they're keeping us busy while they're searching!"

The four divers exchanged solemn glances. Could it really be true? They knew Cutter and his team had little respect for them, but could the researchers be manipulating them this way?

Kaz broke the uneasy silence. "Okay, let's say both you guys are right. They're jerking us around, keeping us busy doing nothing, while they're scanning the Hidden Shoals for metal. That still doesn't answer the biggest question — why all this secrecy? These people are scientists working for a top institute. Why can't they just admit what they're after?"

Adriana flipped her wet hair out of her face. "It seems to me," she said slowly, "that there must be something very special about their work."

Dante raised an eyebrow. "A government contract? Maybe top secret?"

"Maybe," she said. "But whatever it is, we're mixed up in it now."

03 July 1665

At first, Samuel blamed the stink of the Griffin on the port of Liverpool. But as they sailed farther, in fair seas or rough, the overpowering stench was still with them. Worse, it seemed to be growing in intensity. It was a mixture of bilge water, cooking fires, the rotting food stores, and livestock smells from the goats, pigs, and chickens that were raised on board to keep up a supply of fresh milk, eggs, and meat for the captain and crew.

Mostly, though, it was the reek of people — two and eighty unwashed men on a long journey under a relentless sun. The acrid odor of seasickness could never be fully swabbed away. And as the barque was tossed by malevolent waves, even the most seasoned sailor would lose control of his stomach. Captain Blade himself was not immune. One time during a spell of rough weather, Samuel barged in on him on the floor of his quarters, retching into his chamber pot.

He leaped to his feet, scorching Samuel with eyes of fire. "You'll not speak of this to anyone, boy, or I'll have you flogged!"

It was not an idle threat. There were floggings al-

THE DISCOVERY

most daily on the crew deck of the Griffin. *Captain Blade insisted on performing these himself, with his bone-handled snake whip.*

*"Ah, it feels good to stretch the old muscles," he would grin as his victim sobbed in a pool of his own blood, his back crisscrossed with angry red stripes. "A man needs some physical activity."*

*A regular recipient of Blade's brand of "physical activity" was old Evans, the sail maker. The over-powering wind gusts of the Atlantic crossing relent-lessly shredded the barque's many sails. Though the silver-haired man labored night and day, sewing until he could barely see his stiff fingers before his failing eyes, he could not keep up with the damage.*

*"I'll hang your courtly self if I don't see the mizzen in its place before the boy brings my supper!" the captain roared. "Courtly" was the ultimate insult on shipboard. A courtly seaman was a landlubber.*

*In Evans's case it was the truth. He was a farmer by trade. His landlord had evicted him from the potato fields that provided his meager living. Evans had grown too weak to work the property profitably, and he had no sons to help him. Going to sea was his only chance to provide for his wife and daughters.*

*In spite of their age difference, Samuel felt a bond with the much older man. Both were non-sailors who had been forced by poverty to the Griffin and its merciless captain. The ship's boy spent most of his free* time in the sail maker's cabin, stitching canvas until his hands bled, substituting his young eyes for the old man's dim ones.

Although Evans appreciated the help, he must have at first suspected that Samuel was the captain's spy. The old man was always saying things like, "Captain James Blade is a right gentleman. Lucky we are to have such a fine master on the Griffin."

Even after a brutal flogging, he had nothing but praise for the instrument of his agony. As Samuel poured seawater over the man's whip-scarred back to prevent infection, Evans would whimper, "'Tis a fine captain who takes such a personal interest in the affairs of his crew."

Samuel said nothing. He had never known his own father, and longed for the moment that Evans would trust him with his true thoughts.

Late one night, as the two struggled to darn a foresail so pockmarked by mending that it resembled a ragamuffin's wardrobe, the moment finally came. By the dim flicker of a waterlogged oil lamp, Evans said in a matter-of-fact tone, "He's a proper lunatic, that captain of ours. I hate him, I do."

"Shhh!" Samuel hissed, glancing nervously over his shoulder. Then, in a whisper, "I hate him too. Every time I touch his filthy chamber pot, I want to throw it in his face."

"That whip — I see it in my sleep!" All at once,

*the old man's moist, haunted eyes took on a faraway look. "In my dream, it's wrapped around Blade's white throat. I'm pulling it tighter, tighter. He screams, but I don't stop pulling, squeezing —"*

*"That's mutiny!" Samuel breathed in horror. "It's a hanging offense!"*

*"And then I think of my girls," the old man finished, visibly deflated, "and I remember I have to avoid the noose for their sakes." He added earnestly, "But this old body is not strong enough to survive another flogging. I'm telling you true, Samuel. I'll die under James Blade's lash."*

*The weather continued wild and dangerous. Two and a half months into the perilous crossing, a storm sank the* Viscount, *an eighteen-gun brigantine in their small fleet. The* Griffin *picked up four and thirty hapless sailors, adrift in the rough seas. The rest simply slipped beneath the waves and were seen no more. Captain Blade clung to the ratlines through the entire operation, cracking his whip into the wind and rain and hurling abuse at rescuers and survivors alike.*

*There were now more than one hundred souls packed onto the barque. Conditions were more than cramped; they were unsafe. Fever spread like wildfire through the seething mass of humanity. Six men had already died, including the ship's carpenter, whose responsibilities included replacing damaged or rotten*

wood in the leaky hull. The Griffin *sat low in the wa-*
*ter. Samuel was ordered away from the sail maker's*
*cabin to join the army of pumpers in the unbreathable*
*air of the reeking bilge.*

*He was returning, bowed down with fatigue, from*
*several hours below, when he heard the distant cry:*
*"Sail, ho!"*

*It was Evans, perched high in the rigging, where*
*he had been struggling to mend a tear in the square*
*topsail at the tip of the mainmast. From that vantage*
*point, he had spied another ship on the horizon.*

*Captain Blade poked his head out of his quarters.*
*"One of ours?" he called.*

*Evans squinted. "I can't tell, sir!"*

*Blade stormed down to the main deck. "Are you a*
*seaman or a gooseberry, mister? Is it one of our fleet?"*

*Samuel tried to jump to the old man's defense.*
*"He doesn't know ships, sir! He's just a farmer who*
*went to —"*

*Thwack! The big emerald flashed in the sun as the*
*captain brought the bone handle of his whip down*
*hard on Samuel's forehead. He collapsed to his*
*knees, seeing stars.*

*"You'll earn yourself a flogging if I have to come*
*up there!" Blade bellowed at his sail maker.*

*But Evans was paralyzed. His pale, nearsighted*
*eyes could not recognize the distant vessel, and his*
*fear of the captain prevented him from guessing.*

THE DISCOVERY

"You'll be right sorry you troubled me!" Blade strode to the ratlines and began to climb, not quickly, but with the authority and balance that comes from decades spent on shipboard.

It was a nightmare, Samuel reflected, watching the captain close in on the quaking sail maker. His friend's words came back to him: "This old body isn't strong enough to survive another flogging. . . ."

He flung himself at the ratlines, scrambling like a spider, shocked at first at how fast and good he was at it. The chimneys, he thought, arms and legs working efficiently. If I can make it up Sewell's chimneys, I can make it up anything!

The captain bellowed with rage as he pulled level with Evans. "Why, you worthless maggot, don't you recognize your own flagship? I'll flog you till there's nothing left but a handful of your rotting teeth!"

The angry green of the emerald flashed in the sun. At first, Samuel thought Blade was going to lash the poor farmer right there on the ratlines. It was a hor-rifying prospect. Surely Evans would lose his grip and fall. Then he realized that it was the old sail maker who had snatched up the whip, and was at-tempting to wrap it around Blade's neck.

"No!" Samuel cried, but he knew it was already too late. Under maritime law, even touching the cap-tain was a capital crime. No matter what happened now, poor Evans would hang.

*"Mutinous — scum — " With great strength, Blade managed to pull himself free. He brought down his clasped hands full force on the sail maker's crown. Evans went rigid for a moment, and then let go of the rope. Horrified, Samuel watched his only friend plunge to his death one hundred feet to the deck below.*

*The effort of the savage blow had overbalanced the captain, and, with a terrified scream, he too lost his purchase on the ratlines.*

I'll not help him, *Samuel resolved as his master plummeted toward him.* I'll not save the murdering —

*Yet the action was pure instinct. As the captain fell, pawing desperately at the rigging, Samuel reached out and grabbed his belt. He would not have been able to hold on, but he slowed the acceleration of the drop just enough for Blade to snatch the webbing of rope. The cruel captain hung on, gasping for breath and whimpering with panic, as crewmen surrounded the sail maker's broken body beneath them.*

It should be you, Captain, lying down there dead, and Evans up here with me, consigning your black soul to the devil! *Samuel thought, biting back tears. Aloud, he just said, "You all right, sir?"*

*Gingerly, Blade hoisted himself up to regard his cabin boy. "You're my lucky angel, boy," he groaned wearily. "Aye, you're a lucky one, Samuel Higgins."*

# CHAPTER NINE

Slowly but surely, Kaz, Adriana, Dante, and Star began to fit into the routine at Poseidon Oceanographic Institute. They continued to dive with Cutter and his crew aboard the *Ponce de León*, tagging underwater caves and trying to keep a low profile while they snooped.

"We don't want them to think we're on to them," Star advised. "No matter what they're up to."

Dante was all for the interns minding their own business. "If it's top secret or something," was his reasoning, "then it should stay that way."

"We're just curious," Kaz insisted. "It's not like we're spies."

"And who has a better right to know?" Star added. "They're messing up our summer program. The least they can do is tell us why."

So they continued with their busywork and kept an eye on the team from San Diego, although there was little to see. According to Captain Vanover, a magnetometer looked pretty much like a sonar, so the tow fish itself yielded no clue. Cutter spent most of his time belowdecks, his head buried in reams of printouts. Reardon could have been any fishing bum on a Caribbean vacation. He seldom left the stern and his rod and reel. Captain Hamilton ran the boat, period. Marina was the only one who had much interaction with the teen divers.

"If anybody's innocent on Cutter's team, it has to be her," was Adriana's opinion. "She's just a friendly, interested mentor."

"Who looks like a supermodel," finished Kaz.

"You don't have to be a photographer to recognize *that* thing of beauty," Dante agreed.

Star shook her head. "You guys are such losers."

It was not the first piece of ribbing Dante had taken on the subject. When he printed his second batch of pictures, more than half of them were of Marina. To make matters worse, the developing was so off that her perfect skin matched the bright orange of the fire coral in the reef shots.

"Stick to purple water, Romeo," was Adriana's opinion.

The interns kept their suspicions to themselves, saying nothing to the other institute people for fear of word getting back to Cutter. When they did ask questions, they kept them general, omitting any reference to the team from California.

"Why would a ship tow a side-scan magnetometer?" Adriana asked Captain Vanover in the cafeteria one night.

"Depends who's on board, and what he's looking for," came the reply. "A mag is basically a fancy metal detector. Geologists say most of the world's mineral ore is under the sea."

"Mining companies use them?" asked Kaz.

"Sometimes. But the salvage people love them too — anybody who wants to track down something big underwater. How do you think they found the *Titanic*? The military is also a big user. They're always going after stuff — equipment and ordnance they lost in the drink."

Dante shot the others a meaningful glance. Could that be the mysterious assignment — top secret work for the navy, searching for a sunken submarine or even a lost nuke?

"But around here," Vanover went on, "a lot of the mag scans are done by treasure hunters."

"Treasure hunters?" repeated Star.

"Sure," the captain told them. "A few hundred years ago, these waters were the money highway. And they say at least half of it is lying under the seabed somewhere."

Adriana nodded wisely. "In the sixteenth and seventeenth centuries, the Spanish shipped billions in treasure from the New World back to Spain."

"A lot of those ships never made it to Europe," Vanover explained. "Hurricanes, reefs, pirates. That's why a mag comes in handy. Gold and silver are *metals*. If a galleon went down in the area, its cargo would show up on the scan."

Dante was amazed. "And that works? You just tow it around till you get a hit, and bring up millions?"

The captain laughed. "It's a little more complicated than that, Dante. First of all, the sea is a big place — three quarters of the earth's surface, remember? Second, most of those wrecks are under thousands of feet of ocean, far too deep for any diver to reach them. But even if a wreck is located in shallow water, it's not like there would be a boat full of gold bars just sitting there in the sand. Those old ships were made of wood. Most of that would be gone by now, eaten little by little by microscopic worms in the water. And pretty much all that's left is buried in coral, which is another problem. It's against the law to destroy a living reef."

"In other words, forget about it," concluded Kaz.

"Most treasure hunters search for decades and never find much," Vanover agreed. "But there are exceptions. A man named Mel Fisher excavated two galleons off the Florida Keys, and

THE DISCOVERY

brought up hundreds of millions in gold and gems."

Dante whistled. "He's got it made!"

"Not necessarily," said the captain. "Who owns sunken treasure? Now the government's suing him, and he's up to his ears in lawyers."

"A hundred million bucks can hire a lot of lawyers," Dante pointed out. "That's not just rich; it's *rolling*."

Huge money — that was Dante's secret dream. Not that most people didn't want to get rich. But for an artist, a big pile of cash had a special meaning — freedom. He could pursue his craft without having to worry about selling pictures or making a living.

A financially secure photographer wouldn't have to learn color. Which had one definite advantage in Dante's eyes.

No diving.

Dante was the weakest diver in the group, but even his meager skills were improving. This was true for all of them, if for no other reason than the huge amount of ocean time they were logging.

"You learn to dive by diving," was Star's opinion. "Even a baboon would get better if he spent as much time underwater as us."

When it came to scuba, Star held on to her

praise the way a miser holds on to his pennies. To listen to her, the only people who had ever gotten it right were herself, English, and Jacques Cousteau, probably in that order.

It bugged Kaz. *She thinks we're all useless,* he reflected resentfully. *I probably saved her life in that plane, and she never even said thanks.*

In fact, Star was very much aware of Kaz's development as a diver. His technique was raw, but the Canadian's natural athletic ability gave him amazing strength, stamina, and body control. He could also hold his breath for a year! One time Adriana got her tether line tangled up in a stand of sea fans. In the process of cutting herself free, she accidentally sliced through her air hose. Now she had to "buddy breathe" to rise to the surface — with her partner, Kaz, sharing his regulator.

It was a tense moment for any diver, but Kaz remained calm, just as he had in the German bomber. Star watched the ascent anxiously, ready to offer help. None had been required. From what she could tell, Kaz barely needed more than a breath or two on the way up. How would some rink rat learn to do that?

The one thing that Kaz could not seem to get used to was sharks. With the water acting as a magnifying glass, even a small reef shark seemed

THE DISCOVERY

pretty intimidating, with a mouth large enough to bite your hand off. And, of course, there was still an eighteen-foot tiger shark around somewhere — unless that whole Clarence story was a goof cooked up by Vanover to pull everybody's chain.

*Some goof,* Kaz thought to himself. He liked the captain. Around Poseidon, Vanover was the only person who seemed to take the summer interns seriously, except maybe Marina.

But Bobby Kaczinski didn't find sharks very funny.

The teen divers took off every fourth day to outgas — to let their systems expel residual nitrogen. It gave them a chance to get to know one another above sea level. The strange turns their internship program had taken seemed to have forced the four closer together. It was something that might never have happened if the summer had gone off as planned.

The institute had mountain bikes for them to borrow, so they explored Saint-Luc's other villages and swam at the many beaches and coves that ringed the small island. Even off the reef they spent much of their time in the water. It was the only way to beat the relentless heat.

Star was awkward on the bicycle at first, until Kaz suggested that the others slow down so she could keep up. Then, somehow, the girl with the limp put on a burst of speed that nearly flattened him. They spent the hours that followed panting to keep up with her on the dirt roads.

"Now I know how to get something done around here," commented Kaz. "Just tell Star she can't do it."

"Maybe we should dare her to air-condition the island," gasped Dante, struggling up a hill at the back of the pack.

As they circled Saint-Luc's west coast, a new skyline began to appear — massive offshore oil-drilling platforms that stretched into the Caribbean like a series of colossal croquet hoops.

"Man," breathed Dante, "look at those."

To see anything man-made in a place as remote as Saint-Luc was jarring. Huge towers of concrete and steel soaring hundreds of feet out of the sea seemed almost fake — clever forgeries merely painted onto the horizon.

"This must be where English works," said Kaz in a small voice. To slip beneath the waves at the feet of such massive pieces of equipment — it was nothing short of terrifying. But for English, it was probably no big deal. The sea did not intimidate Menasce Gérard.

It wouldn't dare.

THE DISCOVERY

# CHAPTER TEN

Marina Kappas surveyed the light chop that frosted the Caribbean, a frown on her exquisitely formed lips. "It doesn't look too bad on the surface. But I'll bet there's a current a few feet below."

"Yeah, whatever." Star yawned and jumped off the dive platform.

Marina turned to the three remaining interns. "You'll be tethered to the Brownie, but without an anchor line, you can drift without knowing it," she said in concern. "And you'd better watch out for Star. Sometimes confidence can work against you."

Kaz flipped down his own mask. "We'll keep an eye on her." He added quickly, "But don't tell her I said that."

Dante hit the waves with a splash, bit down on his regulator, deflated his B.C., and sank. Sure enough, the current kicked in a few feet below the surface. The unseen force was subtler than wind. And yet it was relentless, propelling him slowly but irresistibly backward.

DIVE

*Don't panic*, he told himself, remembering his certification training. *Just keep descending.*

The advice turned out to be correct. By thirty feet, the manhandling of the ocean began to weaken. That was when he noticed something unusual.

*Where are all the fish?*

The reef was empty. The coral was still there — with its growth of anemones and sea fans. But the permanent traffic jam of fish that characterized the Hidden Shoals was just plain *gone*.

He shot a questioning look at Adriana. His partner shrugged, mystified.

The disturbance came from above. At first, it seemed like portable rapids — a fast-moving wave of violently foaming water.

He tried to swing his camera around to get a shot of the phenomenon, but he spun too hard, twirling himself on a diagonal axis like a globe. Peering through the lens of the Nikonos, he saw a blurry panorama, and then —

Two eyes and a protruding snout staring right back at him!

He nearly jumped out of his wet suit. Then he recognized the creature in front of him.

*A dolphin!*

A whole pod of them, in fact, scouring the

reef in a cacophony of high-pitched squeals and clicks. Dante tried to guess at their number, but the sea mammals were moving too fast — faster, in fact, than he'd ever seen anything travel in water. There were at least twenty of them, maybe thirty, diving and swooping as they streaked past.

His visitor circled him with a lightning spin-o-rama, and darted off to join the group.

*No wonder the fish cleared out. This is a hunting party. They're not gone; they're hiding!*

He began shooting pictures. Dante had seen dolphins only at aquariums and theme parks. These appeared similar — Atlantic bottlenoses. But the show tanks of Sea World could not begin to demonstrate the *personality* of these animals. Fish eyes were blank and staring. But the expression of a dolphin sparkled with charisma, even humor. The face that had scared Dante out of his wits wasn't a threatening one. On the contrary, it had been almost mocking, as if to say, "Man, you're a lousy swimmer. What are you doing in my ocean?"

*I need a video camera,* he thought to himself. Still pictures would never do justice to the dolphins' playfulness. He squinted at a small dark object that appeared to be swimming along with the pod. It was a conch shell, batted from snout to snout. A toy!

*They're practically people!* He wondered whether the dolphins would consider that a compliment.

A practiced bump from a bottlenose floated the shell directly into Kaz's hands. The boy lobbed it back into the pack only to have it expertly volleyed to Adriana.

*They're not just playing,* Dante marveled. *They're playing with us!*

The game lasted maybe thirty seconds before Dante bobbled and dropped the shell, earning a squeaky reprimand from a five-foot cetacean. To interact with these creatures, so alien yet so strangely human, was something he would never forget.

But Star was not ready to say good-bye to their new friends. With a Herculean double kick of her flippers, she came up behind a dorsal fin and latched on to it. The dolphin seemed surprised at first, and then sped up, carrying the girl along for the ride. Suddenly, Dante felt his safety line go taut. And then he was flying through the water at spectacular velocity.

Shock soon turned to amazement. Since the four divers were connected via the Brownie, Star's dolphin was towing them all! He could see Kaz and Adriana, sailing along with him. Kaz's arms were spread like airplane wings. Those maniacs were *enjoying* this!

THE DISCOVERY

*Like it's some kind of underwater roller coaster.*

The other dolphins kept pace with them as the reef accelerated to a blur.

*But is it safe?*

Dante never saw the coral head swinging out to meet him.

# CHAPTER ELEVEN

*Wham!*

Dante bounced off the tower of living lime-stone like a rag doll. The jolt halted the Brownie on the surface, and yanked Star off her purchase on the dolphin. The ride was over. The streaking pod disappeared from view a few seconds later.

The divers gathered around Dante, who hung in the water, dazed but unhurt, the Nikonos dangling limply from its arm harness.

Star peered into his mask, fearing that the collision had knocked him unconscious. But his eyes were open and alert, fixed on the seafloor.

For Dante, it was like studying a pixelgram — that moment when your brain makes the connection, and you plunge into the depths of 3-D. It wasn't even a real image — more like the echo of one, formed by thousands of layers of coral polyps growing over an object long buried, long forgotten.

He deflated his B.C. and began to descend to the bottom. The others followed, confused. They didn't see it, *couldn't* see it.

THE DISCOVERY

In his excitement, he nearly fumbled away his dive slate. He scribbled the word that was pounding in his brain, revving his heartbeat up to the danger zone:

ANCHOR.

They stared at him blankly.

*What are you, blind?* he wanted to howl. *Right there — in front of your noses!*

The same condition that held color tantalizingly out of his grasp revealed the presence of the anchor in the subtleties of light and texture and shading. The others would never see it. He had to *show* them.

But how? Coral was like rock; it *was* rock beneath the living layers at the surface.

A few feet away, the reef gave way to sandy bottom. He began to dig, burrowing with both hands. Instantly, the crystal-clear water was murky with mud and silt.

Star, Kaz, and Adriana watched him, their bewilderment evident. Had Dante's collision scrambled his brain? Why was he using the ocean floor as a sandbox?

Kaz touched his arm, but Dante shook it away. He was a man on a mission, tunneling down to the lost anchor. *How big do they make these things? If the top is long enough, then it should be right about —*

His glove struck something hard. "Got it!" he cried into his regulator.

He had stirred up so much silt that the sea was churning brown. He took Kaz's gloved hand and pressed it against ancient iron.

Star removed a fin and fanned the water clear above the buried object. They could make out part of a thick shank topped with a sturdy ring. A small black disk floated beside it, disturbed by the digging action.

*A chip off the old metal?*

Dante stuck it in his dive pouch — proof of the anchor's existence. But there was another problem: How would they ever find this spot again?

Then he remembered the marker buoys. He clipped one around the iron ring, and sent the balloon shooting for the surface. They followed it up, carefully matching the pace of the slowest of their bubbles.

A few bold fish watched them ascend — the advance scouts venturing out of hiding to make sure the dolphins were gone. The reef was returning to normal.

The divers broke into the chop and swam a short distance to the Brownie. The *Ponce de León* was almost upon them, a silhouette against the brilliant sun.

"Over here!" panted Star, waving her arms.

THE DISCOVERY

"We found something!" added Dante.

Marina jumped down to the dive platform to help them aboard. "I don't see a lot of markers."

"Not a cave," Dante exclaimed. "An anchor!"

"You're kidding!" Cutter came running, Reardon hot on his heels. Soon the four divers stood dripping on deck.

Adriana pulled off her flippers. "Is that what you're looking for? With the magnetometer?" She added, "We know you're not taking sonar readings."

The three scientists exchanged a meaningful look. Finally, Marina spoke. "Our tow fish can do both — side scan mag and sonar. When we publish our map, it's going to come with an overlay page of mineral deposits under the reef. That's what the mag is for."

"What about this anchor?" Reardon put in gruffly.

"Dante found it," Kaz explained breathlessly. "Most of it's buried in coral. You can tell it's really old."

"I got a piece of it," added Dante, fumbling in his pouch.

Cutter frowned. "A piece of anchor?"

"More like a chip." The photographer pulled out the small black disk. It was irregular in shape, but generally round, about three inches in diameter. "Is there some way to get it analyzed? You know, find out how old it is?"

A gasp escaped Reardon, which Marina extinguished with a stern look.

Cutter spoke up carefully. "I'm telling you this now, because I know how embarrassed you were when word got around the institute about that German plane. Guys, you just found the anchor of the *Queen Anne's Revenge.*"

Adriana gawked at him. "*Blackbeard's* ship?"

"Don't you remember the movie? Harrison Ford played the diver who spotted the anchor buried in the mud."

"You're not saying — " Star's eyes narrowed. "Another film prop?"

Cutter nodded. "It took the location people three weeks to plant it deep enough on the bottom."

"That anchor wasn't in mud," Kaz pointed out. "It was in coral."

"Coral grows fast," put in Marina. "Especially on something hard like an anchor. How old is that movie — seven or eight years?"

"But the *Queen Anne's Revenge* didn't sink in the Caribbean," Adriana pointed out. "It went aground off the Carolinas. Why shoot the film here?"

THE DISCOVERY

Cutter shrugged. "On-screen, water is water. You can't tell the latitude by looking at it. Hollywood people like to work where the sea's nice and warm and crystal clear. It's easier and cheaper."

Dante regarded his anchor chip with chagrin. "Worthless." As he reared back to pitch the black disk into the sea, Reardon bulled forward and snatched it out of his hand. "Mind if I hang on to this?" he asked. "I'm a big Harrison Ford fan."

Star looked disgusted. "Is there anything else we should know about before we make total idiots out of ourselves? Did Steven Spielberg recreate the lost continent of Atlantis over by the oil rigs?"

Marina laughed. "Don't be embarrassed. You kids are doing beautifully, and you're turning into top-notch divers. Don't let yourselves get obsessed with sunken anchors or crazy discoveries. You'll just end up disappointed."

"Right," agreed Cutter. "Anything of value in these waters has been salvaged decades ago. There's nothing left to find down there."

Throughout the conversation, Chris Reardon did not take his eyes off the small black disk.

*11 August 1665*

The Griffin's *store of fruit had long since gone rotten, and was maggot infested besides.*

*"Eat it, young Samuel," ordered York, the ship's barber. "The maggots too. They'll keep the teeth in your head."*

*Samuel closed his eyes and took a tiny bite of the moldy apple. He could feel the wormy insects moving on his tongue, and quickly swallowed, choking back his nausea.*

*As barber, York was in charge of much more than cutting hair. He was the* Griffin's *sole medical man, apothecary, and dentist.*

*"Scurvy takes the teeth first," he lectured. "Then the mind. Then your life."*

*It was true. At the start of the crossing, each crewman aboard the ship had been allotted a small quantity of fruit. Those who had not jealously hoarded their shares were now suffering deeply from the disease. Toothless, their bodies bent from pain, they stumbled around the barque, struggling to perform their duties. Many more had given up trying,* and hung in their berths, eyes wide with vacant stares. Of two and eighty seamen and four and thirty Viscount survivors, only sixty men — barely half — remained. Now, nearly four months out of England, the rest had succumbed to scurvy, fever, and the relentless assault of the Atlantic. The gut-wrenching stink of death joined the mix of overpowering smells that made up the reek of the ship.

The funerals were becoming commonplace — two or three a day now. Normally, a body would be wrapped in a shroud for burial at sea. But sewing the shrouds was the office of the sail maker, and Evans was long gone. Samuel was struggling to take over the old man's duties, but it was all he could do to keep the Griffin's patchwork canvas aloft. So the dead were dispatched naked to their final resting places.

"It makes no difference to the sharks," was Captain Blade's opinion. "A meal's a meal, wrapped or no."

The cruel seaman never missed a flogging, yet never attended a single funeral. "A captain has more important things on his plate than feeding fish," he told Samuel.

An hour did not pass in which Samuel neglected to curse himself for saving his master's life on the ratlines. His hatred of the captain grew stronger, not weaker, as the barque approached the New World.

But even as resentment swelled inside Samuel,

*James Blade had begun to warm to the cabin boy who had stopped his fall that fateful day.*

*On the surface, there was no difference. The captain continued to treat him as a slave who was unworthy of even the slightest consideration. But it was Blade who had ordered the barber to keep an eye out for the young seaman the crew now called Lucky.*

*Never mind that the men of the Griffin avoided York like an evil spirit. He was most often seen covered in gore, sawing an unfortunate sailor's leg off. His newfound "friendship" with Samuel only served to make the boy feel like even more of an outcast. And he had James Blade to thank for it.*

*Samuel's feelings for the captain were not helped by the information he acquired on bailing duty in the ship's bilge. As he battled the pumps and the stench, he overheard some sailors chortling over the day when the hold would be piled high with gold and silver. Soon, they said, the Griffin would wallow low in the water from a cargo of plundered Spanish treasure, and all aboard her would be rich.*

*Samuel pounded back to the captain's quarters as soon as his shift was over, ignoring fatigue and the cramping of his muscles. He found Blade at the small desk, examining his rutter — the secret diary of a ship's pilot who had sailed this route before. No map, no chart, no instrument was as vital to a safe voyage as a good rutter.*

THE DISCOVERY

"Sir!" he cried. Distraught, he related what he had heard from the pumpers in the hold. "It can't be so, can it, Captain? Tell me we're not — common pirates!"

"Pirates?!" The bone handle of the snake whip came down on Samuel's head with devastating, murderous force. The last thing he saw before the captain's cabin went dark was James Blade, his cheeks suffused with purple rage.

Samuel awoke to a stinging pain so great it seared his very soul. He was in the barber's surgery. York was pouring seawater over a bloody gash on the boy's crown.

"A friendly piece of advice, young Samuel," the man said, a trace of humor in his voice. "Never say 'pirate' to Captain Blade. A right good thing it is that he's taken a liking to you."

Samuel tried to sit up, but the torment was too much. "We are pirates," he mumbled bitterly. "Thieves. Murderers too, probably."

"Listen to me, boy," York ordered. "We're patriots, with the full backing of the king of England. There are papers on board signed by the Merry Monarch himself in proper London. They give us the right — no, the responsibility — to attack and disrupt enemy shipping in the Indies."

Samuel frowned. "How does it help England if we steal their treasure?"

"*Gold buys ships, boy. And trains soldiers, and equips them with muskets and cannon,*" the barber explained. "*We're at war, Lucky, and wealth is power. The Royal Navy can't waste a ship on every stinking fever-hole in the New World. That's our lot — the patriots, the privateers! We're legal as a magistrate, flush with letters of marque to raid the scurvy Dutch.*"

"*But —*" Samuel was confused. "*But they were talking about Spanish treasure, not Dutch.*"

"*True that is,*" York agreed. "*And a beastly nuisance to us that His Majesty, God bless him, called a truce with the cursed Spaniard. But the ocean is large, and the courtly affairs of Europe far distant. Mistakes are made, you see my point? A Spanish ship looks much like a Dutch ship in the heat of battle, and treasure is treasure, no matter whose dead hand you pry it from.*"

He put an arm around the cabin boy's shoulders, and Samuel winced from the stench of decay on his blood-spattered smock. The barber's pockmarked face was barely an inch from his own, his breath as foul as the rest of him. "*And in this part of the world, Lucky, no treasure shines as bright as Spanish gold.*"

THE DISCOVERY

# CHAPTER TWELVE

Kaz stumbled through the darkness of 4:45 A.M. along the boardwalk that connected the Poseidon compound to the small marina. There was little moon. Only a handful of stars flickered through the overcast to light his way.

A dull clunk — his dive bag, falling to the dock. As he bent down, groping through the gloom, his knife slipped from its scabbard and planted itself with a *boing* tip first in the weathered planking. It could just as easily have been in Kaz's foot.

With a groan that was overwhelmed by a yawn, he gathered up his gear. Hockey players lugged a lot of equipment too. Why was he so discombobulated this morning?

"Kaz! That you?"

Dante beckoned from the harbor lights. Kaz gathered up his things and hurried over. "Where's the boat?"

"Gone," the boy told him.

"You're kidding!" Squinting, he took inventory of the various research vessels and launches that

DIVE

bobbed by the dock. There was no *Ponce de León*.

"Maybe it's in for service," suggested Dante. "Like, change the oil — "

"Rotate the tires," Kaz added sarcastically.

"You know what I mean. Boat stuff."

"What boat stuff?" Star came into the light, her dive bag draped over her shoulder.

Adriana was right behind her. She did a quick scan of the harbor. "Not again. I thought all this was behind us."

"It could be a maintenance problem," put in Dante.

"Yeah, well, I want to hear that from Cutter." Star dumped her gear on the dock and marched back up the boardwalk toward the institute. Her limp added an ill-fitting wobble to her almost military gait, but the others followed without comment. All too well they recognized the look of determination on the slight girl's face.

Only Kaz ventured a discouraging word. "You know, if the boat's being serviced, Cutter's probably grabbing some extra sleep."

"I don't care if he's in a coma." Star strode purposefully up to the small cabin and rapped on the door.

The team leader wasn't home, so they tried

the main lab area, where Cutter, Marina, and Reardon shared a small office.

"Tad?" The door was slightly ajar. Star pushed it open and turned on the light.

The room was deserted, the desk hidden under piles of maps and data printouts. The only other object on it was a drinking glass filled with what appeared to be water. In the bottom sat a small metal disk.

"Blackbeard's anchor," said Dante sarcastically. "Coming soon to a theater near you." But when he took a step toward it, he noticed a sharp chemical smell coming from the clear liquid. And when he peered into the glass itself, he saw that his artifact had *changed*.

The strong solution had eaten away the black coating. Now the piece gleamed shiny silver. Even more amazing, the thing was stamped with a design — a worn pattern, perhaps a coat of arms.

Dante was thunderstruck. This wasn't part of the anchor at all. It was a *coin!*

He turned to the others. "Guys — is that what I think it is?"

Kaz peered into the glass. "Silver, right?"

"Definitely," said Star. "It's pretty crude, but I guarantee that's some kind of money."

Adriana stepped forward, eyes alight. "Not just money. That's a piece of eight!"

Dante stared at her. "A piece of *what*?"

"Spanish money," she explained excitedly. "From hundreds of years ago! They have lots of it at the British Museum. In the seventeenth century, this silver piece was the most common coin in the world. Eight reals — a piece of eight."

Dante perked up. "Is it worth anything?"

"What do you think?" Star asked sarcastically. "It's a three-hundred-year-old coin."

"It's living history," Adriana amended. "This coin was made from silver pulled out of the mines of South America by descendants of the Incas. You can't put a price on that."

"Fifty bucks?" prompted Dante. "A hundred? More? Man, I almost chucked it overboard!"

Kaz's eyes narrowed. "But Reardon wouldn't let you. He practically leaped across the boat to get it off you."

"He knew," Star agreed bitterly. "And so did Cutter. That anchor wasn't any movie prop. We found something, and they're trying to steal it from us."

"We'll steal it back!" Dante decided.

"Brilliant," approved Kaz. "And what about the anchor down there? You can't just hide that in your underwear drawer. We have to get it on official record that this find is *ours*. Let's go to Gallagher."

When Dr. Geoffrey Gallagher arrived at his office promptly at eight that morning, he found the four teenage interns fast asleep on his doorstep.

"Good morning," he said loudly enough to startle them awake. He noticed with some annoyance that his cameraman was filming the four as they scrambled to their feet.

Kaz found his voice first. "Dr. Gallagher, we have a problem. We found this coin — "

"A Spanish piece of eight — " Adriana put in.

"An anchor too," added Dante. "I spotted it first. I thought it broke off the anchor, but it turned out to be a coin — "

Star cut him off. "But Chris Reardon stole it — "

"Well, we gave it away," Kaz took up the narrative, "but we didn't know it was a coin then. We thought it was part of a movie prop — "

It was the truth, but it was coming out in a scattered jumble of half sentences and interruptions as the groggy four struggled to give voice to their disorganized thoughts.

Gallagher grimaced in perplexity. At least, he noted, the cameraman had stopped filming these babbling youngsters. It was obvious that they had nothing to add to a scientific documentary.

He pulled himself up to his full six feet. "What you young interns don't seem to understand is that this institute is actually dozens of independent projects, headed by dozens of different scientists. I make it possible for these projects to function, but I have no authority within the projects themselves."

They looked blank, so he simplified his language. "Your boss is Mr. Cutter, not me. If you have anything to report, you report it to him."

"But that's the whole problem — " Kaz began.

At that moment, Dr. Gallagher noticed that the camera's red light was on again. He gave his most public smile. "You young people are the future of the oceanographic community. You are an asset to Poseidon."

And he and his cameraman entered the office, shutting the door in their faces.

Angrily, Kaz reached for the handle.

"Forget it," grumbled Star. "The guy's a dolt. All he cares about is looking good on video."

Discouraged, they straggled back to the dock to retrieve their diving gear.

Dante sat down on a weathered piling. "Some summer this turned out to be," he

THE DISCOVERY

growled. "I feel like getting on the next catamaran to Martinique and the first flight home. I should tell them to stick their internship. It's not like I'm pumping out thousands of great pictures."

"I'd leave too," Adriana said quietly, "but there's nowhere to go. My parents are in Saint-Tropez or Corfu or wherever the in place is to go this year."

Star folded her arms in front of her. "I'm not a quitter."

"None of us are quitters," Kaz retorted. "We're just talking, okay? Don't tell me you're not disappointed with how this internship's been going."

"I should be the most disappointed of anybody," grumbled Dante. "Technically, that's *my* coin they ripped off. I'm the one who found the anchor."

Star looked at him curiously. "There's another thing I've been wondering about. How did you see that? And you spotted the plane too. How come you see things other people don't?"

Dante looked away. "Maybe I have better eyesight than the rest of you guys."

"You've got terrible eyesight," Adriana put in. "You think the ocean is purple."

"No, I don't," the photographer defended himself. "That was a darkroom error."

"Or those scuba tanks," Kaz persisted. "You thought a red sticker was a green sticker."

"I got confused — " Dante managed weakly.

"Between red and green?"

When it finally came out, it cascaded from him in an avalanche. "Don't you get it? To me, red is green, and green is red, and they're both gray! I'm color-blind! The great photographic prodigy is living inside a black-and-white movie!"

The others were stunned.

Kaz was first to find his voice. "How does that help you pick out an anchor buried in coral?"

"You guys look at a reef and see a billion different colors. But to me, it's all a super-detailed charcoal sketch. I focus on shading and texture, rough and smooth, raised and flat. To you, that anchor was invisible. But to me, the shape under the coral was as obvious as a person under a blanket. I couldn't see it directly, but I knew it was there."

Adriana spoke up. "But why would you take color pictures if you can't see color? How could you ever hope to get it right?"

Dante shrugged unhappily. "I don't know. I guess I figured I could learn to fake it or something — connect certain shading to certain colors. But it's no use. Some handicap for a photographer, huh?"

THE DISCOVERY

"That's not a handicap," Star said sharply. "That's a *gift*. You see what other people can't. Poor you."

As they sat on the dock, feeling sorry for themselves, the sound of an approaching engine caught their attention. It was the *Hernando Cortés*, with Captain Vanover at the wheel. He tooted the horn twice and waved at them.

Adriana raised an eyebrow. "You know," she began thoughtfully, "Gallagher won't listen to us, but what about the captain? He always takes us seriously. Maybe we should tell *him* about the coin."

"And maybe he'll steal it from off Cutter so he can keep it for himself," Dante put in cynically. "Vanover's nice, but so is Marina. And she lies to our faces. Who knows who you can trust around here?"

"Agreed," said Kaz. "This is between us and Cutter. We'll keep it to ourselves."

The *Cortés* moved smoothly into its berth, and the hulking figure of Menasce Gérard leaped over the gunwale and tied up the vessel. He did not look in their direction, and they were not sorry.

Vanover called to them from the cockpit. "Morning, guys." He noticed their diving equipment piled up on the dock, noted the absence of the *Ponce de León*, and looked disgusted. "Not again."

Kaz nodded. "They stood us up. We were here by five. They were already gone."

"That tears it! Load up your gear and get on board. I'll take you to Cutter."

When English came back from the harbormaster's office, he was dismayed to find the four teens aboard, and Vanover preparing to cast off.

The dive guide was annoyed. "Captain, *pourquoi* — why these teenagers again?"

"Relax, English," the captain soothed. "We're just a taxi service. Cutter blew them off, and I'm not going to let him get away with it this time."

English looked suspicious. "No diving?"

"Not with us," Vanover promised. "We'll radio the office and get the *Ponce's* location. There and back, that's all."

# CHAPTER THIRTEEN

The *Cortés* was seven miles out of Côte Saint-Luc when they heard the blast.

"Thunder?" asked Dante. There wasn't a cloud in the sky.

Vanover and English exchanged a look, and the captain cranked up the boat's speed. On the open water, a boom like that usually meant an engine explosion.

English took over the helm, and Vanover rushed belowdecks to the radio. "This is the *Cortés* calling the *Ponce*. Bill, we just heard a whale of a bang. Are you and your people all right?"

There was no answer. The captain repeated the message. Still nothing.

English leaned on the throttle, and the research vessel surged ahead.

The four young divers braced against bulwarks as the chop tossed the racing boat. Their expressions were sober. Had something happened to Cutter and his crew?

At last, the *Ponce de León* appeared, a speck on the horizon.

Vanover studied it through binoculars. "Well,

it's in one piece," he reported. "And I don't see any fire."

English maintained top velocity. "And the people?"

"Nobody yet," said the captain.

They were four hundred yards off the other vessel's starboard bow when the radio crackled to life. Bill Hamilton, captain of the *Ponce de León*. "This is the *Ponce*. Braden, is that you?"

"What's going on, Bill? Is everybody okay over there? Why didn't you answer our hail?"

Tad Cutter's voice came on the line. "Things got kind of crazy around here. You wouldn't believe the engine backfire we just had."

"That was a backfire?" Vanover exclaimed. "It sounded like a bomb!"

"We're checking the engine now," Cutter went on. "But I'm pretty sure we're all right. Thanks anyway, Braden."

"Not so fast," said the captain. "I've got a surprise for you, Cutter. Four surprises, actually. You left a little something on the dock this morning."

"Oh, yeah, the kids. We got an early start today. I didn't have the heart to wake them."

"Yeah, well, they're awake now. And they're coming over."

"Not a good idea," Cutter warned. "My compressor's down, so they can't dive."

THE DISCOVERY

"No problem," Vanover assured him. "I've got a few charged scuba tanks. We'll come alongside, put them in the water from our platform, and they'll ride home with you when you're done."

There was a very long silence. Then, "Sounds like a plan."

By this time, the two boats were close enough together that Kaz could see Cutter, Marina, and Reardon on the deck of the *Ponce de León*. Reardon was in the stern, checking the fishing line that seemed to be his foremost concern aboard the research vessel. If Kaz had not been preoccupied with struggling into his tropical suit, he might have noticed that Reardon's hair was wet. The bearded man had been in the water, and recently.

The *Cortés* idled one hundred feet astern of the *Ponce de León*, and the four divers took to the waves.

"Remember" — Vanover's parting words — "you have every right to be here. You didn't pick Poseidon; Poseidon picked you. Don't be afraid to tell that to Cutter."

Floating on the surface, Star muttered, "There are plenty of things I intend to tell Cutter."

"What's the point?" sneered Kaz, treading water. "He lied to us before; he'll lie to us again."

"Hi, guys!" Marina beckoned from the deck

of the *Ponce de León*, beaming and waving. "Come aboard! We're moving off!"

"In your dreams," muttered Star. "I'm going down to see what they've been up to." She flipped her mask over her nose and mouth. "Who's with me?"

"Me," volunteered Adriana.

"But what are we supposed to tell Marina?" asked Dante.

"Tell her we didn't hear," Star said. "Her voice doesn't carry so good. I might never hear her again." She bit down on her regulator, deflated her B.C., and disappeared below the surface. Adriana followed.

The water was dark and murky — almost opaque. What had happened to the clear blue Caribbean?

As Star continued to descend, she kept one eye on the fluid kick of Adriana's flippers slightly above her. It would be easy to lose track of her partner in this silt.

Silt. That's what it was. But what force could stir up so much of the stuff? An engine backfire? Not likely.

Forty feet. Where was the bottom?

A curious barracuda peered at them through the pea soup and darted quickly away.

Sixty feet. How deep was it here? The visibility was so bad it was impossible to tell. There was almost no light now. Star felt isolated, disoriented. Only the direction of her bubbles told her which way was up.

Suddenly, her flippers scraped something unseen. The reef! She valved air into her B.C. to make herself neutrally buoyant, and grabbed Adriana before the girl hit bottom. The two squinted at each other in the gloom. Cutter and company may well have been up to something, but the girls weren't likely to find evidence of it with the ocean in this condition.

They swam along the seafloor, following the line of the reef from a few feet above it. And then, quite abruptly, the coral spine was no longer there.

Star gawked. This was no natural feature. It was almost like a crater in the reef — a circular zone maybe a dozen feet in diameter.

She finned ahead and peered down. The hole was filled with chunks of broken coral of all sizes, from boulders to gravel.

The realization almost took her breath away. Cutter's "backfire" — dynamite! An explosion big enough to break the coral and send clouds of muck and silt billowing in all directions!

Her initial reaction was outrage, followed quickly by bewilderment. Why would a bunch of oceanographers — scientists! — dynamite a living reef? This detonation meant the deaths of tens of millions of polyps, an environmental disaster that would take decades to regenerate. It wasn't just despicable; it was illegal! Coral was protected around the world.

But mostly, it flat-out made no sense. What was to be gained by such mindless destruction?

All at once, the shape came together, a familiar image concealed by the rubble that had been the reef. A dark form amid the lighter, multicolored debris: a ring, cross, and double hook — Dante's anchor. The marker buoy had been removed, but there was no question it was the same artifact.

*They're after our discovery!*

Star felt a pinch on the sleeve of her wet suit. Adriana, coming to the same conclusion.

Everything fell into place. No scientist would dynamite coral. But Tad Cutter was no scientist. It explained the magnetometer, and why Cutter kept his interns busy tagging caves when he took them out at all.

And it explained why he and his people had instantly recognized the Spanish coin for what it was.

Cutter, Marina, and Reardon may have worked for Poseidon, but they were treasure hunters!

THE DISCOVERY

A sweep of Adriana's flipper stirred up the pebbles of shattered coral below them. Star caught sight of something else in the swirl of movement — something smooth rather than jagged, and stark white. She reached into the debris and picked it up — a hilt or handle, perhaps eight inches long. It was carved and polished — and definitely man-made.

A meaningful look passed between the two scuba masks. Had Dante and his sharp eyes inadvertently led Cutter and his team to exactly what they were looking for?

# CHAPTER FOURTEEN

It was the first time Kaz had ever seen Marina Kappas angry.

"They had no right to dive! I ordered them aboard!"

"We couldn't hear you," Kaz called up to the *Ponce de León*.

"I want them *now*!" she exploded. "You go down there and get them. We have a schedule to keep."

Kaz dipped his face mask in the water and popped right up again. "Cloudy today. Let's go down the anchor line. It'll be easier to stay together."

He and Dante began to kick their way around the stern of the boat.

"Hurry!" Marina exclaimed peevishly. "We don't have all day!"

A sharp ringing buzz cut the air. It took Kaz a few seconds to identify the sound — Chris Reardon's unmanned fishing reel, playing out at light speed. Reardon's special bait, squid parts mixed with cold pizza, had hooked something big.

It happened before Kaz could even bite down

THE DISCOVERY

on his mouthpiece. The thousand-pound Mylar line wrapped around him, pinning his right arm to his body. He was dragged below the surface, keenly aware of a force many times his own strength.

Fighting off panic, he used his free hand to fumble his regulator into his mouth. He squinted through the murky water and got a bead on the dark shape at the end of the line. It was a huge grouper, four hundred pounds or more, hooked and fighting wildly. In the creature's mad struggle for its life, it was pulling Kaz straight for the bottom, its desperate gyrations tugging the Mylar ever tighter around the helpless diver.

*I'll never fight it,* he thought, the water rushing past him, the big fish just a blur. *My only hope is to cut myself free.*

His dive knife was in a scabbard on his right thigh. He could just reach it with his left hand. As his glove closed over the hilt, the big grouper abruptly changed direction. Kaz was yanked after it like a puppy on a leash. In agony, he felt the knife slip through his fingers. His last hope, swallowed by the churning sea.

*No,* he reminded himself. *There's still one chance. Something has to stop that grouper.*

And something did. At first, Kaz thought it was a submarine — it had to be, something so big. But then the huge torpedo-like shape opened a gaping mouth. And when it snapped shut, half the grouper was gone.

The Mylar line went slack, but Kaz made no attempt to shrug himself loose. He was paralyzed with a fear that dated back to his very early childhood. For he knew, as surely as if the big fish had been wearing a neon name tag, that this was the eighteen-foot monster tiger shark the locals called Clarence.

Still sinking slowly, he watched the enormous jaws savage the grouper in a cloud of blood and tattered flesh. The blood looked green at this depth. *The color red is filtered out by seawater. . . .* His scuba instructor's voice echoed in his head, repeating the words in an endless loop. Kaz was powerless to stop the lecture. His mind had shut down. Terror was in charge.

He had left home, family, hockey, everything that was familiar, to travel two thousand miles to the Caribbean — to die.

He barely noticed the moment that he bumped into the seabed. It was almost a comfort. A place to hide while the big shark circled overhead, snapping violently at the bloody scraps around it. To Clarence, blood in the water meant food. The predator already had no memory of the grouper it had just devoured. It never gave a

THE DISCOVERY

thought to its last meal; its next one was the main concern.

Kaz huddled on the sandy bottom, trembling with dread. No plan was taking shape in his mind, no strategy for survival. Even the inescapable fact that his air supply wouldn't last forever could not penetrate his overpowering compulsion to hide from nature's perfect killing machine.

Dante broke the surface and spit out his regulator, gasping in the fresh air.

"Shark!" he tried to yell. It came out a high-pitched wheeze.

He looked around desperately. He was closer to the *Ponce de León* than the *Cortés*, but he instinctively began thrashing toward Vanover's boat. When it was a matter of life and death, you went with the people you trusted.

Something bubbled up out of the water directly in his path, and he screamed in shock and fear.

Star pushed her mask aside. "Not so loud," she warned. "Listen, we found out what Cutter's — "

"*Clarence!*" Dante bellowed right in her face.

"Who?"

"The shark!"

Adriana hit the surface, and this time both Dante and Star recoiled.

"Where's Kaz?" Star asked.

"He's on the bottom and he's not moving!" Dante wailed. "I couldn't get to him! The shark — "

Star was already kicking for the *Cortés*, shouting, "*Captain!*"

Both Vanover and English were on the dive platform to pull the three out of the water.

"What's going on?" the captain demanded. "Where's Kaz?"

Chest heaving, Dante sobbed out a breathless explanation. "The shark didn't bite him," he babbled on, "but I think he's too scared to come up!"

English was already strapping on a scuba tank.

"It sounds like old Clarence," Vanover decided. "You'd better take the shark cage."

The dive guide scowled. "I am not a canary, me."

"The kid could be injured, even bleeding," Vanover argued. "You'll need the cage because of him."

English grunted his agreement.

They spent precious minutes unfolding the titanium cage and attaching it to the *Cortés's* electric winch. English climbed inside and pulled the door shut. The clang sounded like the closing of a prison cell.

Vanover swung the cage over the gunwale. "One tug for down, two for up, three for stop." He hit the winch, and the guide disappeared into the sea.

Menasce Gérard was as much at home in the ocean as on land. In his commercial work with the oil rigs, he often descended to depths of a thousand feet or more — thirty atmospheres of pressure. He feared nothing down here and viewed the cage as an inconvenience, almost an embarrassment. Why was he surprised that those American teenagers had brought him to this?

The poor visibility was unexpected. But, *alors*, this made perfect sense. No single shark could disturb so much silt. But whatever *had* done it might very well attract a large predator like Clarence.

He peered through the bars, looking for the shark and the young diver, but there was no sign of either. When the cage hit bottom, he gave a triple yank on the signal rope, the sign for stop. Then he opened the steel door and ventured out.

He had no weight belt, so maintaining depth was a struggle. He could do it, but not forever, and the effort would surely deplete his air supply quickly. He had to find Kaz right now.

The cloudy water made the search difficult. The minutes fell away. How many? Even a veteran diver couldn't judge. Too many.

He passed directly over the boy and almost missed him in the gloom. Kaz lay flat against the sand as if attempting to bury himself in it. At first, English mistook the blackness of the boy's wet suit for a large sea fan that had fallen over.

Kaz nearly jumped out of his skin when the dive guide grabbed him under the arms and pulled him upright.

Menasce Gérard did not waste words anywhere, especially underwater. "Come," he said into his regulator.

Kaz grabbed the big man's arm and did not let go. Now connected to a weighted diver, English was able to lead the way efficiently along the bottom toward the cage.

It might have been underwater radar, or even a sixth sense, but English knew instantly when the shark began pursuing them. A quick glance over his shoulder revealed nothing. But the predator was coming, concealed by the swirling silt. English could picture the eighteen-foot monster with the cold black eyes.

He spit out another word: "Faster." He still couldn't see Clarence, but he was aware of a dark shape behind them, and it was growing larger. They kicked like machines, propelling themselves toward the cage and safety.

Kaz did not risk a look back, but there was horror behind his mask, and the desperation of the hunted.

The shadows ahead began to resolve themselves into the straight lines and right angles of the cage. But the shark was visible too now, and gaining. Its sweeping tail powered the attack as it closed the gap, mouth slightly open, lethal arsenal at the ready.

With a burst of speed and strength that surprised even him, English finned for the cage and thrust Kaz inside. He scrambled in himself, and grabbed the door to swing it shut.

And then the great mouth exploded out of the shadowy deep with appalling violence.

# CHAPTER FIFTEEN

Jaws the size of a small desk clamped down on the bars of the still-open door in a shriek of bone on metal. The powerful head began to shake relentlessly. The cage tossed, its occupants rattling around like backgammon dice in a cup.

The tugging from the struggle must have reached the surface, because the cage began to rise. The shark remained clamped on the gate, stubbornly trying to bite through the two-inch titanium. English braced himself against the rear slats, kicking frantically with his flippers at the flat blunt snout.

Hanging on to the bars to avoid being catapulted out the opening, Kaz knew a panic he would not have imagined possible. He saw that the only thing keeping them alive at this point was the tiger shark's own stupidity. For if the beast had the sense to let go of the door, it would have been able to poke its head inside the cage and reach them.

The glowing dial of his Fathometer watch showed that the surface was still forty feet away.

When the cage rose above the waves, he wondered if he and English would still be in it.

Aboard the *Hernando Cortés*, Captain Vanover bent over his electric winch, which was groaning and vibrating.

Dante looked worried. "Does it do that all the time?"

"Shouldn't," the captain frowned. "Not to reel in a cage and two divers."

Star peered over the stern. "I can't see anything. No, wait — "

The others rushed to join her at the gunwale.

The ocean was boiling, churning up white water from the depths.

Adriana drew in a sharp breath. "Holy — "

The cage broke the surface, and with it rose the tiger shark, a writhing mass of muscle and fury as thick as a redwood. It was still doggedly clamped on to the bars of the door, being winched from the water up past its huge triangular dorsal fin. Now, hoisted out of the element that was its home, the beast went completely berserk, twisting and thrashing as its snapping jaws punished the tempered steel.

Vanover grabbed a long pole and began beating at the shark's enormous head. Star hefted another and jabbed sharply at the white underbelly. Dante bounced a soda can off a pectoral fin. Nothing seemed to have any effect.

Kaz remained cemented to the bars, still breathing out of his regulator, although he hung six feet above the water.

Bellowing French curses, English shrugged out of his scuba harness, reared back with the compressed air tank, and brought it down full force on the shark's obsidian eye. The force of the blow caused the monster to open its vice-grip jaws. It fell back into the sea with a mammoth splash that rocked the boat and sent a torrent of water over the four spectators on deck. It took two menacing laps of the research vessel, its dorsal fin slicing the waves. Then it finally disappeared.

The captain swung the cage over the gunwale and lowered it to the deck.

English hauled Kaz out and yanked the regulator from his mouth. "You are all right, boy? You are in one piece?"

Kaz nodded. His knees felt wobbly, but he was determined not to collapse. "You — you saved my life!"

The dive guide's response was an elaborate shrug that was very French. "But next time," he added pointedly, "you like excitement, you ride the roller coaster, oui?"

The radio burst to life in the navigation room be-

THE DISCOVERY

lowdecks. Tad Cutter's voice: "What's going on over there? Was that a whale? Is everybody okay?"

Rolling his eyes, Vanover dragged himself down the companionway. "Everybody's fine, Cutter," he said shortly. "One of your interns almost got eaten. Nothing for you to concern yourself about." He severed the connection.

"Hey — " Adriana pointed to the cage. There, pressed into a corner, its skin matching the steel-gray of the bars, cowered a small octopus. "Mr. English — here's the octopus we owe you."

The big guide reached in through the bars, drew out the terrified creature, and spoke directly to it. "You are lucky I'm in a good mood." And he tossed it back into the sea.

It was the only time the four interns had ever seen him smile.

It was decided that the teen divers would ride back to Côte Saint-Luc harbor on the *Hernando Cortés* instead of switching to the *Ponce de León.*

"The last thing you kids need is face time with Cutter and his crew," said Vanover grimly.

Kaz nodded his agreement. "Reardon's probably still sore about losing that grouper. I'll bet he has no idea that his stupid fishing line almost turned me into the catch of the day."

Vanover regarded him seriously. "I've seen too many divers pretend it never happened by making little jokes like that. What you went through — that's as scary as it gets. Here's what you have to decide: Was it a knockout punch? Some guys can shrug off an experience like that and strap on fins the very next morning; others never put a toe in the water again. Your job, Kaz, is to figure out which one you're going to be." He headed up the companionway, leaving them alone in the galley.

"He's right, you know," said Dante. "How are you ever going to be able to dive after today? I don't know if *I* can, and it didn't even happen to me."

"That's just plain dumb," scoffed Star. "Today was a freak accident. Even if you do run into a big shark like that, chances are he'll look right through you and keep on swimming. To quit diving because of this would be like refusing to drive a car because you almost got into an accident once."

"Yeah, but Clarence is still out there somewhere," Dante reminded her.

She shrugged. "The captain says he's been around for years. People hardly ever see him, and even when they do, it's no big deal. Kaz just happened to be there when he was feeding and there was blood in the water."

THE DISCOVERY

"Even so — " Dante began.

"I'm still diving," Kaz interrupted suddenly.

Adriana was wary. "You probably shouldn't make up your mind right away."

"I'm still diving," he repeated. The decision had come to him suddenly, unexpectedly. It was something Star said — "a freak accident." How had the doctors described Drew Christiansen's catastrophic injury? *A freak accident. A one in a million shot.* To consider what happened as anything more than pure wild chance was the equivalent of blaming Drew's paralysis on Kaz.

There was no more extra danger of shark attack in these waters than there was likelihood that a body check from Bobby Kaczinski would put another boy in a wheelchair.

The more he thought about it, the more it made sense to him. "Don't worry about me. I'll be fine."

"You're tough, rink rat," Star said with grudging approval.

"Now, listen. You're not going to believe this, but Clarence was not the top news story today."

"That's because it wasn't *your* head he was practically chewing on," Kaz retorted.

"Seriously." Star persisted. "First off, all this didn't happen at some random spot on the reef. We were directly above the anchor back there."

"We saw it," added Adriana. "The whole thing."

"That's impossible!" Dante exclaimed. "It's buried under tons of coral."

"Not anymore." Star informed him, "because Cutter blasted the reef to smithereens. That's why the ocean was cloudy — from the dynamite."

Kaz shook his head. "Scientists don't destroy coral. They *love* coral. Every day is like take-a-polyp-to-lunch day."

"That's exactly why we've been having so much trouble trying to figure this thing out," Star told him. "Why would a scientist steal our coin? Why would a scientist waste our time tagging caves? The answer is: Cutter, Marina, and Reardon aren't scientists. They're treasure hunters."

"Treasure hunters!" Kaz exclaimed. "It all adds up. They sure aren't oceanographers. Did you catch what Cutter said over the radio? 'Was that a whale?'"

Dante was skeptical. "But if treasure's what they're really after, why would they bring in four kids on summer internships? Wouldn't we just be in the way?"

"I think we're kind of a smoke screen," Adriana put in. "Remember, Cutter's people don't work at Poseidon, Saint-Luc. They're from the head office in California. It's the perfect cover —

they come here and nose around the Hidden Shoals, acting like it's for our benefit."

"And they keep us out of their hair," Star added, "by sending us after caves nobody cares about."

Kaz nodded slowly. "And they picked *us* because we wouldn't be good enough to interfere with their discovery."

"If they make a discovery," Dante added.

"They already did," said Adriana. "Or at least, you did."

Wordlessly, Star reached into the pocket of her cargo shorts and drew out the artifact she had pulled from the wreckage of the coral — the carved white handle. "The anchor, the silver coin, and now this, all in the same spot. Are you going to tell me there isn't a wreck down there?"

The two boys' eyes widened as they stared at the gleaming whalebone hilt. A pockmark of coral growth obscured its main decoration — a large dark stone inset in the delicate pattern. Directly above it were etched the initials JB. The old English script was as sharp as if it had been carved only yesterday.

JB. Was that some poor shipwrecked sailor, dead for hundreds of years?

*28 August 1665*

*The cruel crack of Captain James Blade's whip was familiar now. The percussive snap of oiled leather slicing into lacerated skin, the agonized howls of the unfortunate seaman, the evil green flash of the huge emerald embedded in the handle of the captain's favorite implement of torture.*

*Today's victim was Clark, the bosun's mate. But in the man's piteous complaint, young Samuel Higgins could hear the cries of Evans the sail maker, the only person on this earth who had ever befriended an orphaned cabin boy. Old Evans, now long dead, like so many others on this terrible crossing.*

*The captain was rearing back for another brutal lash when the shout was heard from the rigging.*

*"Land, ho!"*

*And, mercifully, the flogging was over. The celebration was unlike anything Samuel had ever seen — a mad scramble for the gunwales, all eyes straining to drink in the narrow green-brown ribbon barely visible on the horizon. After four long months at sea, suffering harsh treatment and privations, watching*

**THE DISCOVERY**

more than half of their numbers succumb to malnutrition, fever, and scurvy, the weary crew of the Griffin had reached the New World. On a boat with a stench fouler than the filthiest sewer in Liverpool, the tattered seamen danced and cheered like children on May Day.

The captain peered through his long spyglass and emitted a bellow of triumph. "Portobelo, by God! Just a few miles down the coast!" There was a roar of approval from the assembled throng.

York reached out a dirty hand and ruffled Samuel's unruly hair. "To traverse the great sea and strike land a cannon shot from your destination! Aye, boy, that's like firing a musket ball half a league straight through a keyhole! You're a lucky one, Samuel Higgins. Well named, you are."

Praise from the ghoulish barber always made Samuel's skin crawl. But the feeling quickly dissipated, swept up in the joy of their arrival. Land! The endless voyage was finally over.

He ran his fingers through the few copper coins in his breeches — meager wages for these long months at sea, yet still more money than he had ever held in his thirteen years. "Clean water," he said aloud. "That's what I'll ask for first. And bread — fresh baked, with no maggots in it."

"Are you feebleminded, boy?" York cried in disbelief. "That little town there is the western terminus of the Spanish treasure fleet, the richest place in all Creation. We're not here to visit, Lucky. We're here to plunder their treasure and burn their city to the ground!"

THE DISCOVERY

# DIVE

*For Spencer and Harrison Newman*

*29 August 1665*

*The sword was the smallest that could be found aboard the* Griffin, *yet thirteen-year-old Samuel Higgins could barely lift it with both hands.*

*"But what am I to do with this, sir?" the cabin boy asked in alarm.*

*York, the ship's barber and surgeon, regarded him sternly. "We're going into battle, Lucky. You won't be picking your teeth with it."*

*Samuel was aghast. "Me? I'm to join the fight?"*

*The word had spread like wildfire through the English privateer fleet that the invasion of Portobelo was at hand. This was what they had crossed the perilous Atlantic for, losing fully a third of their number to scurvy, fever, and the malevolent sea. At the end of this day lay riches beyond their wildest dreams.*

*In a secluded inlet, forty miles north of the treasure city, the nine remaining privateer ships lay at anchor. Each vessel was manned by a skeleton crew. The majority of the English seamen were loaded onto a flotilla of twenty-four canoes. These had been car-*

THE DEEP

ried all the way from Liverpool for exactly this purpose — a sneak attack on Portobelo.

Hugging the coast, the canoes were paddled south, rushed along by the fast-moving current. Each narrow craft was about forty feet long and equipped with a small sail. The assault force totaled about five hundred in number. They were led by the captain of the Griffin, the dreaded corsair James Blade.

"Row, you scurvy scum!" the captain roared. "We reach Portobelo before dawn, or your bodies will lie at the bottom of the bay!"

Struggling with a heavy oar, Samuel knew this was not an empty threat. Over the course of their terrible journey, he had seen Blade strike, flog, and even hang his crew. And the cruel captain had murdered Evans, the sail maker, Samuel's only friend aboard the barque. The memory of that good man's terrible end still caused the boy to well up with suppressed anger.

By the time they had covered the forty-mile distance, Samuel's hands were raw and bleeding. He wasn't sure he would be able to clutch his sword, much less defend himself with it.

Blade indicated a pattern of flickering lights in the moonless blackness ahead. "The torches of Santiago Castle! Muffle the oars! We'll take those fancy dons by surprise!"

No sooner had the words passed his lips than giant signal fires flared, illuminating the stone fortress before them. There was a flash, followed by a huge explosion. A split second later, a cannonball sizzled over their heads, close enough for Samuel to feel its hot wind. It struck the water behind them, sending up a steaming geyser.

"To the beach!" howled Blade, standing in the bow, a cutlass in one hand and his bone-handled snake whip in the other. "If you want to line your pockets with Spanish gold, first stain your swords with Spanish blood!"

The battle had begun.

# CHAPTER ONE

Perhaps one diver in a thousand would have noticed the faint glimmer on the ocean floor. Dante Lewis spotted it immediately.

*Silver!*

Heart racing, he deflated his buoyancy compensator (or B.C.) vest and began to descend toward it, passing towering coral formations and clouds of sea life.

The Hidden Shoals off the Caribbean island of Saint-Luc boasted some of the most spectacular colors on the face of the earth — the brilliant turquoise of a parrot fish, the electric magenta of red algae, the neon yellow of a snapper's tail, the shimmering violet of a school of Creole wrasses.

Dante perceived none of it.

That wasn't exactly true. He could see everything — and far sharper than the average person. But only in black and white and shades of gray.

The promising thirteen-year-old photographer was *color-blind*. That was why he had accepted the diving internship at Poseidon Oceanographic

DIVE

Institute. Not to *learn* color — his brain wasn't wired for that. But maybe he could learn to detect it, figure it out from the clues he *could* see — light, dark, and shading.

He checked the Fathometer on his dive watch to see how deep he'd gone. Forty feet.

So far, the plan was a dismal failure. Descending in full scuba gear, Dante swung around his Nikonos underwater camera to snap a picture of a flamingo tongue — a rare spotted snail, supposedly orange on peach. To Dante, it appeared gray on gray.

*Everything is gray on gray,* he reminded himself glumly. *And it always will be.*

Sixty feet. He looked down. The glint of silver was still far below.

Dante felt he was stuck on a backward island in the middle of nowhere for the whole summer. There was nothing to do but dive, an activity that he wasn't much good at, and liked even less. He had almost gotten himself killed at least once already.

And for what? Gray fish, gray plants, gray coral.

But there was money in these waters. From centuries of sunken ships. Dante and his companions had already found an antique Spanish piece of eight. His brow clouded. The three-hundred-year-old coin had been stolen from them by their supervisor, Tad Cutter. The interns would not make the mistake of trusting the slick Californian again.

Eighty feet. It was deeper than he had ever been, but he barely gave it a second thought. He was completely focused on reaching the source of the glimmer.

And then his flippers made contact with the soft sandy bottom. He peered down at the object that had drawn him to the depths.

A 7UP can.

His disappointment surged like the clouds of bubbles that rose from his breathing apparatus.

*Stupid,* he berated himself. It was crazy to believe that every glint in the ocean was some kind of lost treasure. *But it would have been sweet to snag a pile of silver and rub it in Cutter's face!* The institute man had done a lot more than swipe one little coin. He and his team had taken over the wreck site it had come from.

*They're probably over there right now, digging up our discovery!*

It was a huge rip-off, no question about it. Yet the whole business didn't seem to bother Dante right then. Instead he felt pretty good. A dull, pleasant fatigue, like a runner's high.

Funny — he was normally pretty nervous on a

dive. Underwater seemed like a place that people simply weren't meant to be. But now he was starting to feel confident. Fearless, even.

A curious lionfish ventured close — a mass of spines and fins and stripes.

*It's an underwater porcupine in designer clothes!*

In some remote corner of his mind, it occurred to Dante that he should take a picture. But he made no move for the Nikonos tethered to his arm. Instead, he reached out to touch an elaborately striped fin.

The attack came from above, knocking him backward. His dive partner, fourteen-year-old Star Ling, grabbed him linebacker-style around the waist, driving him away from his quarry. She shook a scolding finger in his face, then whipped out a dive slate and scribbled: POISON!

Dante squinted at the message, his vision darkening at the edges. He could see all the letters, but for the life of him, he couldn't put them together to read the word. What the young photographer didn't realize was that he was experiencing nitrogen narcosis — the rapture of the deep. Under deep-water pressure, the nitrogen in air dissolves in the bloodstream, producing an effect similar to drunkenness. In diving lingo, he was "narced."

All Dante registered was that he was having a fine time, and here was Star, ruining it. The lionfish had gotten away, leaving Dante sweating from his efforts.

*Who needs a rubber suit to dive in boiling water?*

Before Star's horrified eyes, Dante unzipped his lightweight tropical skin suit and began to peel off the thin material. In his narced state, he had forgotten that the wet suit was not for warmth; it was for protection from the sting of coral and other venomous sea life.

She grabbed him and held on. He fought back, the upper half of the wet suit flapping from his waist.

That was when she saw the shark.

# CHAPTER TWO

It was a bull shark, seven or eight feet long, although it looked even bigger through the lens of the water. It was not Clarence — the teen divers had already had a run-in with the eighteen-foot tiger shark of local legend. But Star was an expert diver, and she knew bulls could be aggressive. Especially if this one mistook their struggling for the thrashing of a wounded fish.

"Calm down!" she barked into her regulator, tasting salt water.

Dante was too impaired to heed the warning. His eyes were barely open, mere slits behind his mask.

The predator was only a few feet away, close enough for Star to see the peculiar remora fish clamped to its underside, attaching itself to feed on scraps of prey.

Star was torn. Should she swim away? But what about her partner? She was there for him, and he for her.

Onto the scene burst a blur of black rubber, a six-foot-five body formed by rigid discipline into the shape of a torpedo. It was Menasce Gérard, a hulking native dive guide with the unlikely nick-name English. Propelled by the powerful kicks of his flippers, he swam into the shark's path. In a single motion, he pulled the dangling camera off Dante's arm, wheeled around, and brought it down with all his might on the bull's flat snout.

The shark reared up, shocked. Clearly, a bonk on the nose was the last thing it had ex-pected. It turned abruptly and swam off, roiling the water. Out of the storm appeared a smaller fish — a foot long, with a round suction cup on its back. It was the remora, dislodged from its host during the commotion. It darted back and forth, searching in vain for the bull's pale under-belly. Finding nothing, it panicked and clamped onto Dante's bare chest.

That got Dante's attention. He cried out in shock, blowing a cloud of bubbles into English's face. He tried to pluck the remora from his skin, but the hold was too strong. Even the guide couldn't seem to yank the fish free.

English gave the signal to surface, but Dante was focused on his new tenant. "Get off me! Get off me!" He swallowed water, putting himself in a choking frenzy.

The guide took hold of Dante from behind, crossing his arms in an iron grip. Unable to reach his own B.C., he shot air into Dante's until they both began to rise. Star joined the shaky ascent.

They surfaced about twenty yards from the R/V *Hernando Cortés*, their dive boat. Symptoms of narcosis disappear as a diver rises, so Dante was no longer dazed. Now he was hysterical. "Pull it off! Pull it off!"

Doubting the boy could even swim in his frantic state, English towed him Red Cross–style to the *Cortés*. The other two teenage interns, Bobby Kaczinski and Adriana Ballantyne, hauled him onto the dive platform.

Adriana gawked at the fish fastened onto Dante. "What's *that*?"

English scrambled up beside them. "Remora!" he exclaimed, trying to work his hands under the creature's suction cup.

"You're hurting me!" cried Dante.

Star was last out of the water. She kicked off her flippers and approached Dante. She walked with a limp — the result of a mild case of cerebral palsy — although underwater the condition disappeared. Hefting her dripping air tank, she began smacking the remora with the flat bottom. Dante staggered backward, flopping down on the deck. "What are you trying to do, kill me?" he gasped.

"Silence, you silly child!" ordered English in his French Caribbean accent. This was not his first run-in with the four teens, and he was not in the mood to be understanding. "We do nothing, you complain! We do something, you complain louder!"

"But what if it's stuck on forever?"

"What's all the commotion?" Captain Braden Vanover peered down from the flying bridge. Spying the fish attached to Dante's chest, he exclaimed, "Oh, jeez!" and disappeared below.

He returned a moment later, carrying a bottle of Jamaican rum and a hypodermic syringe. He dipped the needle in the liquor, drew up some dark brown liquid, and injected it into the remora, just behind the gill slits.

The gray fish dropped to the deck, flipping wildly on the olive-painted planks. English expertly kicked it back into the sea.

Then he wheeled his furious attention on Dante. "You were maybe trying out for the *Sports Illustrated* swimsuit issue, monsieur? Why do you take off the wet suit at eighty feet?"

"He was narced," supplied Star.

"It wasn't my fault," Dante defended himself. "How was I supposed to know that crazy fish was going to stick on? It could happen to anybody."

"If it was not you, then it would not happen!" the guide seethed. "All of you — you attract the troubles like the giant magnet!" He turned to face Vanover. "I am finished with these American teenagers. I am not MTV, me! The next time they dive with you, you will find another guide!" He peeled off his dripping wet suit and stormed below.

"I'm Canadian," Kaz called after him. If English had heard, the big man gave no sign.

The four interns exchanged agonized looks. Their internship was a sham — a smokescreen for Tad Cutter's treasure hunting. Scuba trips with Captain Vanover and English were all that kept this summer from being a total bust. Now they were gone too.

"Well," the captain said slowly. "You've heard the bad news. Anybody ready for the good news?"

"We could sure use some," said Adriana.

"The office just radioed in. The PUSH team wrapped up their research a few days early. The next project doesn't start down there for another week. The station is yours if you want it."

# CHAPTER THREE

The Poseidon Underwater Self-contained Habitat, or PUSH, was a subsea lab built right onto the Hidden Shoals proper, sixty-five feet beneath the waves. There, scientists called aquanauts could live and work for days at a time, spending almost every waking minute diving.

For Star, it was a dream come true. "The only problem with scuba is it's over too fast. But on PUSH, when your air runs low, you just swim to the station, switch tanks, and swim back out again. And there's no decompressing because you don't have to return to surface pressure. Home is right there on the reef."

"Home is an underwater sardine can," Dante said sourly.

"Even when you're not diving, it's still awesome," Star went on. "Because you're under sixty-five feet of water. Look out the window, and you're right in the thick of things."

"We'll be in the thick of things, all right," grumbled Dante. "Every time you crook your finger, you'll be picking somebody else's nose."

The four were in the cabin the two girls

DIVE

shared, watching Adriana pack for their undersea sojourn. The girl gazed bleakly from the stacks of color-coordinated designer outfits to the tiny watertight bag about the size of a kindergartner's knapsack. Anything that wouldn't fit had to be left on dry land.

"This is impossible," she complained. "If I take the rust shorts, then I'm stuck with the matching sweatshirt. And it's so puffy, it fills the whole bag!"

"Rust?" repeated Dante. "Is that supposed to be a color?"

Adriana nodded. "It's between taupe and burnt sienna."

"Well, thanks for clearing that up," Dante said sarcastically. "Just pack any old thing. We're going to be so sick of looking at one another that you could wear a rabbit suit and nobody would notice."

"And bring your toothbrush," added Star. "We'll be breathing recycled air, but I doubt the $CO_2$ scrubbers can do anything about bad breath."

It was important not to forget anything. Once they had been at the station for half a day or so, a return to the surface meant seventeen hours in a decompression chamber.

As soon as their bags were packed, the four

took advantage of their last chance to e-mail family and friends from Poseidon's computer lab. PUSH had computers linked by wireless telemetry to the outside world. But the connection was expensive, so there were strict rules against using it for personal correspondence.

Kaz replied to messages from his parents and Steven Allagash, his sports agent. Kaz was a hot prospect to make it as a professional hockey player. They called him the most promising young defenseman to come out of the Toronto area in twenty years.

That was *before*.

He sent just one more e-mail, to a boy named Drew Christiansen. The two were not friends. In fact, Kaz couldn't understand why Drew didn't consider him Public Enemy Number One after what had happened.

The Ontario Minor Hockey Association finals, game six. Kaz could still feel the contact of the body check as he drove Drew away from the net. It was a clean hit — even Drew agreed on that. A freak accident, according to the doctors. Trauma to the spinal column.

In that terrible instant, Drew Christiansen and Bobby Kaczinski were both out of hockey for good.

Drew had no choice in the matter. He would never walk again. And Kaz wanted nothing to do with a sport that could turn him into an instrument of destruction. That was why he had applied for the Poseidon internship. Diving in the Caribbean, it had seemed at the time, was the opposite of hockey in Canada.

He felt more than a little ridiculous e-mailing "How I Spent My Summer Vacation" to this stranger whose life he'd ruined.

*But I'm not going to pretend it didn't happen* —

"Hey, guys," called Adriana excitedly from another workstation. "I've got an answer from my uncle!"

Adriana's uncle Alfred Ballantyne was an antiquities expert. She had e-mailed him a photograph of an artifact Star had brought up from the shipwreck site — an elaborately carved whalebone hilt.

Adriana dropped her voice to a whisper as the others gathered around. They hadn't told anyone else about the artifact. If word of their find got back to Tad Cutter, they had no question that the treasure hunter would try to take it from them, just as he'd stolen their piece of eight, the Spanish silver coin. There was no way to be sure who they could trust at the institute. The only safe course was to trust no one.

Adriana pointed to the body of the message. "Right here."

**. . . I don't think your artifact is the hilt of a sword or dagger, since there is no evidence of a guard or cross-piece. My best guess is that it is the handle of a walking stick, or perhaps even a whip (popular on ocean voyages for keeping both the crew and the rats in line).**

**I can't identify the stone because of the coral encrusting it, but I'm sure you noticed the letters JB carved just below there. These are the initials perhaps of the artisan, but more likely the owner. Above you'll see a design depicting a sprig of thistles. You'll recognize this as the symbol of the Stuarts, British monarchs who ruled in the seventeenth and early eighteenth centuries. Therefore, the item must have been crafted in England at that time. . . .**

"Whoa," breathed Kaz. "That thing is one heavy-duty museum piece."

"And to think I've got it stashed in my under-wear drawer," added Star.

"Yeah, but he doesn't tell us how much it's *worth*," put in Dante, who tended to view these artifacts in terms of dollars and cents. "Scroll down. Let's see what else he says."

"Oh, that's about the carving in English's window," Adriana told him. "I sent Uncle Alfie a picture of that too."

The native dive guide's cottage window displayed a large fragment of what once had been a huge carving of an eagle. It was apparently some kind of family heirloom. English refused to talk about it.

Adriana scrolled down.

. . . **Your other specimen presents somewhat more of a puzzle. One possible explanation for its European origin is that it may have broken off a ship. Old wooden vessels were festooned with elaborate sculptures, which their superstitious makers believed would ward off bad luck, evil spirits, hurricanes, fever, and pirates. The eagle may be of English style, so perhaps that's why your friend is called English. . . .**

"Friend," snorted Kaz. "With friends like him, who needs Ming the Merciless?"

"Hi, team." Marina Kappas was working her way between the rows of computer desks toward them.

Instantly, Adriana closed her e-mail program. Marina was on Tad Cutter's crew of treasure hunters. On the surface, she was affable, outgoing, and seemed genuinely concerned about the teens' well-being. She was also flat-out gorgeous, which scored a lot of points with Kaz and Dante. It had far less effect on the girls. And all four had to bear in mind that, beautiful or not, friendly or not, as Cutter's colleague, she was on the other team.

"I hear they've stolen you away for a few days at PUSH," Marina went on. "We'll miss you guys."

"I can tell," Star said sarcastically. "There's something about getting up at four in the morning to take off without us that shows you really care."

Cutter and company had been avoiding their interns since day one.

Marina shrugged. "Workaholics. Tad and Chris are crazy when they're on a project. Hey, you're going to love PUSH. Not much elbow room, but really fascinating."

The four exchanged a meaningful glance. Marina Kappas didn't care if they were fascinated or not. She just wanted them down on the station, out of the way, leaving her team free to continue the search for sunken treasure — with no prying eyes to watch them.

# CHAPTER FOUR

The bow of the R/V *Francisco Pizarro* cleaved the light chop of an otherwise flawless Caribbean. It was the interns' first ride with Captain Janet Torrington, whose job it was to deliver them to PUSH for a five-day stay.

The captain was telling them about Dr. Igor Ocasek, the scientist who would be sharing the small station with them.

"The thing about Iggy is that he's a genius, which means half the time he seems as dumb as a box of rocks. When his mind is on a problem, you can be three inches in front of his nose, screaming your lungs out, and he has no idea you're even there."

"What is he studying?" asked Adriana.

Torrington shrugged. "His specialty is mollusks, but right now I'd have to say he's a Doctor of Tinkering."

"Tinkering?" Kaz echoed.

"You know, fiddling with stuff. Retooling, refitting, rewiring. He can improve anything. Iggy designed a better *paper clip* last year, if you can believe it. Superior ergonomics, whatever that is. It's up in Washington now, patent pending."

As they approached the Hidden Shoals, Torrington slowed to a crawl, and the *Pizarro* began to pick her way gingerly through a minefield of marker buoys. These indicated coral heads towering so close to the surface that they presented a hazard to shipping. It was no joke. A living reef concealed a limestone core strong enough to rip open the hull of a boat.

Kaz pointed at the outline of another vessel undulating in the heat shimmer on the horizon. "Isn't that the *Ponce de León*?" Tad Cutter's boat.

Dante frowned at the silhouette. "I thought he was spending all his time over the wreck site."

"That *is* the wreck site!" Star exclaimed. "I wonder how far away we'll be."

As if on cue, Captain Torrington cut power as the *Pizarro* bumped up alongside the PUSH life-support buoy. She sprang to the gunwale and tied on.

"Last stop, folks. Your home away from home."

The four interns began the process of pulling on their lightweight wet suits.

"This couldn't have worked out better," Star said in a low voice. "It's our perfect chance to check out the wreck site on our own."

THE DEEP

Dante worked the tight arm strap of his Nikonos past his elbow. "I don't know, Star. That looks like a half-mile swim from here. Maybe you can make it, but we can't — not there and back again."

Star shrugged into her compressed air tank. "Then I'll go myself."

Adriana stared at her. "Alone?" The buddy system was practically carved in stone for divers.

"Cutter and his crew could be pulling millions of dollars' worth of stuff out of that wreck, and we'd never know the difference," Star argued. "This is the only way we'll find out for sure." She flipped down her mask. "Let's go."

With their watertight bags tethered to their B.C. vests, the four climbed down to the dive platform, stepped into their flippers, and jumped down to the waves.

Captain Torrington waved. "See you next week. Tell Iggy I said hi."

Still on the surface, Star switched her underwater watch to compass mode and took a careful reading of the *Ponce de León*. Just past east-northeast.

They valved air from their vests and descended, slipping easily through the chop. The instant Star was underwater, she felt her disability vanish. Down here, there was no weakness on the left side — or any side. This was the medium that was meant for Star Ling. She was comfortable; she was graceful; she was home.

It wasn't a recreational dive. In fact, all they were supposed to do was follow the buoy's umbilical lines directly down to PUSH.

Star passed through a shimmering cloud of blue-and-white-striped grunts. She was already well ahead of the others. She was used to waiting for them. Kaz, Dante, and Adriana were inexperienced divers. It had baffled the interns at first — why pick a bunch of beginners for a prestigious internship? Now they understood perfectly. Tad Cutter had been betting that novices wouldn't discover his secret plans. He'd also been convinced that Star's disability would keep her from getting in his way.

*Better luck next time, Tad, old pal.*

As she passed a hovering sea horse, the sunlight from above provided an X ray of its pale brown translucent body. *She's pregnant!* thought Star, and then quickly corrected herself. *He's pregnant.* In a rare reversal of nature, *male* sea horses carried the young.

PUSH looked like a giant car engine on the ocean floor. At the center was the station's main living space — a steel tube ten feet wide and fifty feet long. Star floated beside an underwater rack of compressed air tanks as the others joined her.

Since the station's underbelly was mirrored, the entrance seemed like a square hole in the middle of the ocean, a magical portal to dry land sixty-five feet beneath the waves. The feeling of hoisting herself through the opening into the pressurized air was unreal.

A short metal ladder led up to the wet porch. There, the interns shrugged out of their gear.

"Check it out!" Star pointed to a rack of six diver propulsion vehicles, or DPVs. The scooters looked a lot like bombs. In reality, their "tails" were protective housing for the propellers that moved them through the water. "Transportation to the wreck site."

The four unpacked their watertight luggage — nothing wet was allowed past the hatchway that led to PUSH's living area. They each carried an armload of belongings as they passed barefoot through the pressure hatch into the entry lock.

A rapid series of pops, like machine-gun fire, resounded in the confined space. Kaz, who led the way, was pelted by a barrage of hot, stinging projectiles.

He gawked. Popcorn littered the dark industrial carpet. At the center of the chamber knelt a young man with long flyaway hair. He held a blowtorch under an enormous conch shell that was overflowing with popped kernels.

Spying them, he quickly shut off the blowtorch. "Sorry about that. Welcome to PUSH. I'm Iggy Ocasek." Unable to shake hands in greeting, he held out the shell. "Hungry?"

"No thanks." Kaz performed the introductions. "Kaz, Star, Adriana, Dante." The latter two were on their hands and knees gathering up clothing dropped during the snack attack.

"This isn't what it looks like," Dr. Ocasek explained, setting shell and torch on a stainless steel counter. "Poseidon is about to authorize a major study of how mollusk shells conduct heat at depth. I figured, I've got mollusks, I've got heat, I've got depth, I've got — "

"Popcorn?" finished Adriana.

"You learn to improvise down here," the scientist admitted. "And you've got to admit that the shell conducted heat beautifully."

While Dr. Ocasek vacuumed up the popcorn with a handheld portable vacuum, the four interns explored their surroundings. The habitat was laid out like the cabin of a commuter jet. A narrow hallway stretched from end to end, flanked by looming steel walls of switches, dials, and readouts. Bare bulbs provided harsh, unyielding light. There were occasional comforts of home — a microscopic bathroom ringed by a flimsy privacy curtain, a small refrigerator/ freezer, a microwave, a built-in dining booth to seat six.

"Six *hobbits*," put in Dante.

At the far end of the station, bunks were stacked three high on either side of the corridor. It wasn't difficult to spot Dr. Ocasek's berth on the bottom left. It was unmade, with tools, a roll of electrician's tape, bits of cable, and a soldering gun scattered around the sheets. Beside it, the metal wall plate was gone. Through the opening, an electric blanket had been hardwired into the guts of the habitat.

"I guess it gets chilly at night," Star observed dryly.

"That guy's nuts," said Dante with conviction. "If he short-circuits the station, no more air pumps, and we all suffocate."

"He's just eccentric, that's all," soothed Kaz.

"Maybe so, but I'm sleeping with my scuba tank."

Star laughed. "Suit yourself. Come on, let's go find a shipwreck."

# CHAPTER FIVE

The double-tank setup was awkward and heavy, and Adriana struggled to get used to its bulk. The extra air supply made sense, though. Since they didn't have to worry about decompressing back to the surface, PUSH aquanauts could dive for hours at a time.

As Dr. Ocasek swam around to help get the others outfitted with extra air cylinders from the underwater rack, a four-foot moray eel followed him like an adoring puppy. Every now and then, the scientist would reach into his dive pouch and toss the creature a lump of food.

"Peanut butter sandwich," he explained into his regulator.

Peanut butter was the staple on the station. Adriana had checked the tiny pantry and found fourteen jars of the stuff, and precious little else.

*That's how you know when it's time to leave PUSH,* she thought to herself. *When your tongue is permanently stuck to the roof of your mouth.*

At last, all was ready, and the four yanked the trigger handles of their DPVs. The propellers whirred, pulling them forward. As Adriana glided silkily through the water, her awkwardness fell away. It wasn't the speed that astonished her. In fact, she was only traveling a few miles per hour. No, what amazed Adriana was the total ease with which she moved over the coral and sponge formations of the reef. Diving had never been second nature for her, like it was for Star.

Hanging on to the handles of the scooter, she fell into line behind Star, who navigated by the compass on her dive watch. A pair of eagle rays raced her for a while before veering off, wings undulating. Even her breathing was easier — slow, natural breaths instead of her usual gasping sucks on the regulator. Kaz flashed her thumbs-up. Even Dante was grinning. This was the only way to travel.

She felt like a tourist, taking in the scenery and enjoying the ride. Freed from the mechanics of scuba, she vibrated with nervous anticipation. A seventeenth-century shipwreck!

Her brow clouded a little. After two straight summers working with her uncle at the British Museum, the job had fallen through this year. Alfred Ballantyne could only bring one assistant to Syria on his archaeological dig. He had chosen Adriana's brother, Payton. The Poseidon internship had been almost a consolation prize.

But a three-hundred-year-old wreck! That beat

a Middle Eastern dig any day — or at least it would have if it hadn't been for Cutter and the team of treasure hunters.

By the time she noticed the roar, she realized she'd been hearing it for a while already. She peered past Star, trying to identify the source of the noise. But up ahead the water had become murky, almost opaque.

They had seen this effect before. Something was kicking up tons of mud and silt, churning the clear blue Caribbean into a turbulent blind tunnel of swirling brown.

An explosion? Cutter had done this before — dynamiting the reef to get at what was underneath the coral.

But no. The sound was steady, not a sudden blast. And it was increasing in volume. Whatever the source of the roar, it was getting closer.

And then, directly ahead, an unseen power grabbed hold of Star and flung her contemptuously aside.

Adriana froze as she tried to wrap her mind around what had happened. By the time she could react, the irresistible force had pounced on her.

The ocean itself was moving, a deep-water riptide. With overwhelming strength, it hurled her — up, down, sideways? It was impossible to tell.

THE DEEP

Rocks and chunks of flotsam battered her, caught up in the whirlpool. The mask was torn from her face as she whipped violently around. All sensation ceased to be. There was only pure motion, pure speed.

When she struck the coral, the collision sucked the wind out of her and knocked the regulator from her mouth. She lost her grip on the DPV. The scooter fell away, its auto-shutoff cutting power. Everything went dark.

*Am I dead?*

Her next gasping breath drew in a lungful of water. The choking was violent, desperate.

*No — alive —* The thoughts were fragments, half formed, rattling around the darkness of her mind. *Alive — and drowning —*

With effort, she forced her eyes open against the sting of salt water. She flailed for her mouthpiece, finding it at last and biting down hard. The rush of air brought her back to herself. Her body ached and her eyes hurt like crazy.

*Can't close them! Have to see!*

Dante was taking the brunt of it now. Fins windmilling wildly, he spun out of control, striking a mound of brain coral. Was he okay? Where was Kaz? And what had happened to Star?

All at once, the roar ceased. As the silt storm began to resolve itself, Adriana could just make out a silhouette standing near the source of the disturbance.

*Too big to be Star . . . Kaz?*

She reached up to wave, but an iron grip held her arm in place. Strong hands pulled her behind the stout base of a coral head. There crouched Kaz and Star.

*Then who is the silhouette?*

Star scribbled the answer on her dive slate: REARDON.

Adriana squinted. She could make out the stocky diver's beard below his mask. Chris Reardon, Cutter's other partner. The third treasure hunter wielded what looked like an enormous hose, a foot thick or more. Was that what had tossed the interns around like wisps of algae?

Her eyes were killing her. She had to find her mask! Wincing with pain, she searched the bottom. Where had it fallen? And then she spotted it, nestled in a growth of pink anemones.

Reardon hit a switch, and the roar returned. In less than a second, the mask disappeared in the blizzard of silt. Adriana squeezed her eyes shut in an attempt to protect them from the swirling particles that were everywhere in the water.

She was stuck. They were all stuck.

# CHAPTER SIX

Aboard the R/V *Ponce de León*, the noise was earsplitting, far louder than it was underwater.

The device was known as an airlift, but Cutter and his team called it Diplodocus. The long, thick hose stretching over the gunwale of their boat into the water resembled a sauropod dinosaur, its long neck drooping in a lazy arc as it drank from some Jurassic lagoon.

The contraption was basically a souped-up vacuum cleaner, strong enough to suck chunks of coral all the way from the ocean bottom. It was definitely not a toy. It had the power to break up limestone, or to rip a person's arm clean off. Handling the airlift's nozzle was no easy task. Reardon had to dive with weighted boots and a sixty-pound lead belt to avoid being tossed about at the end of the massive hose.

Their work was as exhausting as it was boring, but this was the only way to excavate a shipwreck long buried in a living reef: First, use Diplodocus as a blower in order to blast the weakened coral to bits, kicking up all the mud and artifacts trapped underneath. Then, vacuum up the debris and search for something of value.

That was what Cutter and Marina were doing. The backwash from the airlift was deposited into a huge wire-mesh basket that floated off the *Ponce de León*'s stern. Load by load, the two treasure hunters winched the tons of broken coral on deck, combing painstakingly through it, breaking up larger chunks with hammers.

So far, they had recovered a great deal of items in this way — ceramic cups, bowls, and plates, glass bottles, brass buttons and medallions, rusted metal nails, hinges, pulleys, buckles, musket shot, and cannonballs. Old ballast stones littered the deck of the research vessel. An anchor and the coral-encrusted barrels of two cannons lay out of sight in the ship's hold. They had found every sort of artifact — with one exception.

"Where's the treasure?" roared Cutter, tapping at a lump of coral with half a saucer encased in it. "We didn't go through all this for a boatload of broken dishes!"

"The kids found a piece of eight," Marina pointed out, tossing a ball of grapeshot on top of a pile of the stuff.

"Yeah, one coin out of a king's ransom," Cutter said disgustedly. "*Nuestra Señora de la Luz* was packed with silver and gold. That fleet carried the wealth of Asia and South America for an entire year! Where is it?"

Marina frowned. "Can we be *sure* this is *Nuestra Señora de la Luz?*"

"It has to be. Every knickknack we pull up is Spanish in origin. There was only one galleon lost off Saint-Luc in the mid-seventeenth century. Most of the treasure fleets took the northern route, via Havana and the Florida Straits." He sighed. "I guess we'll just have to dig harder."

He signaled Bill Hamilton, captain of the *Ponce de León*, who activated the winch. The small crane hoisted the basket up off its raft, and another load of debris hit the deck between the two treasure hunters.

Cutter stared. Buried amid the coral fragments was a dive mask.

"Chris!" Marina shouted.

They rushed to the gunwale and peered below. Reardon wasn't technically scuba diving. He was breathing through a long hose connected to a Brownie compressor that floated beside the boat. Marina grabbed the safety line and gave two sharp tugs, the UP signal.

They waited — a breathless wait.

Marina looked nervous. "Decomp?"

Reardon had been on the bottom at sixty-five feet for nearly an hour — long enough to start thinking about decompression. Maybe he had paused during his ascent.

The alternative was too awful to think about: If he had somehow gotten his head caught in the airlift's nozzle . . .

And then Reardon broke the surface with a splash. His swimming was awkward because of his heavy belt and boots, but he managed to struggle to the Brownie.

"What's the problem?" he called.

Seeing the mask on their partner's face, Cutter and Marina exchanged a confused glance.

Marina cupped her hands to her mouth. "Did you see anything down there?"

"Are you kidding?" came the reply. "When that monster's on, I can barely see my hands in front of my face."

Cutter turned to Marina. "This is a popular dive spot. That mask could have been there for years."

She examined the faceplate, molded plastic, and rubber headband. There wasn't a speck of coral, algae, or anemone growth anywhere.

"Yeah, probably," she said. But she didn't sound convinced.

After some frantic searching, the divers were able to locate their DPVs in the murky water. Adriana never found her mask.

It was a tense ride back to the station. The interns barely noticed the spectacular colors of the reef, or the multitudes of creatures that darted around, agitated by the airlift's tempest. All thoughts were riveted to their near miss. No serious injuries, and Reardon hadn't seen them. But it had been close. Too close.

Star's eyes never left the glowing dial of the compass on her dive watch. She led the way until she reached one of the fixed navigation lines that fanned out from PUSH. There they turned left and followed the white rope until the familiar shape of the habitat appeared out of the blue.

Dante was last up the ladder, but he was already babbling excitedly the instant his mouth cleared the water in the wet porch. "Man, what hit us, an underwater tornado?"

He was interrupted by a low, muffled banging.

Adriana started. "What was that?"

But there was the sound again, like someone knocking on glass.

Dante peered out the viewing port.

"Who are you looking for?" Star asked in an amused tone. "The Avon lady?"

And then a loud, tinny amplified voice blared, "No! Over here!"

The four interns jumped. Dr. Ocasek peered

out at them from the round window of the station's decompression chamber.

"Sorry to startle you," the scientist chuckled through the intercom. "I know you weren't expecting to find me in here. I have to rush topside."

In PUSH language, rushing meant getting there seventeen hours later. It took that long for the chamber to bring an aquanaut back to surface pressure without risk of the bends — decompression sickness. The interns would have to go through the same treatment when their stay was over.

"I thought you were here for another week," Kaz said.

"It's kind of an emergency," Dr. Ocasek admitted. "A small explosion in my part of the lab up there. I can't understand it. My experiments hardly ever explode."

"Is it safe for us to stay here on our own?" Dante asked uneasily.

"Oh, they're sending someone else down. I assured them that you kids are totally independent. But you know what a worrywart Geoffrey can be."

"Right," said Kaz. They were certain that Dr. Geoffrey Gallagher couldn't have cared less about the four of them. If Poseidon's director was worried, it was over the bad publicity that would fall on the institute if anything happened to four teenagers on their guest staff. That kind of black eye might even shut down production of the documentary film that was going to make him the next Jacques Cousteau.

They shrugged out of their gear and filed through the pressure hatch into the station proper.

"You've got to be more careful," Star admonished Dante. "You almost spilled the beans in front of Iggy back there."

Kaz was shocked. "You think *Iggy's* in with Cutter and his people?"

"Of course not," Star replied. "But if we keep quiet, there's less chance of word getting back to Cutter that we're onto him. For all we know, Iggy is Poseidon's number one blabbermouth. We don't want him spreading it around that Reardon's down on the reef with something that nearly blew us up."

"I think that thing was an airlift," Adriana said. "Some of the underwater archaeologists at the British Museum use them, but only as a last resort. They're so strong that they sometimes smash more artifacts than they collect."

"They smash innocent by-swimmers too," Dante added.

"We were lucky," Adriana said solemnly.

"How do you figure that?" asked Kaz.

"An airlift works like a vacuum cleaner. We got to Reardon when it was blowing *out*, breaking up debris. If we'd come along when the nozzle was set to suck, somebody could have gotten killed."

"That's our treasure they're vacuuming," Dante complained bitterly. "If they get rich off *our* discovery — "

"They won't," Star promised. "But first we'd better see exactly what they've found over there."

"What are we going to do?" challenged Kaz. "Swim up and tell Reardon we're stealing back our shipwreck?"

"No," replied Star, "we wait till he goes home and *then* steal it back."

"But you know Cutter's schedule," Dante protested. "He's on that reef from the crack of dawn till after dark. The only time to avoid him would be the middle of the — "

The others stared at Star in dismay. Was she suggesting that they navigate all the way to the excavation and back again in the inky blackness of underwater night?

She looked at them pityingly. "They're called lights, guys. Maybe you've heard of them." A broad grin split her delicate features. "And just wait till you get a load of the ocean at night."

THE DEEP

# CHAPTER SEVEN

Kaz peered nervously down at the black water at the bottom of the hatch. He was afraid, no question about it. Not of the usual night hazards — becoming lost or disoriented. Or torch failure, which could strand a diver in a silent world of infinite dark.

No, Kaz's fear stemmed directly from the object of his greatest childhood interest and obsession: sharks.

*Sharks are night feeders.* It was in every single volume of an entire home library dedicated to the sea predators. Did that mean nocturnal divers were in any extra danger? Even the experts weren't sure.

Kaz had never truly understood his lifelong fascination with sharks until he'd come face to face with them in the waters of the Hidden Shoals. That had cleared it all up: He was scared to death of them.

Most of the local sharks were nurse and reef sharks three or four feet long — pretty harmless, if you didn't make them mad. But Kaz knew that larger, more aggressive cousins — bulls, ham-

DIVE

merheads, makos — also prowled these waters. And somewhere lurked Clarence, the eighteen-foot monster tiger shark with a gullet large enough to swallow a filing cabinet whole.

Suppressing his unease, Kaz started down the ladder. "I'll go first," he mumbled, then bit his mouthpiece and let the water swallow him up.

The headlamp in his dive hood created a zone of illumination around him, a funnel-shaped cocoon of light in the great dark sea. He finned away from the station's bulk, adjusting his buoyancy with the B.C. valve. The reef's rush hour was over. But he soon realized that the water was just as crowded with different, smaller creatures. The ocean was alive with millions of undulating blue larvae, each one just a few millimeters long. They hung there, absolutely defenseless, as they were attacked by the thousands by tiny, round, tentacled predators —

*Polyps!* Kaz thought in sudden understanding. *At night, coral polyps dislodge from the reef and go hunting!* He was witnessing the very bottom of a food chain that extended all the way to Clarence, wherever he was.

*Far away, I hope.*

The other interns floated around him now, taking in the night scene. Following Star's lead, they switched off their headlamps. The ocean seemed pitch-black at first, yet as Kaz's eyes adjusted, he began to see the glow of the moon, penetrating through sixty-five feet of water. Light and color shone all around them from the bodies of fish. It was bioluminescence — the emission of light from living creatures. Like a large moving mushroom, a jellyfish glowed pale pink as it pulsed by. Even the plankton was bioluminescent, causing the water itself to sparkle like glitter makeup.

They switched their headlamps back on, and Star led the way to the wreck site, navigating by the compass on her watch. It gave Kaz a giddy feeling of power to outrace the fish, many of which appeared to be asleep. Some hung motionless in the water; others had attached themselves to kelp and sea fans. There were even a few "sleepwalkers."

*Sleep-swimmers,* Kaz corrected himself.

The wreck site was difficult to find. They would have missed it completely if the water hadn't still been a little cloudy from the use of the airlift hours earlier. With their DPVs set on low, they circled the area, spiraling gradually inward, until at last Dante's sharp eyes fell on the coral ditch that was Cutter's excavation.

Adriana emptied her B.C. to lessen her buoyancy. Setting down her scooter, she planted herself on her knees on the bottom and began to sift through the limestone rubble. She worked alone for a few moments while the others hung back, uncertain what to do. Then, noticing their inactivity, she gestured impatiently for them to join her.

Kaz settled himself beside her and began to sort debris. The operation reminded him of the time he was eight when the phone company had busted up the Kaczinski driveway to repair a broken wire. The neighborhood kids had spent days "mining" the blocks of blacktop. It had been a good time, made doubly precious to Kaz by the fact that he was constantly being whisked off to some hockey practice while everybody else had fun.

But here — two thousand miles, sixty-five vertical feet, and two atmospheres of pressure from his home in Toronto — there was an immediacy, a truth to this moment. This was a real shipwreck, pursued by real treasure hunters. And the treasure, if it was there, would be worth real money — millions, probably.

*Enough to change our lives forever.*

It was theirs for the taking — or losing, if they stood by and let Cutter's people have their way. He dug faster.

Gold fever. He remembered the term from a social studies unit on the Klondike gold rush. He could feel himself coming down with the disease.

The oppressive click and hiss of his own breathing was amplified by the scuba gear. It was accelerating, and so was his heartbeat. The moment when he would push aside a block of coral to reveal gleaming treasure underneath seemed so close he could almost taste it. And the compulsion to keep digging overpowered everything, even fatigue.

He could see it in the urgent actions of his fellow divers as well. It was especially obvious in Dante's intense, almost crazed eyes, magnified by the prescription lens of his mask.

They worked tirelessly, moving blocks that would have been far too heavy to handle on land. The increased effort ate up their air supplies, and soon it was time to switch to the backup tanks.

Kaz hurriedly snapped the hose back into place. His first breath drew a mouthful of burning salt water into his lungs. Choking, he fumbled with the connection, desperate to restore the flow of air. He finally got it right, but each convulsive hack drew in more water, causing a chain reaction of coughing.

Star grabbed him by the shoulders. "Are you all right?" she shouted into her mouthpiece.

Kaz tried to signal okay with his thumb and forefinger, but he could not get his breathing back under control. With effort, he narrowed his focus to the bowl-shaped debris field below them. The less he thought about the constant tickle in his throat, the less he was likely to cough. But the search was becoming frustrating. There was nothing here but a pile of rocks.

He frowned. This couldn't be right. The shattered coral was jagged, random. But these rocks were round, and mostly smooth, like quarry stones. What were they doing at the bottom of the Caribbean?

He cast a perplexed look at Adriana. It was hard to read the expression behind her mask, but her eyes were alight with excitement. She pulled her dive slate from the pocket of her vest and wrote: BALLAST.

Of course! She had told them about this. Old wooden ships carried tons of ballast rocks to prevent them from keeling over in rough seas.

*This is it! The ship itself, locked in coral for more than three hundred years!*

Then, as if his realization had opened the floodgates, the artifacts began to come. First, Star pulled out what looked like a lump on a stick. Upon closer inspection, it was a pewter spoon, its bone handle imprisoned in coral. Next, Dante's sharp eyes fell on a fragment of a dinner plate. A brass crucifix was Adriana's first find, followed by a handful of lead musket balls. More cutlery followed — they stuffed dozens of spoons and knives in their mesh dive bags. Dante pulled out another plate, this one intact except for a small wedge-shaped nick in the edging. Star came up with a small glass bottle in perfect condition.

Dante scribbled TREASURE?! on his slate. Adriana shook her head impatiently, digging with both gloved hands. Her face glowed with purpose.

Kaz latched onto a round coral fragment and brought it into the beam of his headlamp. The light flickered, then stabilized, giving him his first good look at the object before him.

A scream was torn from his throat, dispatching a cloud of bubbles to the surface.

There, partially encased in coral, was a human skull.

The skull slipped from his grip and settled back on the shattered reef. The others gawked in revulsion.

*Calm down,* Kaz told himself. *People die in shipwrecks. You know that. This is no great shock.*

But it was a shock. He was here to dive, not to come face-to-face with death.

*It happened three hundred years ago! This is*

*no different from the mummy exhibit at the museum!*

Star was more concerned about Kaz's flickering headlamp. Equipment failure could be even more devastating on a night dive. She checked her air supply. The gauge read 1600 psi, but the others were inexperienced divers, and probably had less. It was a good idea to head home.

Their bags full of artifacts, they returned to their scooters for the ride back to PUSH. Unlike the trip over, Kaz barely noticed the nocturnal life of the reef that was all around him. The horror-movie image of the skull hung before him like a totem of doom. How must it have felt to drown in these waters? Especially for a European sailor, so far from anything familiar?

*We look at that wreck as an underwater ATM,* he thought. *But it's also a mass grave.*

He felt the weight of the items in his goody bag tethered to his belt. Stealing from the dead. Well, not exactly. Nobody from that long-lost ship could have any use for this stuff now. But it didn't feel right.

Dr. Ocasek was still shut away in the decompression chamber, so it was pretty easy for the interns to smuggle their dive bags into the main lock. Adriana spread a towel over the stainless

steel counter, and they placed their dripping artifacts across it.

Kaz stared intently at the coral-encrusted objects as if expecting some hidden discovery to
burst upon him like a sunrise. Then he turned to
Adriana. "Am I excited about this?"

"Of course," she replied with a frown. "All
this stuff is consistent with the seventeenth century.
The cutlery handles are made of bone or wood.
And the workmanship looks a lot like things I've
seen at the museum from the same time period."

"But you're not smiling," Star pointed out.

"It's *Spanish*." She pointed. "Crucifixes,
Catholic religious medallions. See that helmet?
Only Spain used that design — there were sol-
diers on the galleons, separate from the crew.
The seamen couldn't fight, and the soldiers
couldn't sail."

"Then it's definite!" cried Dante. "That's a real
treasure ship! I just hope Cutter hasn't already
boosted all the money."

"But the JB hilt is from England," Adriana reminded him. "My uncle identified it, and he's an
antiquities expert. What was it doing on a Spanish galleon?"

Kaz shrugged. "Some Spanish guy bought an
English walking stick. Or a whip, or whatever
that handle is from."

"Or he could have stolen it," added Star.

"Maybe," Adriana admitted grudgingly. "But in those days you couldn't just go on the Internet and order stuff from around the world. And Spanish colonials were barred from buying foreign goods. An English artifact on a Spanish ship — I don't know. It sounds kind of fishy to me. There's something here we're not seeing. . . ."

*30 August 1665*

*The settlement of Portobelo was ablaze. The bodies of its soldiers and citizens lay strewn about its ruined streets.*

*Samuel wandered through the bloody chaos, the blade of his sword striking sparks as he dragged it across the cobblestones. He did not have the strength to heft it, and certainly not the will. Samuel Higgins had been kidnapped from his family at the age of six, and had lived a life of privation and torment. Yet this was the lowest he had ever sunk in misery. He had not known the true mission of the* Griffin *when he had signed on. Even upon learning the truth, he could never have imagined this frenzied rampage of torture and murder.*

*Sick at heart, he walked away from the mayhem and started back to the beach. He had no definite plan. Perhaps he would sit on the sand and wait for this nightmare to be over. But he had not ruled out walking straight into the sea until the blue water swallowed him forever.*

DIVE

And then his back exploded with pain, and he fell to the street, waiting for death. Surely, this was a musket ball that had struck him down. He turned, expecting to see a Spanish soldier reloading his weapon. Instead, it was the tall figure of Captain James Blade, furling the leather of his whip. Set in the handle, an emerald the size of a robin's egg gleamed cruelly in the sun.

"Going somewhere, boy?"

The true extent of his predicament brought Samuel out of his daze. Walking away in the middle of a battle was desertion — a hanging offense.

"Captain," he said beseechingly, "what use have you for me in this fight — a boy who cannot even lift his sword?"

"I'll kill you myself if you turn your back on your duty again!" Blade threatened. He reached down, grabbed a handful of Samuel's unruly brown hair, and drew the boy to his feet. "These foul maggots call you Lucky. Be they right or be they wrong, they take heart when they see you. And you will be seen!"

So Samuel dragged himself and his sword back to the battle.

Musket fire was heard in the alleyway behind the merchants' houses. A lead ball ripped into the stone wall of the church, missing Samuel by inches. Terri-

THE DEEP

fied, he ran around the corner of the building and stopped short. There in front of him stood a captain of the Spanish garrison.

The officer reared back a double-edged broadsword, preparing to deliver a blow that would slice the cabin boy in half. Samuel raised his own sword in a feeble attempt to ward off the attack. He closed his eyes, waiting for it all to end.

Suddenly, distant drums resounded through the burning town, beating out the cease-fire. It was the garrison at Santiago, signaling the Spanish surrender.

Portobelo was won.

And young Samuel Higgins was still lucky.

# CHAPTER EIGHT

Breakfast the next day was powdered milk and peanut butter on toast. After passing a serving through the airlock to Dr. Ocasek in the chamber, the interns suited up and headed back to the wreck site.

This time, they were careful to maintain a safe distance. As soon as the water turned murky and they could hear the airlift's roar, they retreated to a hiding place behind a coral ridge. There they waited, observing nothing but swirling clouds of silt until their air ran low.

Back at PUSH, the four found Dr. Ocasek out of decompression and all packed up for his return to the surface. "I just talked to topside," he told them. "Jennifer Delal will be coming down in a couple of hours. She's collecting algae samples from the reef."

"We got you a going-away present," said Star. From her mesh bag, she pulled an enormous conch shell nearly two feet long.

"Something to make popcorn in," Kaz supplied. "Just in case you get hungry topside."

The scientist was impressed. "Wow, that's a beauty! I'm going to miss you guys."

They watched through the viewing port as he exited the wet porch. The shell under his arm was larger than the waterproof bag that held all his belongings from a two-week stay. He tossed one final piece of sandwich to his "pet" moray, and disappeared up the tether line. A boat waited at the PUSH life-support buoy to whisk him off to deal with the wreckage of his workspace and his exploded experiments.

On the station, the time dragged. Sick of peanut butter, they tried to make a freeze-dried beef Stroganoff dinner from the pantry. But Kaz forgot to add water before heating. Gray smoke billowed from the microwave, setting off the top-side monitoring sensors.

"Don't worry," came the amused voice of the technician over the emergency wall speaker. "The habitat has air scrubbers that'll take out the smoke automatically. Just don't cook any more duck à l'orange, okay?"

"It was beef Stroganoff," Kaz admitted.

"Listen, nobody comes to PUSH for the fine cuisine," the man assured them. "Just sit tight until Dr. Delal gets there, got it?" He severed the connection.

"What about fish?" asked Dante. "That's

food, right? We're choking on peanut butter, and right outside our window is the ultimate seafood buffet."

Star laughed in his face. "Like you could cut open a fish without fainting."

"I did once," Adriana informed them. "Actually, it was at a resort, so the staff did all the gutting and cleaning. But I watched."

They settled in for a long wait on the cramped station. The water outside the viewing ports darkened from blue to black as night fell. There was still no sign of Dr. Delal.

Adriana sprang to her feet. "I'll call topside."

Star grabbed her arm. "They'll just order us to stay put again."

"Which is exactly what we're doing," agreed Kaz. "So what's the problem?"

"She probably just decided to hold off until morning, and they forgot to tell us," said Star. "Which means we'll sit here all night and lose our only chance to check out the wreck site when Cutter isn't there."

Dante stared at her. "You mean a night dive? Now? When we're all alone?"

"You think some scientist could help us if we ran into Clarence out there?" Kaz said.

"Is that supposed to make me feel better?" Dante demanded.

THE DEEP

Star paced the narrow aisle, her limp exaggerated by the cramped quarters. "We'll give it till midnight," she decided. "Then we dive — Dr. Delal or no Dr. Delal."

At eleven-fifty-five, with no sign of the scientist, they dressed out and shrugged into the awkward double-tank setups.

The fifteen-minute half-mile ride to the wreck site was becoming familiar, Adriana reflected as she clung to the handles of the DPV. There was the coral head that reminded her of the Eiffel Tower, and the colony of tentacled anemones that resembled a field of powder-blue flowers. A little farther along, her headlamp illuminated the "lobster sponge," a titanic red sponge that was used as a hiding place by several clawless Caribbean lobsters.

*I'm starting to recognize the fish too.* The thought seemed crazy. But no — there was the barracuda that was missing the top half of its crescent tail. It was exciting, almost like running into an old friend.

*I wonder if he knows us too —* "Hey, it's those losers on the dive scooters. Who taught them how to swim?"

She became all business when they reached the wreck site. She worked tirelessly, stuffing her bag until it was bursting with coral-encrusted artifacts. The passion of her own efforts didn't surprise her. She loved this stuff. But she was amazed at the enthusiasm the others put into the job. It was backbreaking work, even underwater, where the blocks of limestone weighed much less than on dry land. At such a level of exertion, a diver sucked air at double speed, and soon Star was tapping her on the shoulder. Their backup tanks were down to half full. It was time to return to PUSH.

The trip home was a pleasantly exhausted one. Their DPVs worked a little slower from the weight of bags jam-packed with artifacts.

As she glided through the black water in her cone of light, her mind toyed lazily with the puzzle of the shipwreck. A Spanish vessel, almost certainly. Maybe even one of the fabled treasure galleons — the time period seemed about right. But where was the treasure? Surely Cutter couldn't have it all. That much silver and gold would sink the *Ponce de León*. And how did the bone handle fit in?

*Maybe I'm making a mountain out of a molehill.* She knew, for example, that English cannons were common on foreign ships. Was it really so weird that a Spaniard had acquired an item that had once belonged to an Englishman with the initials JB?

Something was wrong. Up ahead, she could see Star turning around. That was when Adriana realized that she had noticed none of the usual landmarks on the return trip. She checked her dive watch. They had been on the move for twenty minutes, maybe more. They should have reached the habitat by now.

With a feeling approaching fright, she realized they were lost.

# CHAPTER NINE

Frantically, Adriana ransacked her mind for any clue as to where they had veered off course. Somehow, they must have skirted the circle of navigation lines that stretched out from PUSH like the spokes of a wheel. But how far back? And in what direction?

Star tried to quell the panic that was swelling in the group. She gestured emphatically at her headlamp. The message was clear. Search for the habitat, but stay in sight of the others' lights.

*Okay,* Adriana told herself, *you've got air left.* That was if she didn't squander it by breathing too fast. They retraced their steps a few hundred feet and fanned outward, scouring the bottom for the white ropes. The beam of Adriana's torch cast a ghostly oval over the reef, but she saw nothing but coral, sponges, and the occasional fish.

*Come on! Where is it?*

She took a quick inventory of her dive mates, now distant glows in the darkness. How would she even signal the others if she found something? Would a short, sharp shout into her regulator reach them?

*It won't make any difference if we can't find something to shout about.*

She could feel her gas running low now. There was still plenty to breathe, but it took more effort to suck it out of the tank. A check of the gauge drew a wheezing of shock from her. It was under 100 psi — at this depth, three minutes, tops! And she was gasping, devouring what little supply she had left.

*Control yourself!*

It was easier said than done. The full impact of their situation pressed down on her like the immense weight of the ocean. She couldn't shoot for the surface even if her tank ran bone dry. None of them could. The interns had been living at sixty-five feet for three days. Their bodies were saturated with dissolved nitrogen. A quick ascent would bring out millions of tiny gas bubbles, turning the blood into a lethal froth — a case of the bends so severe no one could survive it. Above lay only death.

*But I'll suffocate!*

Her face distorted by horror, she spun around to warn the others. Her panorama of black ocean revealed *two* sets of lights.

*Two?!*

Off to her left bobbed the interns' headlamps. And there, approaching fast from the right, were five more.

A rescue team?

*But how did they know we were in trouble?*

Right then, she didn't care. She pointed her DPV in the direction of the newcomers and took off.

As she closed the gap, she realized that she was advancing toward not a group of rescuers, but a single diver.

*Dr. Delal! She came after all! And when she saw we weren't at the station, she went looking for us!*

The newest aquanaut wore a headlamp and had strapped hand lights to both ankles and wrists to catch their attention in the dark sea. She looked bigger than Adriana remembered her — probably from the magnifying effect of the water.

Adriana drew a shallow, painful suck from her mouthpiece. Her gauge showed zero. She inhaled again —

*Nothing!* Terror twisted her insides. The tank was bone dry!

With two powerful kicks, the aquanaut was upon her. The newcomer wore smaller wing tanks affixed to arms and legs. Confident hands snapped one of the wings onto Adriana's regulator.

*Air!* The metallic tang of that first compressed lungful was the most delicious taste she could remember.

"Thank you!" she panted into her mouthpiece.

Her savior was already steaming for the other three interns. Adriana followed. Even on her scooter, she had trouble keeping up with Dr. Delal's powerful kicks.

Kaz was beginning to panic, his gas supply dwindling. Dante, who was already out of air, was buddy-breathing what little Star had left. Adriana watched their rescuer distribute the wing tanks.

The truth was so awful it made her nauseous. But it was undeniable: If Igor Ocasek's replacement really had stayed topside until morning, they would all be dead.

It was a chastened and bone-weary team of interns that followed their rescuer back to PUSH. When the terror subsided, it left nothing but exhaustion in its wake. Adriana barely had the strength to haul her scooter, her burgeoning dive bag, and herself up the ladder to the wet porch.

She collapsed onto the plastic grating, fighting an impulse to weep with sheer relief. "Dr. Delal," she managed, too weak to pull off her gear, "I don't know what to say."

There was a familiar grunt that definitely couldn't have come from anyone named Jennifer. Up popped the mask to reveal the face of their savior.

It was English.

Menasce Gérard's dark, burning eyes scorched them with fury and contempt. "You!" the six-foot-five dive guide exclaimed. "They tell me only Jennifer is sick, I must go to PUSH in her place. If I know it is for you, I say no."

"Well, we're really glad you decided to come," Kaz said, his voice shaky. "We couldn't find the nav ropes. I don't know what happened."

"We messed up, pure and simple," Star confessed. "We could have died." She swallowed hard. "We *would* have died."

English was not sympathetic. "If you stop doing these idiot things, you do not have this problem! Night diving is not for the kindergarten. *Careful* — you have maybe heard this word before?"

"Sorry," mumbled Kaz.

"I am not Superman, me. I cannot always be there when you play dice with your lives. And for what?" He tossed a disgusted glance at Adriana's mesh bag, seeing the lumps of coral but not the artifacts they concealed. "Rocks. *Fou!*" He peeled off his dive gear and stormed through the pressure lock.

Dante set his tanks on the EMPTY rack by the compressor. "Is it just me, or is that guy always there every time we look like morons?"

"Thank God for that," Kaz said feelingly. "How many times has he saved our necks?"

Adriana stepped out of her flippers. "Do you think he's right? Are the night dives too risky?"

Star shook her head vehemently. "We just got cocky, that's all. We made it okay a couple of times, and we let our guard down."

"Down here, you only get one mistake," Dante pointed out.

Star nodded gravely. "You're right. It was my bad, and it won't happen again. English is right. He won't be there for us every time."

"I don't want him *any* time," Dante said plaintively. "Don't get me wrong — I'm grateful. But he hates us."

"He doesn't hate us," argued Star.

"Ask him!" Dante insisted. "He doesn't even try to hide it."

"We'll stay out of his way," soothed Adriana.

"Down *here*?" Dante shrilled. "The guy takes up half the station! We couldn't stay out of his way if we shrank to the size of Barbie dolls! Face it — we're locked in an underwater sardine can with an unfriendly giant."

# CHAPTER TEN

Menasce Gérard peered through the viewing port as the four interns set out from the station, gliding easily on their DPVs. He took careful note of the direction of their bubble trails, just in case he had to rescue them again.

He snorted. English was the most talented diver on an island of talented divers. His work on the oil rigs was difficult and dangerous, calling for great strength and skill at staggering depth and pressure. Why was a man like him playing nursemaid to a group of spoiled American teenagers?

He turned away from the viewing port. With a pop, his head shattered the bare bulb on the low ceiling. *Mon dieu*, this habitat was not built for a man his size! It was the interns who had brought him to this underwater dungeon, *merci beaucoup*.

As he brushed the glass fragments from his short hair, he noticed the crimson on his fingers. He began rummaging through the stainless steel cabinets in search of an adhesive bandage. An open cut was the last thing a diver needed. Even the slightest smell of blood in the water could attract sharks.

A lump of coral toppled from a cabinet and fell at his feet. Ah, yes — last night's souvenirs. Then he noticed the ancient piece of cutlery protruding from the small block. He examined the other contents of the locker, marveling at the artifacts inside. Those teenagers had found something! Was there no end to their mischief?

Within minutes, he was pulling on his wet suit. He selected a scooter from the rack, stepped down to the top rung of the ladder, and disappeared into the waiting water.

The interns cut power to their DPVs, gliding to a halt at the crater of shattered coral that was the wreck site.

Where was the boiling silt storm? More to the point, where were Reardon and the controlled devastation of the airlift?

Where was the *Ponce de León?*

Valving air into her B.C., Star ascended to forty feet — as high as she dared to go without risking decompression sickness. Sharp knives of sunlight cut the turquoise water, and she could clearly make out individual swells on the surface. Cutter's boat was nowhere to be seen.

After fumbling around in the pitch-black, skulking by headlamp, this felt almost like a promotion. Soon they were harvesting artifacts at greater speed than ever before, enjoying the excellent visibility and natural light.

Dante's sharp eyes made out a rounded edge. The photographer deftly plucked a pewter serving dish out of the debris and stuffed it in his bag. It was a nice find — the best of the day so far. But Dante wasn't satisfied.

*Where's the money?*

A Spanish galleon — the richest kind of shipwreck in the world. And what had the interns managed to salvage so far? Plates. Cups. Spoons. What were they supposed to do, have a tea party?

Of course he understood the archaeological value of these items. The stuff was a window back in time, three hundred years, maybe more.

Archaeology. That was Adriana's gig. Dante snorted into his mask — easy for her not to care about getting rich. She was rich already, or at least her family was. Dante might *need* that money someday. Photography probably didn't pay very well — black-and-white photography, anyway. And he was doomed to that specialty.

But with this treasure, or a share of it, he wouldn't have to care about that.

He finned away from the excavation, scanning the area. Maybe they were looking in the wrong place. Galleons were big, weren't they? What if they were working on the opposite end of the wreck from where the treasure had been stored? They could be salvaging some kind of seventeenth-century cafeteria while millions in silver, gold, and jewels lay a few yards off.

But where? And if the treasure lay buried under coral, how would they ever get at it? Cutter was the one with the airlift and the dynamite. Cutter had a boat that could winch anchors and cannon barrels up to the surface.

He stared at the reef's rocky rind, poring over every bump and contour. Surely, there had to be some sign, some hint of a man-made shape encased in the living limestone.

He found nothing.

He kicked through the murky haze stirred up by the efforts of the others, swimming to the far side of the wreck site. Here, coral gave way to sand and mud bottom.

*Now that's searchable.*

Expelling air from his vest, he dropped to the seafloor on his hands and knees and began to dig. Almost immediately, he was lost in his own silt cloud. As he labored, it occurred to him that if he'd thought to look here, so had Cutter.

Exhausted, and sucking far too much air, he

sat on the bottom in a remarkably dry-land pose, elbows on his knees, chin resting on his knuckles.

The picture came into focus gradually, as silt resettled itself, and the murky water began to clear around him. He blinked in surprise.

He'd always imagined the shoal as a broad plain, but really it was more of a mountainside here. Not far beyond the wreck site, the seafloor sloped sharply downward, falling off so quickly that Dante could not make out the bottom.

*This is where the Hidden Shoals end. It must drop to deep ocean from here.*

He increased buoyancy and lifted off the sand, peering into the abyss. As he floated free of the silt, the downward slope came into perfect focus. That was when he saw it.

It was far below on the incline, right at the point where the exhausted rays of sunlight succumbed to the permanent darkness of the deep. He could just make out the shadows of —

Of what?

He couldn't be sure. But it was definitely something. Half-buried objects, scattered along the distant slant as if they had bounced off the back of a runaway truck.

Could this be the treasure?

*If I could only get a closer look . . .*

Dante finned to the edge of the plateau, and

angled his direction down, paralleling the slope of the bottom. Valving air out of his B.C. made descent easier, and he focused all his concentration on the faint hints of debris far below.

When he felt the tug on his leg, he yelped into his regulator, fearing the jaws of some prehistoric sea monster. No, it was another diver, waving a scolding finger.

*Star?*

He peered into the newcomer's mask and recoiled in shock. Oh, no! It was English, clinging to a DPV! The guide must have followed them. They were caught.

Dante held up a finger — one minute.

English shook his head vehemently. He pulled out his slate and scribbled: TOO DEEP.

PUSH aquanauts were supposed to maintain depth between forty and eighty feet. Dante checked his Fathometer. Almost ninety.

*But I just need to see it!*

Dante wheeled and continued to kick down the incline. English sprang into action. Dropping the scooter, he lunged forward, latching onto the boy's slim torso. Dante took evasive action, rolling out of his grasp. As English struggled to hold on, he accidentally yanked the boy's weight belt clean off.

Now suddenly buoyant, Dante shot upward. Desperately, he fumbled to deflate his B.C. to slow the ascent, but couldn't find the valve.

*If I surface now, without decompression, the bends will kill me!*

English's glove snapped out of nowhere and put an iron grip on his ankle. At last, Dante emptied his vest. Neutral again, he clamped himself onto the guide's arm and did not let go.

The weight belt floated to the sandy slope.

*Clang.*

The unmistakable sound reverberated under water, carrying even more clearly than it would have through the air.

*Wait a minute. Lead weights hitting wet sand don't clang.*

English heard it too. Both divers descended to the spot where the belt lay. The guide removed a flipper and shoveled through the mud and silt.

Dante spotted the dark object immediately. It was just below the sand, barely buried. The two wrested it free of the shoal, and English hefted it in his arms. It was about the size of a lampshade, dark with rust, and eaten through in about half a dozen places. But it was unmistakable — a brass bell.

The thoughts sparked instantly in Dante's

brain: Adriana! She had to see this! Old ships had bells, didn't they? Adriana would know if this was from a Spanish galleon.

A white-toothed grin penetrated English's perpetual scowl. He reached down and handed Dante his discarded weight belt. Dante reattached it, and the two kicked away in tandem, holding the bell between them like a trophy.

The dive guide's smile disappeared as they crested the slope. He took in the sight of the other three interns, busily harvesting artifacts from the ruined reef. They looked up at his approach, as though receiving his white-hot anger by telepathy.

Seething, English passed off the bell to Dante and swooped over the reef, examining the destruction. The strokes of the underwater pencil against his dive slate reverberated like gunshots.

YOU DO THIS?

Kaz blustered his denial, and wound up choking on salt water.

They were a hundred percent innocent, but how could they ever explain the whole story down here, where more than a syllable or two was impossible?

Star drew out her slate and wrote a single word: CUTTER.

English's stark expression plainly said he did not believe her.

At that moment, all explanation became unnecessary. Sixty-five feet overhead on the surface, a dark shape moved into position. Minutes later, an anchor dropped, settling on the reef ten yards away from them.

The *Ponce de León*.

The four interns retrieved their scooters and purred off to the ridge of coral that had served as their hiding place before. English followed, but his eyes never left the shadow of the research vessel above them.

They watched from the cover of the ridge as two dark figures descended through the filtered sunlight — divers wearing weighted boots instead of flippers. Chris Reardon and Tad Cutter. Instead of the long serpentlike tube of the airlift, each man carried what looked like a futuristic weapon, connected to the surface by a hose.

Kaz stared. What were those things? Dynamite charges? Spear guns? He did not have long to wait. The moment Reardon's boots thudded to the bottom, he positioned the six-inch blade against the unbroken reef at the edge of the excavation. With a monstrous roar, the device began pounding at the coral, smashing it to pieces.

Kaz gasped. A jackhammer! They were widening the search area!

Cutter's machine blasted to life, working on

the other side of the gash. Within seconds, the two treasure hunters disappeared inside an enormous cloud of silt and powdered coral.

Soon the interns couldn't see anything. But there was no question that the operation was proceeding. The vibration of the jackhammers seemed to rip at the very fabric of the ocean. At that, it was nothing compared to the vibrations of outrage emanating from Menasce Gérard. To a native islander, this wanton destruction of the living reef was nothing less than a crime against nature. It took every ounce of self-control he had, learned from a lifetime of diving, to hold himself back from physically attacking them.

Star understood his agitation. She scribbled on her slate and held it up for him to read: TREASURE HUNTERS.

His expression thunderous behind his mask, English indicated Dante, who was close by, still hugging the bell. Their mesh bags bulged guiltily. The irony almost cut Kaz in two: *If Cutter's the treasure hunter, how come we have all the treasure?*

Mastering his anger at last, English turned his DPV back in the direction of PUSH and beckoned the others to follow.

They did not break free of the cloud kicked up

by the jackhammers until they were a third of the
way home.

The wet porch rang with anxious voices.

"We didn't do anything to that coral!" Star
pleaded their case. "Cutter broke it up with
dynamite! We were just nosing around."

"This never was a real internship," Kaz continued. "The whole thing was a sham — a smokescreen to hide the fact that they were looking for
a shipwreck."

"And they found it," Dante added. "Actually, *I*
found it. But they stole it. And now they're digging up half the ocean looking for the treasure."

"It's the truth, Mr. English," Adriana said
earnestly, "whether you believe us or not."

"I believe you," the guide said gravely.

They were struck dumb. It had never occurred
to them that Menasce Gérard might take them at
their word.

"Oh," said Kaz, surprised. "Great. So what
happens now?"

The giant ignored him and pulled off his dive
hood, checking the security of the Band-Aid on
his head.

Dante spoke up. "You know — what's our
next move? How do we stop Cutter?"

English shrugged hugely, his massive shoulders blotting out all view of the pressure hatch that led to the entry lock. "It is not my job for save the world, me."

"You mean you're just going to let him steal everything?" Dante protested.

English raised both expressive brows. "This is *my* property on the bottom of the ocean?"

"Well, shouldn't we at least call the cops?" asked Star. "That reef is protected, and they smashed it. They're smashing it *right now!*"

English laughed mirthlessly. "The cops — you refer to seven Saint-Luc men with the asthma. They cannot dive, so they are the cops."

"What about the government?" Adriana prompted.

"The government is eight thousand kilometers away, in Paris. The local magistrate is on Martinique, and would not know coral from corral, the place where you keep the horse." He looked earnestly into their faces. "*Tiens*, I agree with you. This is a terrible thing — a waste. But this is not my business. I am a diver. Justice is for someone else. A judge, *peut-être*."

Dante hefted the bell. "Well, here's one thing Cutter's not going to get. What do you make of it, Adriana?"

She took it from him. It was heavier out of water, about the weight of a small TV. "It's the ship's bell, all right. We can try to clean off some of this rust. I think these things were engraved, so we might be able to identify the ship."

"For what?" grumbled Dante. "So Cutter can know whose gold he's getting rich on?"

"For historical value," Adriana insisted. "We know the artifacts are Spanish. Maybe the Spanish government keeps online archives we can check." She turned to English. "Do you think?"

"Why do you look at me?" the dive guide said, almost defensively. "What do I know about the Spanish treasure, me? A Frenchman named English."

The interns were taken aback. That was almost a *joke*! Humor from the implacable Menasce Gérard. It didn't seem possible.

"You know, you never explained that," Star ventured at last. "Where your name comes from, I mean."

"*Exactement,*" English agreed. "I never explain you this thing."

He turned away to shrug out of his wet suit. And for a moment it seemed as if the subject was closed. But then the enormous guide spoke again.

"My ancestor was English," he said, his back still to them. "From the shipwreck."

"Really?" Adriana was impressed. "How long ago?"

The famous shrug. "This is maybe, I think" — he paused, searching for the right word — "baloney? A rumor in the family. Here, *aux Antilles*, so many boats sink over the years, everybody think his ancestor sail with Columbus."

Kaz regarded English intently. "I know you don't like us because we don't belong at the institute. But now maybe you understand that it isn't our fault. We're not properly qualified because Cutter wanted us that way. He picked us because we're not great divers, and he picked Star because he thought she would be handicapped."

The guide tossed his wet suit onto the drying rack. He said, "You get better." And he ducked through the pressure hatch, leaving them alone.

The four interns stared from one to the other. First humor and now this. Had English actually said something *nice* to them?

# CHAPTER ELEVEN

The old ship's bell, after more than three centuries at the bottom of the Caribbean, now sat in a glass tub, soaking in a mild acidic solution. On the other side of the lab area, in PUSH's entry lock, Adriana pounded the keyboard in search of clues to the identity of the mysterious galleon.

The lists and numbers that passed across the screen astonished her. The web site was maintained by the Spanish government. It contained a complete archive of every ship that had ever sailed to and from Spain, including its cargo. There were passenger manifests and bills of lading all the way back to the fifteenth century.

*If that wreck is what we think it is, it has to be in here somewhere,* Adriana reasoned.

Outside the viewing port by her shoulder, a lobster hunt was in progress. English was leading Star, Kaz, and Dante on a search for a dinner that was worthy of their last night on PUSH. Seafood was on the menu; peanut butter most definitely was not.

She got up from the chair and knelt down in front of the bell. Using a long-handled soft brush,

THE DEEP

she dabbed gently at the coating of rust on the brass. A cloud of reddish-brown particles flaked off into the surrounding liquid.

She squinted at the mottled surface. Was it getting cleaner, or was that just wishful thinking? She could make out faint lines of engraving, but nothing was clear enough to read.

She glanced up. Outside the porthole, Dante had cornered one of the clawless Caribbean lobsters in a rock crevice, and was trying to coax it out.

"Stay in there, kiddo," she advised the creature. "He wants to cook you." With a self-conscious laugh, she realized she had spoken aloud.

Dante lay on the rocks, his head almost completely inserted in the opening. As he reached out to grab, a huge dark shadow fell over him.

Adriana gaped. An enormous manta ray came flapping down to take a look at the diver with his head in a hole. Frantic, she banged on the window with both fists, hoping the concussion of her knocking would carry through the water. Perhaps it did, because Dante emerged with his captured lobster to find the twenty-foot wingspan of the devilfish looming over him.

Adriana couldn't hear anything, but it was

plain that Dante was screaming his head off. He spat out his regulator, and howled a cloud of bubbles that seemed to have no end. Star and Kaz tried to come to his aid, but Dante was out of control.

English finned onto the scene, with bubbles pouring from him as well. Adriana felt a stab of fear. The guide was afraid of nothing. Just how dangerous was this big beast that hovered like an alien spacecraft?

Then she realized that English was not in the grip of terror. He was laughing.

Somehow they managed to get Dante calmed down. He was inconsolable, though — in the excitement, his lobster had made its escape. With sign language, English instructed the others to watch. Then, astoundingly, he climbed right onto the manta's expansive back.

Adriana stared through the viewing port. The monster just hung there and allowed itself to be mounted, great wings undulating slightly. Then, with a nudge from its rider, it took off, sailing gracefully over the reef, bearing English like some begoggled jockey. It was out of Adriana's view almost immediately, but she could see the others watching with undisguised awe.

She returned her attention to the bell, and

brushed a little more. The solution was now growing cloudy with rust particles, and the engraving was definitely beginning to appear.

*1!* But no — there was a crosspiece on top! *T, then!* She dabbed the brush gently but firmly, holding herself back from scrubbing. If she ruined this artifact, she would never forgive herself.

T-O-L-L — no, the second L was an E!

Outside the habitat, the manta flashed by, this time with Star on its back. What was this — a carnival? Manta rides: fifty cents?

*Concentrate! You're so close to cracking this!*

She kept on working the soft bristles, and more engraving began to appear.

Another O. No, wait! It was a D! T-O-L-E-D — it could only be one word: Toledo!

*Of course! All the great metalworks in Spain were in Toledo! This bell was made there!*

The exhilaration of discovery had her dancing around the tiny room. But she quickly returned to the bell. There had to be a date there, and she was going to find it.

Star, Kaz, and Dante clattered onto the wet porch, whooping and exchanging high fives.

"That was awesome!" Star crowed ecstatically. "Like riding a pterodactyl underwater!"

"It was so *tame!*" marveled Dante. "Who

knew something that big and ugly could be so friendly?"

"Is that any way to talk about our dive guide?" Kaz grinned.

"You know what I mean!"

All at once, Adriana appeared at the pressure lock, smiling from ear to ear. She said, "*Nuestra Señora de la Luz.*"

The three stared at her.

"What are you babbling about?" asked Star.

"That's our galleon! It means 'Our Lady of the Light.' It sailed from Cádiz in 1648, and was lost at sea in 1665 on its fifth Atlantic crossing!"

"It says all that on the bell?" asked Dante incredulously.

Star was disgusted. "Sometimes you ask the dumbest questions! How could it say when they sank? You think they were engraving it while they were going down?"

"There are two inscriptions," Adriana explained breathlessly. "One says 'Toledo,' which means the bell was made at the metalworks there. And the other is '1648,' the year it was cast. I checked the old Spanish records. Seven new galleons were launched between 1648 and 1650. One of them burned in the harbor, and took the dock and half the town with it. One's on display at the Maritime Museum in Barcelona.

Two disappeared looking for the Philippines, which puts them ten thousand miles from here. Two were sunk in naval battles off the coast of Europe. That leaves just *Nuestra Señora de la Luz.*" She quivered with excitement. "It was part of the 1665 treasure fleet — the only ship that never made it home. According to the rest of the fleet, it disappeared in a hurricane in the French West Indies — right around here!"

"Then that's the only ship it can be!" Kaz exclaimed.

"And Cutter's taken it from us," added Star bitterly.

"Hold on a second," Dante interrupted. He turned to Adriana. "Did you say *treasure* fleet?"

"You won't believe it!" she crowed, eyes shining. "The web site showed the bills of lading. *Nuestra Señora* was a floating Fort Knox. You know that piece of eight we found? There were seven hundred thousand of them, freshly minted from South American silver! There were tons — *tons* — of gold! Chests piled high with pearls and precious stones! The total estimated value of that cargo today is one-point-two *billion* dollars!"

The whoop of celebration that escaped Dante was barely human.

"What are you so excited about?" asked Star.

"A billion bucks, and we've found nothing but a bunch of spoons and plates!"

"I think I know where the real thing might be!" Dante babbled excitedly. "If you go past the wreck site, the seafloor falls away to deeper ocean. The bell came from the top of that slope. But when I looked, I could see stuff scattered way, way down there, almost out of sight. The treasure's there! I know it!"

Adriana looked thoughtful. "It's possible, you know. *Nuestra Señora* went down in a hurricane. Heavy seas could have separated the cargo and dragged it off the shoal."

"We have to get to it before Cutter figures that out!" Kaz exclaimed urgently.

"I see," came a cold voice behind them.

They wheeled. English stood at the pressure hatch to the wet porch, scowling at them. Every inch of his six-foot-five frame radiated deep disapproval. He tossed a dive bag crawling with live lobsters onto the stainless steel counter.

"So. Monsieur Cutter, he is the treasure hunter. And you are not? You cry for the destruction of the reef, and then you drool over gold like common bank robbers! You do not fool me!"

Star was genuinely distressed. "That's not how it is!"

But English was carved from stone. "I have ears, me. I am not *stupide!*" With lightning speed, he reached out a hand and nudged an escaping lobster back into the bag. "Pack your gear. After dinner, we go into decompression. Then our association is at an end. Once we are topside, I do not know you."

The lobster was delicious, but the four interns very nearly choked on it. The click and scrape of cutlery on their plates resounded in the steel-trimmed galley. There was no conversation. Every time English cracked a shell, his expression plainly said he would have preferred to be snapping one of their necks.

It was painful, but not nearly as torturous as the endless stay in the decompression chamber. The only reading material was a small library of scientific journals. Every time one of the teens spoke, the dive guide would soon extinguish the conversation with a look that would have melted the polar ice cap. Kaz made an attempt to start a word game, but the other three were too intimidated to join in. Sleep was reduced to a handful of claustrophobic catnaps. The metal floor of the chamber was painful, but not half as much as the burning of the twin laser beams of English's eyes.

Over seventeen agonizing hours, the device

brought them back to surface pressure, giving their bodies a chance to expel the excess nitrogen they had absorbed during their time at sixty-five feet.

At long last, they wordlessly gathered together their tiny pieces of luggage, their bags of artifacts, and the *Nuestra Señora* bell, and started up the habitat's umbilical to the PUSH life-support buoy. Sunlight had never seemed so overpoweringly brilliant. There, waiting for them, was the *Hernando Cortés*. Captain Vanover was on the dive platform to haul them aboard.

"Hey, you guys, how was it? Iggy said you were having a blast!"

Star kicked off her flippers. "Yeah, well, Iggy left," she said pointedly.

Vanover frowned. "Huh?"

English surfaced behind them, deliberately swam away from the platform, reached up to the forward gunwale, and hoisted himself aboard. He peeled back his hood, stepped out of his fins, and stormed below, without a word to anyone.

# CHAPTER TWELVE

To tell or not to tell. That was the question.

One thing was certain: The interns had come up against a brick wall. Now that their stay at PUSH was over, they no longer had access to the wreck site. And they definitely had no way to investigate what Dante had spotted on the deepwater slope at the edge of the Hidden Shoals.

The next morning, in search of privacy, the four signed out bicycles and took to the dirt path that connected Saint-Luc's tiny villages.

"We need help," Kaz concluded, propping his bike up against a rock. "And that means we have to spill the beans to somebody. Who do we trust?"

Star laughed mirthlessly. "My mother, but she's not here."

Adriana adjusted her kickstand. "It has to be the captain," she reasoned. "English hates us, Gallagher ignores us, Cutter's the enemy, and Marina's with Cutter."

"We can't trust anybody," Dante said flatly. "Not with a billion dollars."

DIVE

"Then it stays down there," Kaz argued. "And what good is that?"

Dante squinted out over the vast expanse of ocean visible from high ground. "How well do we really know the captain? So he's a nice guy — so what? He could be in cahoots with Cutter. Or he could use our info to buy his way on to Cutter's team."

"Maybe," Star nodded. "But I don't think so."

"Let's put it to a vote," decided Kaz. "Who says the captain's in?" He raised his hand. Adriana was next, followed by Star.

Dante was distraught. "Do you guys realize how many zeroes there are in a billion?"

"If you're so good at math," Star pointed out, "then you know you've already lost this election."

Painfully, Dante's hand crept up to join the others. "I hope we're not sorry about this."

"You're absolutely positive you've found *Nuestra Señora de la Luz*?" asked Captain Vanover.

They sat on aluminum folding chairs, sinking into the sandbar where the portable restaurant was located. *La Mouette*, translation "The Seagull," was established every morning at low tide in six inches of water on the soft shoal about a hundred feet off the beach at Côte Saint-Luc. It could only be reached by rowboat or motorized launch. And it had to be dismantled every afternoon before high tide. But the spot could not be more spectacular, with gentle whitecaps breaking all around, and thousands of gulls and pelicans lighting on the glistening water.

The captain had invited the four interns to be his guests at lunch. They were ignored by Dr. Gallagher, avoided by Cutter and his crew, and despised by Menasce Gérard. Someone, he felt, had to be nice to them. "People have been looking for that ship for three hundred years."

"We're positive," Adriana confirmed. "Every single artifact we took from the wreck was Spanish — all except for the JB hilt, which someone must have stolen or traded for, I guess. And according to the Spanish records, there's only one galleon it could be."

"If you're right, you're rich," said Vanover.

"Or Cutter is," added Dante mournfully.

Vanover scowled. It had been hard for him to believe that Tad Cutter, a Poseidon scientist, was abusing his credentials in order to hunt for treasure. But earlier that day, Menasce Gérard had said the same thing. "I should have listened to you the first time you told me he was up to no good. But I don't think he's found any more than you have yet. I'd notice if the *Ponce de León* had a heavy load in its hold. She'd wallow to the gunwales."

"Then there's still time," urged Kaz. "Come with us when we tell Gallagher! He won't listen to us, but he'll have to pay attention to one of his own captains."

Vanover took a bite of his seafood stew and chewed thoughtfully. "We could try that. But what good would it do? Poseidon fires Cutter — and then what? He'll just find another boat and keep digging. Right now you have a real advantage over him. He doesn't know that you know."

"And he doesn't consider us a threat," added Adriana.

"He doesn't consider us at all," Star said bitterly.

"That's a plus," Vanover pointed out. "Right now he must be banging his head against the wall, wondering where the treasure is. In his wildest dreams, he'd never believe you kids are as close to it as he is."

"Maybe even closer," Kaz told him. Slowly, he explained Dante's sighting of what looked like a trail of scattered objects, and his idea that the treasure might lie down there. "It's just a theory," Kaz finished, "but Dante's never been wrong about what he sees underwater."

The captain sat forward. "How deep was it?"

"I was at ninety feet when I spotted it," Dante replied. "And it's hard to judge, but it looked a whole lot farther away than the surface. English was with me, and he didn't see anything."

Vanover whistled between his teeth. "Sounds like two-fifty, three hundred feet. Out of diving range — at least, with standard scuba. But we might still be able to take a look."

"How?" asked Star.

"Don't ask me." Vanover sat back and grinned. "Ask an old friend of yours."

Dr. Igor Ocasek was thrilled to see them, and even happier to be asked for his expertise. "I'm kind of at loose ends while my lab is being repaired," he explained.

The problem: how to examine a seafloor too deep for conventional diving.

The solution: lower a video camera to three hundred feet, and look around from the safety and comfort of the R/V *Hernando Cortés*.

The eccentric scientist was already making notes before they had finished telling him what they wanted.

"You'll require floodlights at that depth," he decided, "so there should be some kind of mounting platform. And weights for stability. Let's see

— four wide-angle cameras will provide a three-hundred-and-sixty-degree sweep. Three hundred feet of coaxial cable — no, better make it four hundred. Wouldn't want to be caught short if we have to go deeper —"

"Don't you want to know what we need it for?" asked Kaz in amazement.

"Mmmmm."

And then there were six people on the face of the earth who knew about the mysterious objects on the edge of the Hidden Shoals.

The more the information spread, the greater the chance that someone would betray the secret. But the interns had no choice. Dr. Ocasek had to be aware of what he was looking for.

When they told him, he hardly even looked up. One-point-two billion dollars was the same as one-point-two cents to a man who cared only for science.

*30 August 1665*

*If Samuel had thought the surrender meant the end of the bloodshed, he was sorely mistaken. Now in firm control of the settlement, the privateers went completely berserk. For nearly four months they had been trapped aboard ship — mistreated, malnourished, and, on top of their discomfort, bored to the brink of insanity. Now this sealed cauldron of frustrated energy boiled over onto the hapless citizens of Portobelo.*

*The cruelty was beyond imagination. As the towering sails of the privateer fleet moved into the captured harbor, screams rang out from every house in the shattered town. Even the church was no sanctuary. Torture and murder became an entertainment. Looting followed naturally, as the dead had no use for possessions. Every ring, every bracelet, every cross, even of base metal, found its way into an English pocket.*

*Samuel was assigned to York to help with the wounded privateers. The barber was in his customary condition — blood-soaked. The saw he used for his*

DIVE

terrible amputations looked like a utensil from a slaughterhouse.

Samuel hated any time he was forced to spend with York. But today it was a mercy, because it kept him away from the plunder and carnage all around him.

Right now York was attending to Patchett. The chief gunner had sustained a sword slash to the shoulder. It was almost a stroke of good luck. A few inches lower, and the man would certainly have lost his arm to York's saw. But a shoulder could not be amputated. It had to be treated, and the treatment was this:

The barber brought out a small tin from the pocket of his greasy vest and handed it to Samuel. As Patchett howled in agony, York reached filthy fingers into the wound and separated the torn flesh. It was Samuel's job to pour the contents of the tin into the long cut.

Samuel lifted the tin and recoiled in revulsion. Instead of healing powder, the container was crawling with maggots.

"Sir!" he cried. "The worms have eaten the medicine!"

York roared with laughter. "The worms are the medicine, Lucky! They'll eat the bad flesh and leave the good intact. Now pluck out four lively ones and drop them inside."

Samuel did as he was told, then ran behind the back of the Casa Real and vomited until there was nothing left to come up.

Then the shouting began, Captain Blade's voice louder than any other. Samuel followed the sound, fully aware that he should probably be running in the opposite direction. The throng of privateers was assembled in front of the large storehouses at the waterfront. The wealth of the New World was collected in these buildings — precious metals from the mines of the natives to the south, and unimaginable riches from the Orient. The treasure was carried overland by mule train from Panama on the Pacific side of the isthmus to this very spot. Here it waited for the great galleons to convey it to the Spanish king.

Samuel had heard the sailors of the Griffin speak of this place on their journey. It was, quite simply, the richest acre on the face of the earth.

The huge doors had been thrown open, revealing the contents of the legendary storehouses. Even from a distance, Samuel could see that they were all empty.

He had witnessed many displays of ill temper and homicidal rage during his time as James Blade's cabin boy. But never had he seen his captain in such a state. The mayor of Portobelo cowered on the ground before him, offering information in exchange for his life.

"The galleons, they leave — four days since! Take all treasure! We hide nothing! I swear!"

Captain Blade drew out his lash, and the mayor shrank away in terror. The whip cracked — not at the pitiful Spaniard, but over the heads of the privateer crew. It was a call to attention.

"Back to the ships, you scurvy rats! Those galleons are wallowing low with our treasure! Keep your swords handy, lads! The killing's not over yet!"

THE DEEP

# CHAPTER THIRTEEN

By the light of the moon, the *Hernando Cortés* chugged quietly out of Côte Saint-Luc harbor, just before eleven o'clock. There were no witnesses. But even if the departure had been observed, it was unlikely that anyone would have been able to identify the apparatus lashed to the foredeck.

The thing looked like the window display of a camera store that had been struck by lightning, fusing cameras and floodlights into a tightly packed mass.

"Does it work?" asked Adriana timidly.

Dr. Ocasek seemed vaguely surprised at the question. "It worked perfectly in my bathtub."

At the wheel, Vanover brayed a laugh. "Don't worry. If Iggy built it, it'll fly." He frowned as the vessel bounced through the oncoming waves. "Choppy tonight. We could be in for a rough ride."

When they reached the coordinates of the wreck site, Vanover cut their speed. They proceeded slowly until the sonar told them that they were passing over the point where the Hid-

DIVE

den Shoals sloped down to deeper ocean. Dr. Ocasek's camera array was then winched up and over the side. As it disappeared beneath the surface, the floodlights came on. Everyone gasped. The illumination was so powerful that the sea lit up like an aquarium. The light dimmed as the contraption descended. But even at the search depth of 250 feet, the watchers could still make out a faint glow coming from beneath the waves.

The four interns rushed below to the closed-circuit monitor Dr. Ocasek had set up in the salon. The screen was split in four, one quadrant for each camera.

Dante frowned. "There's nothing."

The screen showed swirling water and an occasional sea creature staring in surprise at this bizarre mechanical intruder.

"We're off the reef," Dr. Ocasek reminded him. "That's where the densely packed marine life is."

"But where's the bottom?" asked Star.

"I'm not sure," said Dr. Ocasek.

"Picture a mountain," came Captain Vanover's voice through the two-way radio from the wheelhouse. "Our cameras are sort of floating in space beside it. This slope might not bottom out flat for two or three thousand feet."

Kaz felt his eyelids beginning to droop. Fifteen minutes of staring at nothing was taking its toll on all the interns as the clock ticked on past midnight. This was turning into a big bust. How could anyone find something on the slope if they couldn't even find the slope itself?

It came up so fast that they barely had a chance to scream. First a large luminescent jellyfish flashed through the top right quadrant. Then a diagonal wall of sand and seaweed was hurtling toward the camera.

Dante reacted first. "Hit the brakes!" he bellowed at the walkie-talkie.

"Slow down!" cried Adriana.

"Veer off!" shouted Star.

When the camera struck the mud, Kaz flinched, expecting an impact. But of course the boat hadn't struck anything. Only the camera array, 250 feet below the surface, had suffered a collision.

Following Dr. Ocasek's instructions, Vanover reversed course, and the contraption came free of the muddy incline. Two lenses were sand-encrusted, but soon washed clean.

From that point on, no one felt remotely sleepy or bored. The *Cortés* traced slow track lines across the water, allowing the cameras a chance to scan the gradient for five hundred yards in each horizontal direction. Then the winch would lower the array another twenty-five feet, Captain Vanover would adjust course, and the thousand-foot trace would begin again.

Around 2 A.M., while they were lowering the array to 325 feet, a gusty wind blew up in their faces, and rain began to pelt down on them.

"How much longer is this going to take?" yelled Vanover from the cockpit. "We've got weather coming!"

With the rough wave action tossing its umbilical line, the camera array bounced and spun far below them. The pictures were chaotic. Kaz's head pounded as he stared at the screen, fearful that something might go by undetected. The motion of the boat was making him queasy, and he swallowed determinedly, his eyes glued to the monitor. Beside him, Dante, never a good sailor, was hugging his knees and moaning.

Dr. Ocasek was the picture of total focus. "If it's down there, we'll find it," he said calmly.

When the time came to lower the winch to 350 feet, it was obvious that conditions outside had deteriorated even further. The tossing of the deck knocked Adriana flat on her back. Even Kaz, who had superb balance from hockey, had to hold on to cabin tops and bulwarks as the sea manhandled the *Cortés*.

"Get back below!" shouted Vanover from behind the wheel. "I'm turning us around!"

"Not yet!" begged Dante, screaming to be heard over the wind. "I *know* I saw something!"

"No!" boomed the captain. "In these seas, if you go overboard, you're done!"

A wave broke over the bow, drenching the winch and the interns who struggled to man it.

"Just one more track line!" howled Star, shaking herself like a wet dog. "If we give up now, we'll never finish this!"

Vanover hesitated, the driving rain stinging his face. "One more!" he agreed finally. "But then I don't care if you find the lost continent of Atlantis — we're going home!"

Star and Dante sloshed down the companionway, and joined the others in front of the monitor for the last pass.

The ship lurched, and a moment later, the camera array swung away from the slope below. And when the pendulum effect brought the apparatus back into position, there it was in the bottom left quadrant:

The long bronze barrel of a cannon.

All four interns began screaming at the same time. Not one word was intelligible.

Even Dr. Ocasek was excited. "Back up, Braden! Back up!"

"Are you crazy?" crackled the sharp voice through the two-way radio. "It's all I can do to keep us afloat!"

The array bobbed in the current, and for an instant, one of the cameras dipped down to reveal a scattering of ballast stones and other debris half buried on the sandy slope.

Dante was out of his seat, crying, *"Did you see that?"* until a sudden pitch of the boat sent him sprawling into Dr. Ocasek's arms.

"It's more debris from *Nuestra Señora!*" exclaimed Adriana in amazement. "I wonder how it got all the way over here."

Star had an idea. "Maybe the galleon broke in two when it sank. And the force of the hurricane blew half of it off the shoal."

"The half with the money in it!" Dante added breathlessly.

Kaz warmed to the argument. "It would explain why Cutter hasn't found any treasure."

"Hey!" came an angry shout from the radio. Then, "If you guys are finished theorizing, do I have your permission to get us out of here?"

"Go!" urged Dr. Ocasek. "We'll bring up the camera array so it doesn't get smashed to pieces when we cross the reef."

"Okay, but *be careful!* We're taking ten-foot waves over the bow."

By the time they got topside, the deck of the *Cortés* was awash with foam and reeling from the motion of the sea. A stack of safety harnesses came sailing down from the wheelhouse and splashed at their feet.

"Get in them!" boomed Vanover. "And lash yourselves to something permanent!"

The thirty-foot walk to the winch was as tough an obstacle course as Kaz could remember. He clipped himself to the rail and hung on for dear life as Dr. Ocasek started the winch. The cable began to wind up.

Kaz put out a hand as Star stumbled. A second later, his own legs slipped out from under him, and he dangled from his harness, knowing he would have been swept away without it. Star, on the other hand, had kept her feet and was sneering triumphantly down at him.

The winch continued to shudder and groan. Two hundred feet . . . a hundred and fifty . . . The underwater lights grew nearer and brighter as they rose. The violent ocean began to glow beneath them. One hundred feet . . . fifty . . . twenty-five . . .

And then the array, still lashed to its weighted platform, broke the surface. Brilliant as a supernova, it turned night into day, showing the occupants of the *Hernando Cortés* just how much trouble they were in. The heeling of the boat in the troughs and crests of the oncoming seas had turned the dangling array into a hundred-pound projectile. It swung from the tip of the winch's crane arm like a lethal tetherball, smacking into the side of the wheelhouse and shattering a porthole. Then the craft righted itself, sending the contraption across the full beam of the ship, missing Adriana's head by inches.

Kaz grabbed a boathook and snagged the umbilical. But the next movement of the ship ripped the pole out of his hands.

"Heads up!" boomed Vanover as the array sailed back over them.

*Wham!* It connected with the railing, denting it. They watched as one of the cameras, jarred loose by the impact, pitched into the sea.

Kaz picked up the boat hook and swung it at the twisting umbilical. He missed the cable, but the end caught the neck of one of the floodlights and clamped on. The whole array came crashing to the deck.

With a cry like a springing tiger, Dr. Igor Ocasek flung himself on top of his runaway creation, preventing it from sailing off again.

It was 4:30 A.M. by the time the *Hernando Cortés* limped back to Côte Saint-Luc harbor.

Waterlogged and weary, the four interns helped Dr. Ocasek carry what was left of the array back to the scientist's cabin. One camera was missing, one was smashed, several floodlights were shattered, and the whole arrangement was covered in mud from numerous collisions with the sloped seabed.

"Sorry about this, Iggy," Star said sheepishly. "I didn't think we were going to wreck it."

Dr. Ocasek was upbeat. "We found what we were looking for. That's all that matters. The rest was the weather's fault."

"You're not going to get into any trouble for this, are you?" asked Dante nervously.

"Are you kidding?" The scientist grinned. "If I showed up one day and everything *wasn't* broken, Geoffrey would have a heart attack!"

They said good night and trudged off to their own quarters. Kaz and Dante let themselves into their cabin and switched on the light.

Dante went straight to the bathroom and began peeling off his wet clothes. "I've never been so tired in my life! I'm going to sleep for a hundred years!"

"Join the club," yawned Kaz. "The minute I hit that pillow — " He froze.

There in the corner sat the bell of *Nuestra Señora de la Luz*, cushioned by a bath mat. It was partly off the piece of cloth, which meant it had been moved. And, on the terrazzo floor in front of it, facing it, were two sandy footprints.

Maybe their activities weren't such a secret from Cutter after all.

# CHAPTER FOURTEEN

It was almost noon before Adriana awoke, the powerful Caribbean sun threading through the gap in the curtains and all but searing a hole in the center of her forehead. She looked to the other bed. Star was still asleep, snoring softly into her pillow. Divers always snored. It was a side effect of time spent at depth and pressure. Even Adriana had woken herself a few times with a loud snort.

She sat up, yawning and stretching, then caught a glimpse of her hands, and gasped aloud. Thick brown mud was caked under all ten fingernails. Her immaculate, stylish mother would faint dead away!

*Ballantyne ladies see to their grooming.* Adriana had been hearing that since birth. Mother, obviously, had never had to handle a hundred-pound camera array that had scoured the seafloor. To her, the purpose of the ocean was for cruising, and to supply sushi.

She padded barefoot into the small bathroom, and switched on the light. Digging through her

DIVE

toiletry bag, she came up with her manicure set and began to clean her nails.

*Yuck! This job is disgusting. You could plant potatoes in the blob I just excavated from under my thumbnail!*

And then the blob twinkled.

*Huh?* Adriana blinked.

It was a tiny particle in the dirt, about half the size of a grain of sand. It was bright yellow, and when it caught the light, it gleamed.

She looked closer. Not yellow, exactly. More like — gold.

Intrigued now, she spread a tissue on the counter, popped the dirt onto it, and used an eyebrow tweezers to separate the shiny fleck from the rest of the material.

It was very shiny — and soft, too. The sharp tweezers could not cut the particle. Strong pressure just left an indentation.

Her breath caught. This didn't just look like gold; it *was* gold!

She finished cleaning her nails onto the tissue, and examined the results. Only dirt. Head spinning, she sat down on the edge of the tub, trying to sort out her thoughts. The dirt under her nails came from carrying Iggy's camera array. That was mud dredged up from the sloping ocean floor near the second debris field from *Nuestra Señora*. How could it be a coincidence — a tiny piece of gold from the very spot where they suspected a vast treasure lay hidden?

But Spanish gold came in bars, coins, great decorative chains. This was barely larger than a particle of dust.

When the answer came to her, it brought with it so much adrenaline that the feeling was closer to terror than understanding. She leaped to her feet, unable to contain the excitement within one body.

"Star! — *Star!!*"

At a quiet corner table in the Poseidon cafeteria, the four interns met with Captain Vanover.

Dante stared at the tiny fleck on Adriana's fingertip. "That's not treasure! That's a molecule!"

"It's a *gold* molecule," Star said in irritation. "And keep your voice down."

"It *is* pretty small," Vanover pointed out. "I can't explain it, but I guess there's a chance it occurs naturally."

"I thought so too," said Adriana. "But then I remembered something I read on the Spanish government web site. All treasure arriving in Spain from the New World was heavily taxed.

But you could never know how much more was smuggled in to avoid the taxes. And the easiest treasure to sneak past the authorities was gold dust."

"Yeah," said Kaz dubiously, "but *one piece?*"

Star took up the explanation. "Think about what happens when a boat sinks. It creates a whirlpool effect, like the *Titanic*. Something as light as gold dust would get sucked up into the whirlpool, and end up spread out all over the bottom around the wreck."

"So we tried a little experiment," Adriana took up the tale. "We pulled all our muddy clothes out of the hamper. And there was another speck on Star's shirt." Her eyes shone. "We're not wrong about this. The debris field we photographed last night has the treasure in it — the *real* treasure! We can't get at all that dust, but the rest of it is lying there, just waiting to be claimed!"

Dante choked back a whoop. "I can't believe it! We found it! It's ours! Now all we have to do is figure out how to bring it up."

"Not so fast," the captain said seriously. "What we saw last night was at three hundred and fifty feet. And that was just the top of the debris field. Who knows how much farther down the slope the treasure could be? There's no way I can let you kids — even you, Star — dive so deep."

Star's jaw stiffened. "That's not your decision to make! No offense, Captain — you've been great to us. But we're talking about a billion dollars here!"

"It isn't worth a dime if you get yourself killed going after it."

Dante was horrified. "You mean we're just going to *leave* it there?"

"Calm down," Vanover soothed. "There are ways to salvage things from deep water. It's possible, but it's tricky. And you have to know exactly what you're doing. Take it easy. We've got time. Cutter's looking in the wrong place; and he doesn't know that you guys are looking at all."

Kaz and Dante exchanged a worried look. "That's not exactly true," Kaz began slowly. He told the others about finding the footprints on the cabin floor in front of the bell. "We have to assume it's Cutter," he finished. "Who else could it be?"

Star looked alarmed. "That's trouble. If he sees us nosing around the second debris field, we'll be leading him right to the treasure."

Captain Vanover looked like a man who had just made up his mind. "All right — here's what

we're going to do. Poseidon maintains a research sub called *Deep Scout.* I'm going to req-
uisition it, and we're all going down there. If we
can snag a piece of that treasure and match it to
the cargo list on the web site, we can file a claim
on the wreck with the International Maritime
Commission." He made eye contact with all four.
"Then it won't matter what Cutter knows. It'll be
our prize, not his."

# CHAPTER FIFTEEN

If a bubble helicopter married a submarine, their offspring might look very much like the DSV *Deep Scout*. A gleaming sphere made of clear acrylic sprouted from a titanium hull that was pockmarked with lights, cameras, and other instruments. Six folded manipulator arms gave the submersible an almost insectlike appearance.

"Isn't she beautiful?" crowed Captain Vanover.

"No," said Dante with conviction.

"I guess not," the captain conceded. "But she'll take us where we need to go. Besides, this boat is usually booked six months in advance. You kids have no idea how many favors I had to call in and people I had to lie to in order to get us on the schedule on such short notice."

*Deep Scout* sat on the launch deck of its support vessel. *Scoutmaster* was a much larger ship than the *Hernando Cortés* or the *Ponce de León*. It had to be to house the crane mechanism required to place the deep-sea vehicle in the water, and to pluck it out again when the mission was done.

DIVE

Kaz's head was spinning by the end of the handshakes and introductions. "It takes this many guys to run one little submersible?" he whispered.

"Most of these are *Scoutmaster's* crew," Vanover replied. "But there's always a tech on board monitoring the sub's every move. Remember, *Deep Scout* was built to explore the ocean floor at depths of up to two miles." Seeing Dante turn gray, he added quickly, "We won't be going *that* far down."

Vanover left them and climbed the metal ladder to the big ship's towering bridge. It was his job to direct *Scoutmaster's* captain to the correct coordinates where Dr. Ocasek's camera array had spotted the second debris field.

Dante leaned against the rail, observing the beehive of activity. "You think we're going to have to split the money with all these people?"

Adriana was disgusted. "Is that all this is to you? Money?"

"Yeah, well, maybe those of us who don't already have one-point-two billion dollars are kind of looking forward to seeing how the other half lives," Dante shot back.

Her eyes narrowed in anger. "You have no way of knowing how much my family has or doesn't have."

"You don't have to apologize for being rich,"

Dante insisted. "But don't act all superior because you're in this for pure archaeology. It's easy to be high-minded when you don't need the money. I do."

"I don't care about the money," Star put in grimly. "I just want to see the look on Cutter's face when we show up with that treasure. Us — the losers he picked because we wouldn't be a threat . . . the *cripple* who couldn't possibly dive. . . ." Her voice trailed off, but her eyes were blazing. "I just want to see that."

Money. Science. Revenge. Kaz marveled at the different reasons his fellow interns had for coveting this treasure. His mind was on something else entirely — the skull they had unearthed at Cutter's excavation. More than three hundred years ago, people had perished in this shipwreck.

*And we're going to take their stuff because they're in no shape to protect it anymore.*

The logic was ridiculous. All the gold in the world wouldn't help those poor sailors, three centuries dead, their descendants scattered across dozens of generations.

*Besides, if we don't get that treasure, Cutter will.*

His reverie was interrupted by Vanover's call from the bridge. "Show time, folks!"

If *Scoutmaster's* deck was busy and frenetic, the cabin of the submersible was an incredibly lonely place. When the hatch was sealed, the five-inch-thick acrylic bubble blotted out all sound. It was like being shut inside a glass tomb. They were immersed in *Deep Scout's* titanium hull up to chest level. Above that, the sphere created a greenhouse effect. Brilliant sunlight baked the cramped interior.

"It cools off when you dive," the captain promised. He was flipping toggle switches and adjusting dials on a control panel that wrapped around the pilot's chair.

That was the only official seat. The four interns pressed into the rest of the cabin, an area of deck space about four feet wide and six feet long. It reminded Kaz of the famous college prank to see how many students would fit into a Volkswagen.

At last, all was in readiness. "Topside, this is *Scout*," Vanover said into the microphone. "Ready to rock."

It was an eerie feeling — motion, but no sound — as the huge A-frame crane hoisted the vehicle over the side and placed it almost gently in the water. The interns felt rather than heard the waves smacking against the hull. There was a grating sensation as the drop-lock disengaged.

THE DEEP

And then *Deep Scout* sank into the deep of the Caribbean.

Clear water changed from pale turquoise to blue, and finally to blue-black. Vanover activated the outside floodlights, and the dark sea around them came alive. Curious fish circled this strange titanium wanderer, drawn by the rhythmic pings and pops of the submersible's acoustic tracking system. Others, bioluminescent jellyfish and octopuses, gave the newcomer a wide berth.

"Awesome," breathed Star, bathed in the reddish glow of the control panels.

"You never get used to it," the captain told her, his eyes darting back and forth from the undersea panorama to the data screen over his shoulder.

*Deep Scout* was designed to operate miles below the surface, so it reached the slope at the edge of the Hidden Shoals very quickly. Captain Vanover manipulated the thrusters, and they began to track back and forth across the incline, searching for the debris field they had only glimpsed through Dr. Ocasek's cameras.

An hour later, they had still found nothing.

Star was growing edgy. "I don't get it. We have to be in the right place. GPS coordinates don't lie."

"We're going by the coordinates of the

Cortés," the captain reminded her. "Remember, the camera array was at the end of a four-hundred-foot tether, blowing around in a storm. We can't know exactly where it was when it detected the debris." He was trying to sound confident, but the strain was evident in his voice. He had gone out on a limb to book *Deep Scout*. If they came up empty-handed, it could cost him his career.

All at once, Dante lurched forward, bonking his head on the thick acrylic of the sphere. "There!"

"Where?" cried the other four in unison.

"Down there!"

Vanover dumped air from the ballast tanks, and the submersible descended. The Fathometer gave their depth as 344 feet. And suddenly, there it was in the lights — the long bronze cannon.

"Look!" Adriana pointed. "The ballast stones!"

They were scattered along the slanting sea-floor below the corroded barrel, disappearing into the inky depths.

"Wow," Kaz said, nearly overwhelmed. "How far do they go?"

"Only one way to find out." The captain operated the thrusters. *Deep Scout's* nose dipped, and the submersible followed the slope down.

The ballast stones were still there at four hundred feet. And at five hundred. In fact, the spread of debris seemed to be thickening. As they passed through six hundred, they could make out other signs of the shipwreck — plates, bottles, muskets, helmets. Intermingled with these items was something the interns had not seen before.

"Are those *timbers?*" Dante asked incredulously, his face pressed up against the acrylic of the sphere.

Vanover nodded. "Wood can't survive up on the reef, where the worms eat it. But the deeper you go, the sea life is less dense, and the old ships last longer — especially the parts that are buried in sand."

"That's an awful lot of stuff for one ship," observed Star. "Remember, half of it's up on the reef. This debris has to stop somewhere."

Dante saw it first, but a moment later, *Deep Scout's* lights illuminated it for the others. About thirty feet below them, the slope suddenly flattened out before dropping off again. This tilted plateau, seven hundred feet beneath the waves, was the final resting place of the old ship.

Kaz stared. It was uncanny how sure of it he felt. Naturally, there was no abandoned galleon listing there on the shelf. Yet the mound of debris half buried in the ancient sand was shaped exactly like an old boat, bloated by slow collapse over the centuries. As the vehicle drew closer, they could make out anchors and cannons — even some of the wooden spine of a once-proud sailing vessel.

There was only one thing that didn't make sense. "That's a whole ship," Kaz mused with a frown. "Or most of it, anyway. How did a piece end up all the way over on the reef where Cutter's digging?"

"There's no way this is the same boat," the captain decided. "Crazy as it seems, you kids found *two* shipwrecks, not just one."

Adriana's eyes shone with excitement. "Two shipwrecks!"

"No!" Dante was alarmed. "*Nuestra Señora* was the ship with the money! *That's* what we need, not some old garbage scow that happened to sink next door!"

"Besides," put in Star, "what about the gold dust test? That said the treasure was *here*, not up on the reef."

The acoustic tracker *pinged* as the five thought it over.

Captain Vanover spoke at last. "Let's give these manipulators a workout. If we come up with a gold ingot, it won't make any difference what ship we're pulling it out of." Skillfully, he dumped air and worked the thrusters until *Deep Scout* hovered directly over the remains of the old ship. Then he reached for the controls that operated the submersible's mechanical arms.

The shape that exploded out of the darkness was longer than the submersible itself, a living missile of pure speed and energy. Kaz saw the eye first, blank and staring, a shiny black button the size of a clenched fist. He recognized the creature instantly, even before the enormous mouth gaped open, revealing row upon lethal row of crushing, ripping teeth.

Although he was safe behind five inches of solid acrylic, Kaz felt the terror course through his body. For such an array of weaponry could only belong to one fish in these waters.

It was Clarence, the monster tiger shark that had nearly taken his life three weeks earlier.

And before Kaz had time to scream, the two-ton body hurtled into the side of *Deep Scout.*

# CHAPTER SIXTEEN

The vehicle lurched from the collision, tossing its occupants like socks in a dryer.

"It's —" Before Kaz could make the identification, he smacked heads with Adriana and went down hard.

"Clarence!" Dante rasped, picking himself up off the deck. "He's trying to eat the sub!"

"Hang on, people!" ordered Vanover, clinging to the controls. "He can't hurt us in here!"

At that moment, the enormous shark struck the hull again, knocking *Deep Scout* over on its side. Kaz was pressed against the glass, his face contorted with fear.

"Yeah, well, he's doing a pretty good job of it!" Dante cried, steadying himself on the pilot's seat.

The captain fired thrusters in an attempt to stabilize the vehicle. "He can kick us around a bit. He's as big as the boat. But a shark can't bite through titanium. Or bulletproof plastic," he added as the blunt snout the size of a cocktail table pummeled the acrylic sphere.

"I — " Kaz struggled to think rationally despite his terror. "I don't think he's trying to eat us. It's more like he's *fighting* us, pushing us away."

"Protecting his territory, almost," Adriana added.

"That's impossible," challenged Star. "Sharks don't live at seven hundred feet, do they?"

"They shouldn't," replied Vanover. "No food for them this deep. But old Clarence, he's never been your average hunk of seafood. I'm going to set us down on the bottom. Play dead. See if he'll leave us alone."

He worked the joystick, and the submersible banked away from Clarence's next assault. As the ballast tanks expelled air, the vehicle fell abruptly, stabilized, and dropped again, catching the edge of the shelf a few hundred yards past the shipwreck. It bounced once and then plowed to a lurching halt in the wet mud and sand.

Inside the cabin, the shaken crew of five waited breathlessly. What would Clarence do now?

The big shark circled them at a distance, its streamlined eighteen-foot body blinking in and out of the reach of *Deep Scout's* floodlights.

Go away, thought Kaz, trying to will his message through the pressurized bubble. *Once was a fluke, but now you're stalking me!*

The speaker crackled to life, and they all jumped. "*Scout*, this is topside. Braden, I'm reading you at a dead stop at seven-oh-three. Just checking to make sure that's where you want to be."

Clarence was closer now, still orbiting them, crescent tail sculling lazily. "It's a long story, topside," the captain replied. "But we're okay here. Out."

"*Are* we okay?" Dante asked nervously.

The shark approached from the left, sizing up the submersible with glassy, dispassionate eyes. The mouth was slightly open now, and they could see past the ranks of razor-sharp knives clear into the beast's gullet. And then, without warning, the great predator turned on a dime and disappeared into the blackness.

No one spoke. No one dared. It was almost as if saying the words aloud — *he's gone* — might bring the monster back upon them. For several minutes, there was no sound but the hiss of oxygen, punctuated by the pinging of *Deep Scout's* beacon.

Vanover picked himself up off the deck. "Now, let's see if we can snag ourselves a piece of treasure."

"Yeah!" cheered Dante. "We're still right on schedule! Come on, baby, give us some *gold*."

The others ignored him. They had noticed what Dante had not — that while the captain vigorously worked the controls, nothing was happening.

Vanover continued to fill the ballast tanks with air, but the submersible did not lift off the ledge. "Uh-oh."

"Uh-oh?" echoed Adriana. "What do you mean, uh-oh?"

The captain spoke into the microphone. "Topside, this is *Scout*. I've got two full ballast tanks, but she won't budge off the bottom. Can you see any problems from your end?"

The small speaker crackled with the reply. "Negative, Braden. All your readings are normal. Are your thrusters functioning?"

"That's a yes, topside. Request permission to abort mission and drop weights for a quick ascent."

"Abort the mission?" repeated Dante. "But we need a piece of the treasure to take to court!"

"Forget the treasure," Kaz said sharply. "It won't do us much good if we're stuck under seven hundred feet of ocean."

The submersible shuddered as the heavy lead weights dropped to the mud of the shelf. The interns held their breath. *Deep Scout* didn't budge.

It was the first moment that Star felt real fear.

The incident with Clarence had been unnerving, but she had known all along that no shark, not even an eighteen-footer, could penetrate the submersible's husk. But to be trapped on the seafloor in a titanium coffin — that was far more terrifying. Oh, sure, a heavy salvage ship could reach them with a crane eventually. But such vessels were slow and ungainly. It would take hours, even days, to get one in place above them.

She posed the question, although she dreaded the answer almost as much as the awful fate it would surely foretell. "Captain, how much air do we have left?"

"Just under eleven hours," he replied. "That's if you believe the instruments. And according to them, we should be on the surface by now."

"You mean we're *stuck* here?" cried Adriana. "For how long?"

"Anything more than eleven hours may as well be forever," Star pointed out.

"What about these?" asked Dante, indicating a rack of six miniature compressed-air tanks. "We're not stuck. We can swim out!"

Star shook her head. "Not from seven hundred feet. The pressure's more than twenty atmospheres at this depth. Popping that hatch would be suicide. The water would come in hard enough to crush us."

"So there's nothing we can do?" Adriana couldn't believe it. "We just wait around to *suffocate*?"

"Nobody's suffocating," said Vanover through clenched teeth. He fired the rear thrusters, struggling to point the vehicle's snub nose upward. There was a loud grinding sound; the sub shuddered. And then *Deep Scout* lurched clumsily off the muddy shelf, beginning a slow, angled climb.

The cheering in the tiny cabin was deafening.

"Quiet!" barked the captain. Into the microphone, he said, "Topside, this is *Scout*. We're going to need divers in the water. Repeat: divers — as many as you can spare. This is not a drill."

"What's wrong, Captain?" asked Star. "You fixed the problem. We're on our way up."

Vanover pointed to the temperature gauge on the data screen. It read 44.7 degrees Fahrenheit. "The temp should be going up as we climb into warmer water."

Adriana regarded the readout. "It's not changing."

"The probe is in the belly of the sub, behind two fiberglass plates," the captain explained. "I think those plates separated, and we scooped up a load of mud when we landed on the shelf. That's why the temp is staying low — it's packed in cold mud."

"The shark!" Kaz exclaimed suddenly. "Clarence must have separated those plates when he rammed the hull!"

"However it happened," Vanover went on, "it wouldn't take more than half a ton of muck to throw off our whole ballasting system. *Deep Scout's* a simple boat. She sinks when she's heavy; she rises when she's light. The thrusters are just for maneuvering." He took a deep breath. "We're not going to make it all the way to the surface on thruster power alone."

# CHAPTER SEVENTEEN

Star stared at the captain in alarm. "There must be *something* we can do!"

"Everybody strap on an air tank," Vanover ordered. "I'm going to bring her as high as she'll go. When the thrusters start to fail, I'll blow the hatch, and we'll swim for the surface." He turned to the microphone. "Topside, did you catch any of that?"

"Affirmative, Braden," crackled the speaker. "My divers are dressing out right now."

Star showed the others how to strap the small wing tanks to their arms. *It's unreal,* she thought to herself. *I'm so scared I want to throw up.* And yet, outwardly, she seemed totally unruffled, dispensing calm, efficient advice to her companions. "When we're about to crack the hatch, pinch your nose and blow, like you're clearing your ears on a dive. Otherwise, the pressure jump will bust your eardrums." She affixed the last cylinder to the captain's burly arm.

Kaz, Adriana, and Dante nodded, mute with shock and dread.

The steady hiss of air suddenly jumped to a roar.

DIVE

"I'm bleeding as much gas as I can into the cabin," Vanover explained, "building up our pressure so the water doesn't crush us."

Star kept one eye on the Fathometer readout. They were passing through four hundred feet.

*Still too deep.* To stand a fighting chance, they'd need to reach two hundred.

*One-fifty would be better.*

The sub was vibrating dangerously as the captain fought to pull the vehicle out of the ocean's abyss. *He's right,* she realized. The weak thrusters weren't designed to bring *Deep Scout* back to the surface — and certainly not when the submersible was weighted down with a half ton of mud.

*The question is: How high can we get?*

Three hundred feet. "Come on, girl," grunted Vanover, bathed in sweat. "Don't quit on me now."

As they passed through 250 feet, the black of the ocean subtly morphed into an ultraviolet indigo. Proof that the sun was up there somewhere, far above them.

"Divers in the water," came the report through the tinny speaker.

"Pray we'll have work for them," Vanover said grimly.

Two hundred and twenty feet. The first thruster

failed and *Deep Scout* began to veer left, unable to maintain a steady course.

"Everybody flat on the deck!" the captain ordered. "When the sea comes in, it'll bounce us around like Ping-Pong balls!"

As the interns struggled to arrange themselves on the tiny available floor space, the submersible went into a spin, crushing them together.

Vanover clung to the joystick like it was the saddle horn of a bucking bronco. "Ready to blow the hatch!"

Star risked one last look at the Fathometer: 206 feet. Were they high enough?

She never saw the hatch actually open. It was just gone, and Niagara Falls was roaring into *Deep Scout*. She pinched her nostrils and blew hard, but her ears still exploded with pain as nearly seven atmospheres of pressure brought the ocean down upon them. The impact was crushing, a full body blow that plastered her against the deck. The captain was swept out of his chair and flung into the heavy acrylic of the sphere.

Then, all at once, the tempest was over. *Deep Scout's* cabin was filled with icy water — at two hundred feet, even a tropical sea was cold. Shivering, Star bit down on her regulator and began pushing the others through the open hatch. The nitrogen narcosis hit her almost immediately —

an instant, pleasant wooziness that eased the chill and the salt sting in her unprotected eyes. *It makes sense*, she reasoned. *I'm breathing compressed air at incredible depth.*

Kaz was fouled in some wires that had become exposed when the onslaught of the sea had wrenched the data screen free of the control console. Star got him untangled and barked, "Go!" into her regulator, following his clumsy progress out of the vehicle. She hoped the others could figure out that they had to find the surface now. Surely they were just as narced as she was.

Star watched as Dante, Adriana, and finally Kaz began to kick upward. Exhaling a bubbly sigh of relief, Star followed. Yet through her nitrogen haze, she couldn't escape the feeling that she'd forgotten something important, left a key task undone.

As she rose, a shape drifted out of *Deep Scout* twenty feet below her. Arms outstretched, it began to sink slowly.

The realization burned through the fog like brilliant sun: *The captain!*

She did a U-turn in the water, diving against her body's natural buoyancy. With no weight belt, descent was difficult. She kicked hard against the sea's resistance, her compact form tight and vector straight. Fighting the rules of physics, she closed the gap between herself and Vanover. Fifteen feet . . . ten . . . five . . . almost there . . .

That was when she realized that no bubbles were coming from his nose or mouth. The captain was dead.

His eyes were closed. He must have been knocked unconscious when the surging water slammed him against the sphere. His tank was gone too, probably ripped away by the same irresistible force. The laws of science and pressure — harmless and boring on a piece of paper in diving class. But here in real life — brutal, overpowering, deadly.

She grabbed his arm. It was lifeless, a piece of floating debris. There was one more chance. She pulled out her regulator and forced it between his gray lips.

Nothing. The man was gone.

She screamed with grief and sorrow, and didn't stop until her own choking extinguished her voice.

Convulsed with coughs, she didn't notice the explosion of bubbles soaring upward from her regulator.

*Oh, no! The demand valve!*

By the time she bit down on the mouthpiece, she knew that most of the air supply had already escaped. Only deep, wheezing pulls would draw anything from the cylinder. Below two hundred feet, gas went fast, compressed by the depth.

*I've got to get out of here!*

She shot for the surface, careful not to ascend faster than her slowest bubbles. She got two more gulps of air before the tank went empty, and she swallowed hard to force back her thirst for more.

*Don't hold your breath,* she reminded herself. That was a good way to rupture a lung. All gasses expand on the way up, including the ones already in your pulmonary system.

One hundred and fifty feet. *Hang in there!* She knew she might get another inhalation if she could make it to one hundred — the traces of air in the tank would expand to provide one more suck. She checked her watch — 120 feet — and —

Right there, rising out of the bowels of the ocean, her heart stopped. Beside the Fathometer reading, a single word flashed on and off, accompanied by a high-pitched beeping.

*DECOMP.*

Decompression. She had spent too much time at depth. It was no longer safe for her to return to the surface without stopping to give her body a chance to expel nitrogen.

*But I can't stop! I'm out of air!*

# CHAPTER EIGHTEEN

It was every diver's worst nightmare. The choice that was really no choice at all. Ascend to the surface and risk the harmful, even deadly effects of the bends.

Or drown.

Star made the decision in a split second. It was no contest. Drowning was a sure thing. *I'll take my chances with the bends!*

Upward she soared, her feet kicking like pistons. As she passed through eighty feet, she managed to squeeze another fraction of a breath out of her empty tank. Then she swallowed again, fighting back the craving of her lungs. It was illogical, but she could almost feel the nitrogen bubbles frothing her blood into a milk shake as she rose to warmth and light.

*No thinking,* she exhorted herself. *Swim!*

Star broke through the waves to a world she'd thought she might never see again. Two huge gulps of air — pure heaven — and then the important business of yelling for help. "Hey! *Hey!!*"

Gasping, she tried to orient herself. The steely

DIVE

bulk of *Scoutmaster's* stern loomed about fifty yards away.

Strong hands grasped her from behind, and she cried out in shock.

"It's okay!" the rescue diver soothed her. "I'm here to help. Don't worry — it's over."

"It's not over!" she shrieked. "I'm bent!"

"You weren't down long enough," he assured her. "You came straight up."

"I *didn't!*" she insisted. "I tried to save the captain! He didn't make it! Look!" She held her watch under his nose.

The man took one look at the flashing DECOMP signal and spoke into the transmitter in his hood. "Topside, this is Diver Two. I need a chopper evac to decompression — now!" He regarded Star intently. "The captain — where did you see him and how long ago?"

"He was sinking from two hundred," she gasped, fighting hysteria. Sharp pains stung her hips and knees. Nitrogen bubbles, collecting in her joints — classic symptoms of the bends. "He wasn't moving, wasn't breathing. I tried to give him my air —" She began to shiver with cold, the onset of shock. *Hold it together. . . .*

The diver grabbed her gently but firmly and began to kick for *Scoutmaster.*

Staring straight up into the blinding sun, Star wept bitter tears. She couldn't tell if she was crying for the captain or for herself. It was all the same tragedy. A good man was gone forever, and she was face-to-face with the possibility that this accident was going to end her life, right here, today.

And then she was being hauled aboard, first to a dive platform, and then onto *Scoutmaster's* deck.

She looked up, her vision blurred, and saw Kaz — two of him, actually.

"I'm sorry!" she sobbed.

"For what?" he asked. "Are you okay? Where's the captain?"

"Dead!"

"That's not funny, Star!" It was Dante, with Adriana at his side. "Hey, you don't look so hot — "

"I tried to help him. I stayed too long. I'm *bent!*"

She was having trouble breathing now, struggling under what felt like a boulder on her chest.

She was aware of a lot of frantic activity before someone slipped an oxygen mask over her nose and mouth. Faces flashed through her pain, those of her three companions and others too. The last thing she heard before slipping into unconsciousness was the distant rhythm of an approaching helicopter.

For Kaz, the nightmare was happening again. He stood on deck in his dripping shorts and T-shirt, watching the crew preparing Star's inert body for airlift. It brought him back to a hockey rink, not so many months ago. Drew Christiansen on a stretcher. The ambulance, backing in the Zamboni entrance. And the siren.

Today, that mournful wail was replaced by the thunder of the chopper as it hovered over them, lowering its wire-mesh recovery cage for Star.

*Star. How can this be happening to her? She's the best of all of us!*

He choked back tears as he watched the crew lay her down on the padded bottom of the basket. She had saved his life that day. He would not have made it out of *Deep Scout* without her help untangling the wires that had trapped him.

He was here; he was fine. And she —

The crew backed away, and the cage lifted off. Kaz was suddenly overwhelmed by the sheer loneliness of Star's journey — one from which she might never return. Almost before he knew what he was doing, he was running forward. He put both hands on the rim of the basket and vaulted over the side, landing neatly next to her.

THE DEEP

Everyone aboard *Scoutmaster* — the interns and crew alike — was shouting at him. But the roar of the chopper drowned them out. The basket was winched up through the windstorm of the rotor blades and hauled into the cabin.

No time was wasted. The helicopter was racing to its destination even before the hatch was closed.

The paramedic glared at Kaz. "Not smart, kid. You think this is a game?"

"I couldn't let her go alone," mumbled Kaz, holding on to Star's limp hand.

The craft was only in the air eleven minutes. Kaz watched in awe as they closed in on an enormous oil-drilling platform off the west coast of Saint-Luc. When they descended toward the helipad, he got a sense of the vast size of the structure. It was like an entire city, propped up on titanic stilts, hundreds of feet above the Caribbean.

A medical team was waiting for them at touchdown. Kaz joined the stampede with the stretcher. An elevator took them into the guts of the platform, where the infirmary was located.

The double doors were marked RECOMPRESSION THERAPY. A dour-faced, lab-coated technician barred their way.

"She can't come in here. I've got hard-hat

divers in the water. What if one of them needs — "

Before the man could finish, Bobby Kaczinski, the most promising young defenseman in the Ontario Minor Hockey Association, did what he had been trained to do his entire life. Without slowing his pace, he lowered his shoulder and delivered a crunching body check that put the technician flat on his back.

The decompression chamber looked like a huge high-tech steel pipe about the size of a Dumpster.

Kaz got out of the way as the medical team worked on Star. She was hooked up to various monitors, and an IV drip was started. The oxygen was discontinued, and adrenaline administered.

*This isn't happening . . . this isn't Star . . . this isn't our summer. . . .*

The heavy door swung shut, rubber gaskets muffling the clang of metal on metal. The hyperbaric chamber pressed Star and a nurse down to seven atmospheres — the same pressure as 228 feet. According to the dive computer in Star's watch, that was the maximum depth of her unplanned adventure. Over the next several hours, that pressure would be slowly reduced, giving her system a chance to expel the nitrogen that was overwhelming her body.

But was the damage already done? It had

taken half an hour to get her into the chamber. Thirty minutes of deadly bubbles foaming her blood.

He looked to the chief doctor, but the man's face revealed no clue as to how the treatment was proceeding.

*This is what we get for trespassing on the graves of sailors who've been dead for three hundred years.*

First the captain, and now Star. It was too much to bear.

Two hours later, when Adriana and Dante rushed into the infirmary, the doctor's expression had not changed.

"She's okay, right?" Dante asked eagerly. "Is she okay?"

Kaz just shook his head and directed their attention to the chamber's window. There lay their friend, her face chalk-white, still unconscious.

The double doors swung wide to reveal Menasce Gérard, terrible in his anger and grief.

"This is true, this thing I hear?" he demanded, voice booming. "The captain?"

"He's dead," Adriana confirmed in a husky whisper. "Star tried to save him and she — "

The big dive guide strode to the window in the chamber. His fury softened at the sight of Star, and he placed a hand against the glass, as if trying to project his strength across the space between them. Then he wheeled and faced down the other three.

"*Alors* — here is your treasure! Are you happy now? Do you feel rich?"

They could not argue, nor defend themselves.

They could only wait.

THE DEEP

*02 September 1665*

The Griffin *under full sail was a majestic sight. She was a barque, three-masted, carrying twenty-four guns, and built low to the water, much different from the workhorses of the Spanish treasure fleet. The galleons were massive, with towering decks. Loaded down with their precious cargoes, they wallowed in the sea, sitting ducks for the faster, more maneuverable ships of the great naval powers — England, France, Holland. And, of course, the pirates and corsairs.*

*That was why Captain Blade was not overly concerned about the four-day head start the Spaniards had on the privateer fleet.*

*"We'll overtake them, we will!" Samuel heard him boast to his officers. Under torture, the mayor of Portobelo had revealed the route the fleet would be following back to Spain. There would be no usual stop in Havana. Instead, the galleons would veer to the south, picking their way through the notorious Hidden Shoals.*

DIVE

As the privateer fleet navigated this course, Captain Blade ringed his vessel with lookouts and placed dozens of men in the highest rigging to scan the horizon for sails. Even when the skies darkened four days later and the rains came, he would not allow them to abandon their posts.

The next morning, with eighteen-foot waves crashing over the bowsprit, gunner's mate Blankenship was hurled from the mizzenmast as the barque heeled in the violent seas.

Even York felt the need to plead with the captain for the safety of the crew. "Sir, the ratlines are not fit for man nor beast with the sea in this condition! We've lost one already!"

"And we'll lose many more," Blade predicted. "That's what the scum are for. Better to lose a few hands than the Spanish fleet!"

Samuel, who was cleaning up the captain's breakfast dishes and stumbling on the unsteady deck, exclaimed, "But sir — "

York silenced him with a sharp slap across the mouth.

It stung, but Samuel realized the barber had just done him a favor. For if the man had given Blade a chance to deliver the blow himself, it surely would have come from the bone-handled snake whip.

"Captain," York persisted, "what might a lookout

THE DEEP

*spy in such weather? Do you not know the size and nature of this storm?"*

*"That I do," agreed Blade. "'Tis a monster gale stretching a hundred miles in all directions around a pinhole of clear blue sky. Aye, that's the beauty part."*

*Samuel could not contain himself. "Beauty? Such storms destroy ships, with all hands lost!"*

*"Perchance they do," Blade acknowledged. "But if we're in it, so are the Spaniards." He emitted a diabolical cackle. "Die we might, boy. But if we live, by God, we'll all be filthy rich!"*

# DIVE

*For Chris and Kyle Kovalik*

*07 September 1665*

*The black wave curled high above the* Griffin, *and came crashing down on the barque with a roar like a wild beast. Tons of water washed over the streaming deck. As the bow was hammered down, the stern snapped high in the air with enough sudden violence that men were hurled off the ship to disappear into the raging sea. Such was the nature of the great storm that pounded His Majesty's privateer fleet in the autumn of 1665.*

*Young Samuel Higgins was still aboard the* Griffin *when she righted herself. But this was only because he had been lashed to a bulwark by York, the ship's barber and medical officer. York had been ordered by Captain James Blade to see to the welfare of the thirteen-year-old cabin boy. The barber took this responsibility seriously. Seamen who disappointed the* Griffin's *cruel master often felt the bite of his bone-handled snake whip.*

*The sails were down to bare poles, and the captain himself had hold of the wheel. He steered his vessel straight into the wind, howling curses at the gale.*

THE DANGER

"*You'll not stop me, by God! The* Griffin *will yet ride low with a belly full of Spanish gold! No storm can change that!*"

*There was a crash as loud as a cannon shot, and the mizzenmast snapped clean in two. One hundred feet up, the top of the pole — thick as a century oak — began its plunge to the deck below.*

*Samuel tried to run, but the same tether that had saved him from being pitched overboard now prevented his flight. He was trapped — trapped in the path of hundreds of pounds of falling wood. A scream was torn from his throat, but it disappeared into the shrieking of the relentless wind.*

*The hurtling mast struck the tangle of ratlines and rigging, halting its destructive drop less than a handspan from Samuel's head.*

*Lucky. That was his nickname among the crew.*

*But no amount of luck would save him if the* Griffin *foundered in the onslaught of nature's wrath.*

# CHAPTER ONE

Star Ling came awake with a start, and stared at her unfamiliar surroundings. The room was an undecorated stark white, with one bed — her in it — and one chair — empty. An antiseptic smell permeated the air.

*A hospital?*

Investigating a stinging feeling, she noted that her hand was bandaged, and a tube protruded from the taped wrapping. Her eyes followed it all the way up to a plastic bag of clear fluid that hung from an IV pole by the side of the bed. She also felt the pure oxygen being administered through a nasal tube.

*Am I sick?*

There was a whoop in the hallway outside. "She's awake!"

In barged Bobby Kaczinski, Dante Lewis, and Adriana Ballantyne — Star's dive partners. The sight of their familiar faces triggered an avalanche of memory.

Their summer internship at Poseidon Oceanographic Institute had led the four teen divers to the site of a seventeenth-century shipwreck off the

THE DANGER

Caribbean island of Saint-Luc. When their discovery pointed to the existence of a second wreck in much deeper water, they had gone to investigate in *Deep Scout,* Poseidon's research sub.

Star remembered that. And then . . . the accident. She closed her eyes tightly to keep the tears from coming, and knew the answer before posing the hopeful question:

"Did I dream it all? The captain?"

"It was no dream," Kaz confirmed sadly.

Captain Braden Vanover had been their friend and mentor. When everyone else at Poseidon had treated the interns like unwanted excess baggage, he had spoken up for them, taken them under his wing. He had been at *Deep Scout's* controls when the submersible had failed. It was due to his skill alone that any of them had survived.

"Did we kill him?" moaned Star.

"I ask myself that a thousand times an hour," said Adriana in a broken voice. "I haven't got an answer."

Dante was devastated. "It's my fault. I'm the one who found the first wreck — and the trail leading to the second one." Dante's unusually sharp eyesight was the result of his color blindness. He saw only black, white, and shades of gray, but very little escaped him.

"Don't flatter yourself, Dante," Star told him in a voice that was weak, but very much her own. "You're not that important."

He looked down, embarrassed, and mumbled, "It's good to have you back. They said you might not make it. And after what happened to the captain — "

Star had a vision of Vanover's drowned body, sinking slowly. She had not known that he was already dead. Her attempts to save him had drawn her too deep for too long. An emergency ascent had brought on decompression sickness — the bends — the most deadly of all diving hazards.

Star could not remember what happened after that. "Where am I?" she asked.

"Brace yourself," Adriana advised. "You're about sixty stories above the open ocean, in the infirmary of the main oil-drilling platform. They brought you here by helicopter to a decompression chamber."

"Well, it worked," said Star. "Believe it or not, I feel pretty good — except I have to go to the bathroom, big-time!"

She swung her legs over the side of the bed, and stepped down to the floor. The room spun, and she hit the linoleum, face-first.

Adriana screamed loud enough to wake the dead. *"Nurse!"*

THE DANGER

White-coated staff came running.

Star sat up, her eyes wide and frightened. "I can't walk!"

The doctor on duty was the last to appear. "Ah, you are awake."

Two orderlies lifted her bodily and put her back onto the bed.

"Doctor, what's happening to me?" Star cried out. "My legs won't work!"

"Your legs are just fine," he soothed. "It is your brain where the problem lies right now."

"*What?*" Star was aghast.

The doctor explained that the brain controls the body by sending signals along neural pathways. With the bends, the body is invaded by tiny bubbles of nitrogen gas that block some of the pathways. "Your brain will attempt to develop new ones," he concluded. "In some patients, this is more difficult than in others."

"What do you mean?" Kaz asked anxiously. "She'll walk again, right?"

"It is impossible to determine at this time," the doctor replied. "It depends on the individual and the degree of neurological damage."

"But I've got cerebral palsy!" Star blurted. "I limp already!"

The doctor blinked. He hadn't been on duty

when Star had been treated. "And you're here on a *dive* internship?"

"She's the best diver around!" Adriana put in. "I mean, she *was* — " She fell silent.

The doctor considered this information. "It may complicate matters," he admitted. "Then again, perhaps the same tenacity that made you a diver despite the odds will help your recovery. But your diving career is at an end. You understand this, yes?"

No more diving! Right now it didn't seem like such a big deal, in view of Captain Vanover's death, and with her own future in doubt. But diving had always been more than a hobby for Star Ling. Once in the water, she had no handicap. Without her diving, she would be nothing more than the girl with the limp.

*Stop it!* she ordered herself. *Be happy. You're alive! You could be dead like the captain. . . .*

"And now," said the doctor to the three visitors, "I think it is time to let your friend get some rest."

Shattered, Kaz, Dante, and Adriana headed for the door.

"We'll be right outside," promised Adriana. "Just call — "

"Actually," the doctor interrupted, "I believe

THE DANGER

Dr. Gallagher wants you back at Poseidon."

"That would be a first," Kaz said bitterly.

In the fluorescent-lit corridor, Adriana let out a long breath. "Wow."

"She'll walk again," Kaz vowed, convincing himself as much as the others. "Star's tough. I'll bet she's more upset about not being able to dive."

"No diving," echoed Dante. "Where do I sign up? I will *never* dive again. I might not even shower!"

"Like Poseidon would even let us dive," snorted Kaz. "What do you think Gallagher wants with us? To give us the boot, that's what."

"We should just leave anyway," muttered Dante. "Save them the trouble of kicking us out."

"I have no place to go," offered Adriana in a thready voice. "My parents are jet-setting around the Black Sea, and our house is closed up for the summer."

Kaz stuck out his jaw. "I'm not leaving till they force me out. I don't want that treasure anymore, but I'm sure not going to let Tad Cutter take it. If Cutter's team comes up with that loot, I'm going to be right here to shoot my mouth off to every newspaper and TV station from Martinique to Mars!"

Tad Cutter, from Poseidon's head office in San

Diego, was officially the scientist sponsoring the teen internships. But really, Cutter and his two partners were treasure hunters. These people had turned the entire internship program into a smoke screen to cover their hunt for the wreck of the Spanish galleon *Nuestra Señora de la Luz*.

"I don't want that treasure, either," said Dante. "I mean, I still sort of want it. But it'll kill me if Cutter gets it."

"Gallagher thinks he's such a genius," Adriana put in angrily, "but he's too dumb to notice there's a team of treasure hunters right under his nose. That's the guy who's going to make decisions about our lives."

"Gallagher's a total idiot," Kaz agreed grimly. "It's nuts even to waste our time talking about him. Who knows what could be going on in his very small mind?"

# CHAPTER TWO

Dr. Geoffrey Gallagher leaned close to his office mirror and snipped an offending hair from his left sideburn. As the star of the video documentary on Poseidon–Saint-Luc, it was important for him to look his best. Jacques Cousteau may have been a genius, but he was too short for the screen. And those hats! Geoffrey Gallagher would put a new face on oceanography.

He turned around and regarded the three Californians seated on his couch — Tad Cutter, Marina Kappas, and Chris Reardon from Poseidon–San Diego.

"Well, Tad, what happens now?" the director asked. "We send the kids home, and you and your people go back to California?"

Cutter seemed surprised. "Of course not!" With the interns gone, he would have no excuse to remain in the Caribbean to go after the treasure. "It was an accident, Geoffrey."

"You say that like someone dropped a tray in the commissary!" Gallagher exclaimed irritably. "A man is dead; an adolescent girl very nearly lost her life and may never walk again; and an eighteen-million-dollar piece of equipment is lying broken at the bottom of the sea! That's not an accident — that's a catastrophe!"

Marina spoke up. "Nobody's downplaying the seriousness of what happened. But why penalize the interns? You don't know them like we do. They're good kids."

Gallagher found himself nodding, not because he agreed with her, but because Marina Kappas was drop-dead gorgeous. He found it hard to concentrate when she was around.

"If anyone is to blame in all this," Reardon took up the argument, "it's Braden Vanover. He didn't deserve to die for it, but come on! What was he thinking?"

"I agree," said Gallagher. "Which brings up the question of where *you* were when all this was going on. Those kids were your responsibility."

"I didn't want to make a big deal out of it," Cutter admitted, "but Braden kind of hijacked the whole internship project. Come on, Geoffrey. If you were a kid, what would you rather do — drag a sonar tow over hundreds of square miles of reef, or go deep-ocean exploring in a high-tech submersible?"

It was an absolute lie. In fact, Captain

Vanover had taken an interest in the four interns only when he'd noticed that they were being completely ignored by Cutter and company.

But Gallagher didn't know that. He asked, "And the three healthy ones are still interested in diving?"

"Maybe after a few days," was Marina's judgment. "But even if all they want to do is lie around the beach and fish a little, have a heart and let them. They've been through a lot."

"You're right." Gallagher nodded. "Besides, to ship them home would leave the Ling girl here all alone. It would be a public relations nightmare if any of the kids started talking to the press. Better to keep them happy." A vaguely annoyed look came over his face. "I sent for them today. They didn't come. They wouldn't leave their friend."

There was a sharp rap at the door, and Menasce Gérard walked in.

"Hey, English," Cutter greeted him.

No one seemed less English than English, who even had difficulty making himself understood in that language. The six-foot-five native dive guide had that nickname because legend said his family was descended from an English shipwreck survivor hundreds of years earlier. The young man was an experienced diver who worked on the oil rigs across the island. He had

also done the occasional job for Poseidon —
more specifically, for Braden Vanover. English
and the captain had been fast friends.

He ignored Cutter and his crew, and spoke to
the director. "We just came back since one half
hour," he reported in a voice heavy with exhaustion. "We do not find the body."

Marina spoke up. "I'm so sorry, English. I
know you and Braden were close."

The guide silenced her with a single brooding
glance. English knew the true nature of Cutter's
work, and had nothing but contempt for treasure
hunters.

"I dive again tomorrow, me," he went on, still
speaking only to Gallagher. "After that" — he
shrugged — "there is no point."

"We're all praying that you find him," said
Gallagher sympathetically.

"This is *difficile*," English explained. "Very
deep water, much time for decompression, and
not so much time for looking. I ask for use Tin
Man. Then I can search till I find."

Tin Man was the nickname for Poseidon's one-
atmosphere diving suit. This highly advanced
rigid suit maintained surface pressure at any
depth. The diver could descend as deep as necessary, and stay as long as necessary. Physically,
he or she would never have left the surface.

"I'm sorry, English," the director said seriously, "but Tin Man is a vital part of what we do here at Poseidon. Scientists reserve its use months in advance. I'm afraid the answer has to be no."

The big man scorched him with eyes of fire. "*Alors*, I think maybe you do not pray as hard as you say."

# CHAPTER THREE

Star threw off the covers and swung her legs over the side of the mattress. She paused as a sweat broke out all over her body. She'd been in some tough spots — many of them right here on Saint-Luc — but she couldn't recall fearing anything as much as she now feared putting her feet on the floor.

She recalled the doctor's words: "There is no physical therapy for what you have. Your legs are not damaged. The problem is in your brain. Only *you* can make yourself walk again."

Clinging to the bed rail with her left hand, she swung over and balanced herself on the right side with a death grip on the nightstand. Her feet touched the floor. The contact felt normal, familiar.

*So far, so good.* She let go.

The collapse was total. Both legs buckled. In the nick of time, she flung her arms wide and broke her fall.

A second later, Dante's excited voice was heard from the doorway. "I think she's getting better. She's doing push-ups!"

THE DANGER

"Tell me you're not as dumb as the things you say," Star pleaded breathlessly.

Dante and Adriana picked her up off the floor and helped her back into bed.

Adriana was sympathetic. "Still no good, huh?"

Star grimaced in disgust. "I'm lucky I didn't break both my wrists when I went down." She spied the duffel slung over Dante's shoulder. "Hey, thanks — you brought my stuff."

"Not only that," said Adriana with a grin. She unzipped a side pocket and pulled out a paper bag soaked through with grease. From it she took a dripping sandwich on a once-crusty bun. "It got a little soggy," she said apologetically. "We had to wait over an hour for the motor launch to come out to the rig."

Star's eyes shone. "A conch burger! You guys are awesome. The food on the oil rig is just a notch above poison. No wonder English is so crabby all the time. He probably eats his meals here." She attacked the sandwich with gusto while sifting through her belongings with her free hand.

"My dive log," she exclaimed, holding up a well-thumbed diary. Her face fell. "Oh, yeah. Ancient history." She shook out some articles of clothing, a toiletry bag, a Walkman, and a stack of dive magazines.

An ivory-white object about a foot long fell out onto the blanket beside her. "Hey. What'd you bring this for?"

It was a carved whalebone handle that Star herself had found in the 340-year-old wreckage of *Nuestra Señora de la Luz*. The initials *J.B.* were etched above a large dark stone that was obscured by coral growth. Adriana had e-mailed a photograph of the piece to her uncle, an antiquities expert with the British Museum. He had identified it as the handle of a walking stick or whip, definitely English in origin. This was puzzling, because *Nuestra Señora* was a Spanish galleon. Every other artifact brought up by either Cutter or the four interns had been of Spanish origin.

"It's safer here than it is at the Institute," Adriana reasoned. "Remember — Cutter searched our cabins. This could be the one thing he doesn't know about yet."

"Good point," said Star. "On the other hand, who cares? We're out of the treasure business. We're probably kicked off the island, right? What did Gallagher say?"

"That's the weirdest part," said Dante. "We

can stay. We can even dive if we want to — fat chance! Doesn't it figure? Now that our summer's in ruins, Poseidon remembers we exist!"

"They just don't want to be sued, that's all," said Star. She indicated a bouquet of flowers on her nightstand. "You'll never guess who these are from. Gallagher! And he's flying my dad down here, all expenses paid. If I was home, I'd get him to clean my room, too. Jerk!"

"You *should* sue," put in Dante. "That way at least something good would come out of all this."

"I hope you're kidding," said Star darkly. "No one should make money off what happened to the captain."

"I miss him," Adriana said quietly. "It's weird being at Poseidon. I keep expecting to walk around a corner, and there he'll be."

There was a melancholy silence.

Star finished her lunch. "Well, I appreciate you guys coming by. Hey, where's Kaz?"

Menasce Gérard loaded the last of the tanks onto the deck of the *Francisco Pizarro* and hopped on board. He checked the labels again. Deep diving with scuba gear was a complicated affair. Several different breathing gas mixtures were required, and the slightest error would scrap the dive. *Alors,* this was the last realistic chance to find the captain's body. So one checked, and checked again.

Captain Janet Torrington looked down from her position in the *Pizarro's* wheelhouse. "All set, English?"

Before he could reply, running footsteps sounded on the dock, and a frantic voice called, "Hey! Wait up!" Kaz pounded onto the scene, his dive bag bouncing wildly against his shoulder.

He leaped aboard. "I'm going with you!"

English was furious. "You! You are going nowhere! Get off the boat, or I throw you off!"

"Captain Vanover was my friend, too!" Kaz exclaimed.

"*Vraiment?* Is this so? Then I wish he chooses his friends more carefully! Do you American teenagers think this is some Hollywood *scenario,* and you are John Wayne leading the pony soldiers? This is not an adventure, silly child! And when you return to your shopping malls and MTV, Braden will still be dead!"

Kaz matched him glare for glare, and said the only thing that came to his mind: "I'm Canadian."

"*Je m'excuse* if I do not stamp your passport!"

THE DANGER

"Look, you need me," Kaz argued. "I was there when the captain died. I might recognize something."

"Such as what, monsieur? That there was the water all around, and it was very deep? Pah!" The guide dismissed this with a sweep of his hand. "This detective work I do not need."

"You can't know that," Kaz persisted. "If you come back without the body, you'll never know if I might have seen it. And today has to be the last day because he's been down there forty-eight hours already and . . ."

The sentence was too awful for him to finish aloud. At the bottom of the ocean, the captain's body would join the ocean's ecosystem. It would soon be disfigured by the feeding of sea life.

"Do you understand this job you volunteer for?" English demanded angrily. "This is not a fun swim for looking at the fishies! Three hundred feet of water is between us and what we seek. Do you not know that you must wear the equipment that weighs more than you? Do you not know that you must breathe the special gases because air is poison at such pressure? Do you not know that every minute on the bottom means four minutes of decompression, if you do not want to end up like your friend Star, or worse?" He snorted in disgust. "What you do not know about this dive would fill the set of encyclopedias!"

Kaz did not back down. "I'll stick with you every step of the way. I'll do whatever you do. Come on, you've got to let me try."

Captain Torrington raised an eyebrow at the hulking guide. "I don't think he's going to leave."

Kaz played his trump card. "You blame us for what happened to the captain. Fine. If I get into trouble down there, it's exactly what I deserve."

English harrumphed. "I will instruct you how to do this thing. But I hope you pay attention like your life depends on it. Because it does, monsieur."

As the *Pizarro* cut through the chop on an uncharacteristically hazy and unsettled day, Kaz did his best to squeeze years of training into a single thirty-minute boat ride. He thought the parade of equipment would never end. He would be carrying three regulators, five tanks of different breathing mixtures, three lights — one in his hood, one on his wrist, and a backup in the pocket of his buoyancy compensator, or B.C.

"You think this is daytime?" asked English. "At three hundred feet, it is always night."

Kaz soon learned that a mixed-gas dive had

THE DANGER

as much in common with recreational scuba as a polar expedition had with a walk in the park. Even his wet suit would be inadequate. The lightweight rubber was fine protection from the scrapes and stings of a coral reef. But only a thick neoprene shell would insulate him from the bone-chilling cold of the depths.

*I may be nice and warm down there,* he reflected, zipping up the heavy material, *but here in the tropical heat, I'm going to melt!*

English loaded him down with enough gear to flatten a packhorse. Back home in Toronto, Kaz had been a hockey player. He was used to heavy padding and protection. But this was unbelievable. More than one hundred pounds of equipment hung on his fourteen-year-old frame. It was all he could manage to put together a string of stiff-legged steps to the dive platform as Captain Torrington dropped anchor.

The spot was directly over the last reported position of *Deep Scout*.

All at once, Kaz felt fear. Could he do this? His basic dive certification didn't cover a mixed-gas jump to three hundred feet.

English was also loaded down, but he moved on deck with ease and confidence. He noticed Kaz's unease. "It is not too late for change the mind," he said, almost kindly.

Kaz shook his head stubbornly and jumped down to the platform. His knees nearly buckled on impact.

"Bring Braden home," ordered Torrington.

They hit the waves.

# CHAPTER FOUR

A powerful current manhandled Kaz right away. He fumbled with his B.C. to descend from the worst of its strength. But he forgot his heavy gear, and plunged thirty feet in a few seconds, popping his ears painfully. At last, he stabilized. Surprisingly, the extra weight wasn't too bad underwater, although the thick neoprene wet suit gave him the feeling he'd been laminated.

With effort, he kicked over to join English, and the two headed down the braided rope toward an invisible destination. The depth made Kaz dizzy. His previous dives had been over the reef, with the bottom clearly visible when he entered the water. All he could see now was a void, and its infinite blueness grew darker as they descended through clouds of marine life.

Just as Kaz was beginning to feel the unnerving wooziness of nitrogen narcosis, English clapped him on the shoulder.

*Tank change.* Kaz switched his regulator from the compressed air in his wing bottles to one of the big eighty-cubic-foot canisters on his back. He spat out an unnerving mouthful of salt water, and

DIVE

inhaled the metallic tang of tri-mix. Instantly, the drunkenness disappeared. English had prepared him for this. The intoxicating effect came from the nitrogen in air being absorbed into the body. But with tri-mix, much of the nitrogen was replaced by helium. This would be the gas mixture they breathed while at depth.

Passing through 150 feet, English turned on his headlamp, projecting a cone of illumination in the darkening water. Kaz did the same, and the sea came alive around him. But they were still nowhere near the bottom.

Two hundred feet. The length of a regulation hockey rink. On skates, Kaz could have covered the distance in a few seconds. Yet the surface seemed miles away. Even the fish avoided this darker world, preferring to stay within reach of the sun's light.

Hockey. It amazed Kaz how much the memory still stung. The Ontario Minor Hockey Association finals. A hard body check, a freak accident. And a boy named Drew Christiansen was confined to a wheelchair for life. So much had happened — Captain Vanover's death, Star's injury. Yet this was still the recollection that haunted Kaz, that kept him up at night. The sport he loved, that he was good at, had turned him into a weapon.

That was what had brought him to Poseidon

THE DANGER

in the first place. Diving in the tropics — what could be farther from hockey in Canada? That was why he was here, under seven atmospheres of pressure, hooked up to a floating laboratory of equipment, breathing a chemist's concoction of exotic gases.

Two hundred fifty feet. At last, there it was. The sea floor. It was slanted sharply downward. This was the place where the Hidden Shoals dropped off to deeper ocean.

At 270 feet, the divers made themselves neutrally buoyant for the search. Kaz looked around helplessly. Topside, it had seemed like a simple task: Go down to the correct coordinates and recover the body. But now he took in the featureless expanse of the slope. Their headlamps carved ghostly ovals out of the darkness of the sandy incline.

The divers synchronized watches. Kaz knew they had only twenty-five minutes of bottom time. Even that would require nearly two hours of decompression before they could safely return to the surface from this depth. If they stayed down any longer, they would not have enough breathing gas to complete the decomp. Then they would face the same choice Star had: suffocation or the bends.

So there was a ticking clock behind the hiss of his regulator. Kaz played his light over the vast sameness of the bottom. He kept a nervous eye on English, who was criss-covering the gradient with methodical track lines. To get lost down here — Kaz couldn't even bring himself to think about it. But one thing was for certain: It would be a death sentence.

*Less thinking and more searching. You've only got fifteen minutes left!*

He could feel the cold now, too. A wet suit was, after all, wet. The penetrating chill of the ocean made him shiver. Due to the slope of the sea floor, he had to adjust buoyancy to parallel it. He watched the numbers on his depth gauge: 280 feet, 290. Would they reach three hundred? It seemed likely. This incline continued a long way. Aboard *Deep Scout*, the interns had spotted scattered debris in this area, leading down to the second shipwreck at seven hundred feet.

Another tank change. Kaz clipped his regulator into the second big eighty. Down here, gas disappeared at lightning speed, squeezed to practically nothing by nearly ten atmospheres of pressure. *Eleven minutes.*

Kaz's breath caught in his throat as English descended to investigate a dark shape on the

THE DANGER

bottom. But it was a false alarm — an area of black mud on the sandy gradient. Kaz checked his watch. *Four minutes.*

*We let you down again, Captain,* he thought in misery. *All you did was be nice to us, and you paid for it with your life. We can't even recover your body for a decent burial.*

He squandered his remaining time, barely kicking his flippers. What difference would it make if they found him? Braden Vanover, the man, the friend, would still be dead.

His dark eyes awash in anguish and fatigue behind his mask, English signaled their return to the anchor line. The search was over. Kaz began to cry softly, but he followed without argument. They ascended slowly, allowing their bubbles to outpace them.

As they passed through two hundred feet, the faint glow of Kaz's headlamp, weakened by the distance to the slope, fell upon a huge sea fan. It had doubled over under its own weight. Standing upright, the thing would have been seven feet tall.

A rush of adrenaline electrified Kaz's core, radiating outward to his extremities. The memories of that awful day exploded like a fragmentation grenade inside his brain, jump-cut images, a real-life music video: the roar of ocean flooding the dying sub, the struggle to get out, the panicked ascent. And, through the haze of nitrogen narcosis, a dark, murky picture — an enormous sea fan collapsed on the slope, just a few yards away.

Kaz broke off the anchor line, finning for the buckled fan.

"No!" cried English into his regulator.

The guide was going to kill him for this, and Kaz didn't really blame him. This detour could throw off their entire decompression schedule, a deadly risk. But something other than reason was propelling Kaz away from the rope and safety. There was one final slim chance to recover the captain, and Kaz had to take it.

He swam with all his might, gritted his teeth, and looked down.

THE DANGER

# CHAPTER FIVE

The body was so close that Kaz recoiled in revulsion.

Captain Vanover lay upon the slope, still in the street clothes he had been wearing on *Deep Scout's* final voyage. The arms were in an outstretched position, swaying softly, matching the movement of the fan.

*Calm down!* Kaz ordered himself as his breathing began to accelerate. If he hyperventilated, he could inhale the rest of his tri-mix in no time at all.

Swallowing hard, he descended to the corpse. He watched as the face entered the cone of brightness provided by the headlamp. He had been prepared for a horror-movie image, a hideously disfigured carcass. But what he saw was perhaps even more disturbing. Although his complexion was blue and lifeless, Braden Vanover looked very much as he always looked — as if he were about to speak. To laugh out loud and tell them it was all a big joke.

*It's no joke,* Kaz thought tragically.

The eyes were closed. And when Kaz

DIVE

reached out to touch Vanover's arm, the skin didn't feel like human flesh anymore. It was rubbery — the cold smoothness of neoprene.

English approached from above, his face a mixture of sorrow and triumph. Despite his emotions, he did not waste a single second. At this point, every bottled breath was borrowed from their vital decompression time.

The operation was not complicated. Kaz helped English carry the body — it was surprisingly buoyant — over to the anchor line. The guide attached two lift bags to his friend — one under each arm. Then he inflated the bags with shots of air from his B.C. The body rose up the rope as if by magic. It was out of sight almost immediately.

Back on the ascent, Kaz could only imagine the gruesome discovery awaiting Captain Torrington when the corpse reached its destination. As it rose, the air in its cavities would expand. The body had not been deformed in its watery grave, but on the surface it would be bloated beyond recognition.

Approaching one hundred feet, they switched back to compressed air. Kaz was aware of the pleasant drowse of narcosis, but the feeling had faded by the time English clutched the line and signaled for him to do the same. They had

THE DANGER

reached sixty feet — their first decompression stop.

The idea was that a deep diver could avoid the bends by returning to the surface slowly. This would allow absorbed gases to breathe out naturally rather than bubbling into the bloodstream and tissues. It was achieved by making five stops on the ascent.

The sixty-foot stop was short — four minutes of fish watching and thumb twiddling. But the times quickly grew. The twelve minutes at forty weren't so bad, but Kaz found himself staring at his dive watch during the eighteen minutes at thirty. Another problem: Up here the sea was warm, but their heavy neoprene suits were designed for much colder ocean. He was sweating profusely.

Finally, it was time for the twenty-foot stop. Here, the current was a factor once again. Kaz had to cling to the anchor line to maintain his position. It wasn't difficult at first, but the effort required to keep it up for the full thirty-two minutes was physically exhausting.

*The depth isn't what gets you,* he reflected. *It's the decomp that drives you mad!*

He was really dreading their final stop. It was right in the teeth of the current at ten feet. And it was scheduled to last *more than an hour.*

Plodding up the rope was like mountain climbing — inching hand over hand through an overpowering wind. When they reached the ten-foot mark, he held on for dear life, flapping like a flag in the fast-moving water. It was time to switch to their third and final breathing gas — pure oxygen to speed decompression.

*But how can I change tanks in this current? If I let go with even one hand, I'm lost.*

He tried calling into his mouthpiece. "I can't — "

English cut him off. "You *will*." Curling his right arm into an iron clamp around the line, he enfolded the boy in a bear hug with the left. Kaz struggled clumsily with the hoses, fumbling to clip the regulator in place. His first breath brought in only seawater. The coughing fit followed immediately. To be out of control, untethered from the rope, made his stomach leap up the back of his throat.

"Try again!" ordered English, eyes afire. "*Vite!*"

There it was. A clean snap this time, and the clear, strong taste of oxygen. Kaz grabbed the line once more. Sixty-four minutes to go.

The ache in his wrists grew to twisting agony. His fingers stiffened painfully, and then went

THE DANGER

numb. And the heat — he was quite literally swimming in his own perspiration inside the heavy rubber suit. When he dared to look at his watch, only eleven minutes had gone by.

*Close your eyes. It helps the time pass.*

But the darkness in his head only reminded him of the darkness of the deep, filling his mind with images of the captain's lifeless body listing on the slope.

And when he opened his eyes, he was looking straight at Clarence.

Kaz's very being convulsed with terror as he stared at the shadowy behemoth about twenty yards away. What else could it be but the eighteen-foot monster tiger shark of local legend? The sleek, muscular body, longer than many boats; the triangular dorsal fin; the top-heavy crescent tail; the huge, gaping mouth . . .

He was never actually aware of letting go of the anchor line. He felt the manhandling force of the current. But at that moment, his fear of the shark prevented him from realizing just how much trouble he was in. The water was conveying him away from Clarence — that was all he cared about just then.

"Boy!" shouted English, lunging for his charge.

Accelerating in the current, Kaz noticed for

the first time how huge the shark was — much larger than he remembered Clarence. He could also make out pale yellow markings on the dark gray skin, almost like polka dots. The mouth looked wrong, too, limp and floppy. The tiger shark had powerful jaws, capable of snapping a person in two.

The truth came to Kaz in a moment of horror. This wasn't Clarence at all! This was a twenty-five-foot whale shark — a huge but harmless plankton eater.

He had let go of the anchor line — the *life*line — for *nothing*.

Menasce Gérard watched Kaz's receding form disappear in the surging current. He had no doubt that he could catch up to the boy. But then the two of them would be lost, with no way to call for rescue. No, the only course of action was to remain here; to remain calm. He would complete his decompression, return to the *Pizarro*, and then go after the boy.

*Mon dieu*, those teenagers were trouble. Yet he had to admit that without Kaz, they never would have recovered the captain's body. *Oui*, he owed the boy that. His stubborn insistence on joining this expedition was as courageous as it was foolhardy.

THE DANGER

English regarded his watch. He still had more than forty minutes to go, but he could cut that time in half. It was risky, but necessary to rescue the boy.

Twenty nervous minutes later, he broke the surface. Not wanting to risk even a short swim in the powerful current, he hauled himself and his equipment straight up the anchor line, and swung a long leg over the gunwale of the *Pizarro*.

Vanover's remains had already been placed inside a gray body bag on the deck. Perhaps that was best — to remember Braden as he was, not in this state.

But this was a time for action, not reflection.

"That was fast," commented Captain Torrington. "Where's Kaz?"

English kicked away his flippers and flung off his equipment. "The Zodiac! *Vite!*"

Torrington did not ask questions. In the few seconds it took for the guide to scramble out of his dripping wet suit, she had the inflatable raft on the dive platform, ready for launch. She suggested one change of plan. "You must be exhausted. Let me look for him."

English shook his head. "I let him dive, me. He is on my conscience." He tossed the Zodiac into the water and stepped inside. As the outboard motor roared to life, he looked around helplessly. Kaz had been drifting for almost half an hour.

Who could guess how far away the boy might be?

THE DANGER

# CHAPTER SIX

Tired.

Kaz's awareness diminished one wave at a time, until only that single word remained.

He bobbed in the heavy chop, kept afloat by the air in his B.C. But he felt nothing anymore — no motion, no spray, no heat from the blazing sun. He knew only his own exhaustion.

His sense of time had been the first to go. Underwater, fighting the current, he had lost track of the decompression schedule. Terrified of ascending too soon, he'd done the only thing that made any sense — stayed under until his oxygen had run out. At that point, he'd had no choice. He had broken the waves, gasping for air.

He had no idea how long he'd been floating here. Hours? *Days?* The one thing he knew with absolute clarity was that it couldn't go on much longer.

He struggled against the confusion, reciting his name, address, and telephone number — concrete facts to replace his disorientation.

"My name is Bobby Kaczinski . . . I play right defense . . ."

*Then what are you doing in the middle of the ocean?*

It took a moment for him to come up with the answer to that question.

"I'm a diver. I was on a dive, but something went wrong." He could not remember what, just that he was here, and had been here for a long time.

He barely noticed when the roar of the outboard motor swelled over the whitecaps. Nor did he recognize the dark features that loomed over him as he was lifted into the inflatable raft. But the face of his rescuer was the most welcome sight he'd ever laid eyes on.

Adriana and Dante hurried through the narrow streets of the tiny village of Côte Saint-Luc.

They had ridden their bikes back from the oil rig where they'd spent the afternoon with Star. At Poseidon, they'd been greeted by a message taped to Dante's cabin door: *Boy is at my home.*

It was signed Menasce Gérard.

"What's Kaz doing at English's place?" Dante

queried as they passed the bar and grill where they had bought Star's lunch many hours before. "Do you suppose he's got a dungeon in there somewhere?"

"That was no easy dive they went on today," Adriana reminded him. "I'll bet Kaz did well, and English is having him over for dinner. We might be invited, too."

"That guy hates our guts," grumbled Dante. "If he's having us for dinner, it's because we're the main course."

She swallowed hard, afraid to say it out loud. "Do you think they found the captain?"

"I sure hope so. I don't like the idea of him lost down there."

English lived in a tiny cottage in the center of town. The big dive guide answered their knock, scowling as usual. They looked beyond him to where Kaz sat in a high-backed rattan chair, drinking from a steaming mug.

Adriana stared. Kaz's face gleamed with a thick coating of cream covering an angry red sunburn. "What happened to you?"

"Nothing," said Kaz. "I'm okay."

"But how'd you get roasted underwater?" Dante persisted.

"I lost the anchor line during decomp," Kaz

explained. "Drifted for a while. But we found the captain."

"Thank God," Adriana breathed.

English spoke up. "This ointment is the best remedy. There is an old woman in the hills who makes it. Also the tea. Good for the dehydration."

"Don't ask me to describe the taste," Kaz added sourly.

"So what happens now?" Dante asked English. "With the captain, I mean."

"The body will be shipped to his sister in Florida." The dark eyes flashed bitter resentment at them. "You are maybe surprised there is no miracle cure for three days drowned?"

Adriana felt instant tears spring to her eyes. "You blame us for his death, don't you?"

The dive guide didn't answer right away. Then he said, "I blame only the bad luck. But if you do not come to my island, Braden, he is still alive, yes?"

"We're so sorry," she barely whispered. "He was really good to us."

"I think you take your friend and go now." It was not a suggestion; they were being dismissed.

THE DANGER

Kaz stood up. "You probably saved my life —
again."

"It was you who found Braden," English
said grudgingly. He looked over to where Adriana, always the archaeologist, was staring at
the weathered wooden carving of an eagle's
head and wings that hung in a fishnet in the window of the small cottage. "And you, mademoiselle," he added impatiently. "What may I
say that might drive you away from me and my
property?"

Kaz spoke up. "Give her a break."

"This piece," Adriana persisted. "I e-mailed
a picture of it to my uncle, and he thinks it might
be just as old as some of the other stuff we
found."

English sighed. "If I explain you this thing, you
will leave, yes?"

"Please," said Adriana, flushed with embarrassment.

"The story of my supposed-to-be English ancestor — after the shipwreck, he floated to Saint-
Luc on this wood."

The girl's eyes shone with excitement. "Uncle
Alfie said the piece probably broke off a ship,
because the back is all jagged! And the wood
definitely doesn't come from here!"

English was unimpressed. "This is family legend only — probably not true. And now you will do me the favor to go home."

Kaz paused at the door. "It was worth it — going after the captain, I mean. I'm glad we found him."

"I, too, am glad," said Menasce Gérard.

THE DANGER

*08 September 1665*

*Samuel came awake to the strong taste of rum being forced down his throat. He gagged.*

*"Drink it, Samuel," ordered York. "It'll clear your head." Once again the burning liquid was forced past his lips.*

*Choking and spitting, he sat up and leaned back against the bulwark. He would have vomited, too, had there been anything in his belly. For three days, the crew of the* Griffin *had battled the storm. There had been no time for eating or sleeping with the destruction of the ship so close at hand.*

*The storm. That was what was different now. The tempest had passed, praise heaven. The rain had ceased, the wind was down, and the sea was calm. But the* Griffin — *the barque looked like the aftermath of a battle. Ropes and debris littered the deck. The mizzenmast had been snapped in half, and a loose starboard cannon had smashed through planking and partially collapsed a companionway.*

*The cabin boy's eyes turned to York. The barber's white smock was spattered with blood.* Amputations of broken or crushed limbs, *thought Samuel. The pungent smell of burned flesh filled the air. Stumps sealed, wounds cauterized, all to prevent an infection that would very likely come anyway.*

*The feeling of hopelessness that washed over Samuel was becoming more and more familiar. His had not been a happy life — he had been kidnapped from his family at the age of six, and had worked as a chimney sweep before running away to sea. Yet the despair that visited him now was sharper than what he remembered from his deprived childhood. Fear of dying was not nearly as unpleasant as fear of living. The captain and crew of the* Griffin *were privateers — licensed pirates. Murderers, torturers, thieves. The world would have been a finer place had the ship and all hands gone down in the gale.*

*"Any idea where we are, sir?" Samuel asked listlessly.*

*"None at all, sad to say," the barber told him. "Separated from the fleet and leagues off course. 'Twill be a miracle if any of us see home again. Now shake a leg. The captain's cabin needs tidying after the storm."*

*James Blade's quarters were in a frightful state. He was not a neat man to begin with, hurling objects in his terrible temper, and letting dropped items lie where they fell. The storm had added to this disarray. Possessions and bedclothes were strewn about the*

THE DANGER

deck space, and a crystal decanter of brandy had shattered. Books had toppled from the shelving and lay open, the paper soaking up the brown liquid.

Samuel rescued the books first, out of a feeling that they were more precious than anything else in the room. Although he could not understand the strange symbols on their pages, he suspected that the volumes revealed a world less harsh than this one. A world where life held more than suffering, violence, and greed.

Lying in the twisted bed linens was the captain's snake whip, its baleful emerald eye glowing from its setting in the carved whalebone handle. Samuel drew back. This was the object he hated more than any other — almost as much as he hated Captain Blade himself. The image of Evans the sail maker, Samuel's only friend, brought tears to the cabin boy's eyes. The poor old man had tasted this whip many times. Those floggings had brought on the terrible circumstances in which Blade had pushed Evans to his death.

He was about to make up the captain's berth when the cry came:

"Sail ho!"

A ship! The fleet!

By the time Samuel reached the companionway, seamen were flocking to the port gunwale, and an excited babble rose from the deck. Samuel joined the *rush, careful to avoid stepping on the rats that any shipboard stampede was sure to stir up.*

*Captain Blade strode to the rail. "Well, come on, man! Is she one of ours?"*

*"She's square-rigged, sir! I'm looking for a marking."*

*With a practiced flick of the wrist, Blade snapped open his brass spyglass and put it to his eye.*

*"A galleon, by God! She's a Spaniard!"*

*York pushed his way forward. "One of the treasure fleet?"*

*"Aye!" roared the captain. "Storm-damaged and helpless. Take up your swords, lads! This night we'll be counting our plunder!"*

THE DANGER

# CHAPTER SEVEN

Star sat up in bed and swung her legs over the side, her features set in an expression of grim determination.

*I will not be crippled by this. I had a disability before, and it didn't stop me. This isn't going to beat me, either.*

But her legs buckled instantly, and no force of will could straighten them. A flailing arm tried to catch the nightstand, but succeeded only in up-ending the duffel bag that sat there. The pain that came when her shoulder made contact with the hard floor was nothing compared with the anguish in her heart.

*I didn't expect to tap-dance today, but shouldn't there be some sign of improvement? Some ray of hope that I'm getting better? Something?*

Enraged, she picked up the first thing her hand closed on — the bone handle. With a cry, she hurled it with all her might across the room. With a crack, it struck the steel door frame and bounced off.

All at once, her anger turned inward. *Sure,*

*that makes sense. Smash a three-hundred-year-old artifact. That'll help you walk.*

Now the only piece from the shipwrecks that Cutter didn't know about was lying on the floor like a dropped pencil. She had to hide it away before anybody saw it.

Using her arms, which were swimmer-strong, she began to pull herself across the tiles. Panting, she reached for the hilt. It was just out of her grasp.

"Room 224," came a familiar voice from outside in the reception area.

Oh, no, Marina Kappas!

In a desperate bid, Star stretched her body to full extension, snatched up the carved whalebone, and wriggled back toward the bed. There were footsteps in the hall as she stashed the handle back in the duffel, zipped it shut, and shoved it under the nightstand.

Two legs appeared in the doorway. "Star, what are you doing on the floor?" the striking Californian asked in alarm.

"The Australian crawl," Star replied sarcastically. "What does it look like I'm doing? I'm trying to walk, and it isn't happening."

And then a soft voice spoke her name.

For the first time, she looked up. "Dad," she barely whispered.

THE DANGER

So much had happened in the past weeks, but their exotic location had given it a dreamlike fairy-tale quality. Now, to see her father — someone from home, from her real life — brought it all crashing down on her.

It was heartbreaking and terrifying at the same time.

Mr. Ling scooped his daughter off the floor and lifted her gently back to her bed. There he held her and let her cry.

Zipped safely away in the duffel bag, the whalebone handle rested on a pile of wadded-up T-shirts. What Star had been in too much of a hurry to notice was that the collision with the door frame had chipped a piece of coral from the hilt. The stone set in its center now glowed a deep fiery green.

The crane was so large that, when its winch was in operation, the roar was like an airport runway during takeoff. Poseidon Oceanographic Institute had nothing like it. This titanic piece of equipment, along with *Antilles IV*, the enormous ship that supported it, was on loan from Antilles Oil Company. It was normally used to salvage lost drill parts and underwater piping. But today the quarry was *Deep Scout*, the research submersible that had been disabled and abandoned by the late Captain Vanover and the four interns.

Three hundred feet below, oil company divers fastened grappling hooks and lift bags to the crippled sub's hull. And then the powerful cables began to haul *Deep Scout* from its watery prison. The lift bags inflated as the vehicle rose and the air inside expanded.

Minutes later, *Deep Scout* broke the surface, its clear bubble gleaming in the sun. Dripping, it was winched onto the expansive work bed of the *Antilles IV*, where dozens of crew members awaited it.

Far astern, a second, smaller crane was in operation. It was raising the diving bell, which housed the salvage divers. It also acted as a decompression chamber, saving the deep-sea workers the need to make decompression stops in the water.

Inside the bell, the men played cards, read magazines, and snoozed the time away. But one pair of eyes was glued to the porthole, following the progress of the work on *Deep Scout*.

English watched intently as the crew shoveled an endless supply of wet mud out of the sub's belly. *Oui*, this was in agreement with what the four teenagers had told him. Two fiberglass plates had separated, causing *Deep Scout* to scoop up huge quantities of sand and mud from the ocean

**THE DANGER**

floor. The extra weight had made the vehicle too heavy to return to the surface.

English and his fellow divers were used to decomps that lasted up to two weeks, but today their stay was short. After two and a half hours, the bell was opened, and the deep-water crew emerged. By this time, the sub's titanium husk was suspended above the salvage deck. A single technician stood below, examining the vehicle and making notes on a clipboard.

English went to join him, peering up at the short, snub-nosed hull. He spotted the loose plates almost at once.

He pointed. "Here — this was the problem, yes?"

The man nodded. "The temperature gauge is behind there." He frowned. "I can't imagine how the plates came apart. It's never happened before, and this boat's fifteen years old."

The native guide squinted for a better look. According to the interns, the damage had been done by a collision with the shark Clarence. But, *alors*, this seemed unlikely. The attack of a large tiger shark would batter the fiberglass, leaving dents from the rounded snout. These panels were intact except for the locking mechanism, which was bent apart.

A one-in-a-million shot from an angry predator?

No. Then the connection would be bent *inward*. This was bent *outward* — almost as if it had been pried apart. . . .

"Sabotage?" he mused aloud.

The technician laughed. "What for? Who would go after a research sub? It's got nothing but bottom samples and rare algae."

It took a lot to surprise Menasce Gérard, but when his mind made the leap, he was profoundly shocked. Perhaps other missions were seeking sand and algae. But on this occasion, *Deep Scout* had been after sunken treasure.

Who had an interest in seeing that mission fail?

For Tad Cutter and his crew, frustration had begun to set in. They had been excavating the wreck site on the reef, and knew it to be the fabled galleon *Nuestra Señora de la Luz*. They had found a great many artifacts there — dishes, cutlery, medallions, crucifixes, weapons, and ammunition; even huge items like anchors and cannon barrels. There was only one problem. An estimated $1.2 billion in Spanish treasure was simply not there.

THE DANGER

That amount of silver, gold, and gems didn't merely get up and walk away. It was definitely down there somewhere. But where to look for it? That was the question.

The kids seemed to be after the treasure, too, with Braden Vanover helping them. But why had they taken a submersible into deep water when the shipwreck was right there on the reef, a mere sixty-five feet beneath the waves? Did the kids know something that Cutter didn't?

It was infuriating, and not a little worrisome. The Californians hadn't been out on the R/V *Ponce de Léon* in days. Their excavation was a dead end, but what were they supposed to do? Start from scratch?

Bide their time. That was Marina's idea. But how long could they keep this up before Gallagher noticed that they weren't mapping the reef anymore? How many hours could Cutter waste in the Poseidon laundry room, watching his socks tumbling by in the window of the dryer and praying for a jolt of inspiration?

The machine clicked off, and Cutter listlessly began to fold his clothes.

The laundry room door was pushed open so violently that it slammed into the wall, and English burst onto the scene, his face a thundercloud.

"English — what brings you — ?"

The guide crossed the room in two strides that would have been impossible for a normal-sized person. In a single motion, he pulled a large towel out of Cutter's basket, wrapped it around the smaller man's torso, and pulled tight, binding his arms to his sides.

Cutter was shocked. "What's going on, man?"

His rage boiling over, English squeezed harder. "You will tell me how you killed Braden Vanover, monsieur, and I maybe take you to the police alive!"

Cutter was having trouble breathing. "What are you talking about? Nobody killed Braden! It was a sub accident! The shark — "

"*Enough!*" The diver's booming voice rattled every loose object in the room. "I see this 'accident.' Unless the shark is handy with the crowbar, this is no accident! This is *le sabotage*! And who has the motive for this? *You!*"

The look of astonishment on Cutter's face was so complete that English released him at once. Surely such genuine surprise could not be faked.

"You're *serious?*" Cutter was aghast. "Someone tampered with the sub? And you think it was *me?*"

"I am not blind, me," English growled. "Do you think you can hide from me this thing you do? I see the coral you destroy to search for gold. I see you smash the reef with airlift and jackhammer. You do not fool me!"

"Okay, okay," said Cutter. "We're not saints. But we're not killers, either."

English glared at him. "We shall see." He turned on his heel and left as abruptly as he had arrived.

# CHAPTER EIGHT

Chris Reardon was horrified. "He accused you of *murder?*"

Cutter sat back in his chair in the small office space Poseidon had assigned to the team from California. "Pretty much. He said the sub was sabotaged, and that's what killed Braden and got the girl bent. I think — I *hope* — I convinced him we didn't do it."

The bearded man shuddered. "English! I wouldn't want to have that guy mad at me."

"We already do," Cutter said morosely. "He's figured out what we're doing here. For some reason, he's keeping his mouth shut, or Poseidon would have bounced us by now."

"He probably doesn't talk to Gallagher," Reardon observed. "Either that or he knows we haven't found one red cent in that lousy wreck."

Marina breezed into the office, waving a videocassette. "Hey, guys, ready for movie night?"

"It's three o'clock in the afternoon," grumbled Reardon.

"What's that?" asked Cutter.

Marina flashed all thirty-two perfect teeth. "Nothing much — just a copy of the tape from *Deep Scout's* onboard camera."

Reardon was astonished. "How'd you get that?"

"The chief engineer in charge of the investigation — turns out he likes me." She favored her two partners with a supermodel smile. "You want to know what Braden and the kids were looking for? If they found it, it's on here."

Cutter snatched the tape from her hand and popped it into the VCR on the desk. "Shut the door."

The three treasure hunters huddled around the small TV screen. *Deep Scout's* camera was triggered automatically as soon as the sub was in water. The monitor showed a steady descent from pale turquoise water, teeming with fish, to depths beyond the reach of the sun's rays. It recorded the instant when the sub's floodlights came on, and even the reaction of a startled octopus.

A counter on the top right kept track of elapsed time on the dive. Below that was a depth readout. By following the numbers, they could see that the descent to three hundred feet was quick and direct. But then the sub leveled off and began what appeared to be track lines along the sloped ocean floor.

"They're looking for something," Reardon murmured.

"This must be just past the excavation," Cutter decided, "where the shoal drops off."

They watched the sub's lights play back and forth over the sandy incline for a few minutes. Marina hit FAST FORWARD, and they began to scan the tape at greater speed. The search continued for quite a while, and suddenly Cutter hit PAUSE.

"Look at that!"

All three stared. It was badly corroded and half buried in the sand, but it was easily identified: a cannon barrel.

"Keep going," ordered Marina. "Let's see what else there is."

The Californians watched in awe as the ocean bottom gave up its secrets before their very eyes. Beyond the cannon, a vast debris field opened up, stretching hundreds of feet down the gradient.

The silence in the room was total, because none of the three was breathing.

"That's impossible!" Reardon blurted finally. "The wreck is on the reef, under tons of coral! How did this stuff get all the way down here to" — he checked the readout — "five hundred feet?"

"Deeper," amended Marina, her eyes glued to the monitor. "Look."

THE DANGER

It was true. Not only did the debris continue down the slope, but there seemed to be more of it the farther the sub descended.

"This is unreal!" Cutter exclaimed, more as a complaint than anything else. "I'm looking right at it, but I can't believe my eyes."

And then came a full view of what *Deep Scout*'s occupants had seen before the accident. Far below the surface, lodged on a muddy shelf at 703 feet, the debris field came to an abrupt end in the remains of a ship.

To three trained treasure hunters, the sight was unmistakable. Even some of the wooden ribs of the old hull were visible, packed in the wet sand.

"*Another* ship?" Reardon exclaimed in consternation. "That's impossible!"

"Which one is *Nuestra Señora?*" asked Cutter.

"Who cares?" snapped Marina. "The treasure's not up on the reef. It stands to reason that it must be down there."

Reardon stared at her. "Are you going to dive to seven hundred feet?"

"There are ways," Marina reminded him.

"There's a time factor here, too," the team leader pointed out. "We're just finding out about this. The kids have known for a week."

"The kids wouldn't dare," said Reardon. "After what happened to them, they won't even be stepping in puddles, let alone diving."

"Maybe not," said the team leader, "but they can still talk. Braden may be gone, but there are plenty of other people on this island who could find a use for a billion dollars."

Marina hit STOP, and the screen went blank. "Speaking of poor Braden, some of the locals are putting on a memorial service on the beach tonight. We can't miss it."

Cutter turned pale. "Are you crazy? I can't go to that! English thinks I killed the guy!"

"All the more reason why we have to be there," she argued. "We've come so far, and we're so close. Let's not lose sight of the prize just when it's in our reach."

THE DANGER

# CHAPTER NINE

It was not yet dark, but the bonfire was flaming high into the dusky sky over the beach at Côte Saint-Luc. About forty people were in attendance when the three interns made their way in from the road, hanging back where the mangroves gave way to the flat sand.

Dante, whose color blindness also gave him excellent night vision, squinted at the crowd.

"Who's there?" asked Adriana. "A lot of institute people?"

"All I see is English. He's twice as big as everybody else. The second we get there, he's going to give us the boot."

"Gallagher?" asked Kaz.

"I don't think so," Dante reported.

"Jerk," muttered Adriana. "He won't come to pay his respects because fixing *Deep Scout* is going to cost Poseidon money."

The crowd was mixed. There were sailors and scientists from the institute, and quite a few locals as well. The atmosphere was more subdued than a party, but it was no funeral, either. People

DIVE

talked quietly, sharing reminiscences of Braden Vanover, and adding mementos to a small table where pictures of the late captain were displayed. There was even occasional laughter, as the memories were often funny.

As the three teenagers joined the group, the first familiar face they encountered belonged to Marina Kappas.

"Thanks for coming, guys," she greeted them. "It means a lot. What do you hear from Star?"

"She's not good," Dante admitted, dazzled by the dark-haired beauty. "They've got a physiotherapist working with her, but she's still not walking. Mr. Ling wants to take her home to the States."

"What a terrible accident." Marina's voice was warm with sympathy. "Braden gone, and Star — "

"Star will be just fine," Adriana said curtly.

"Come on, Adriana — " Kaz began.

"No, *you* come on!" The girl had never been one to look for a fight. But right now she was picturing Star standing with them. Star had always been suspicious of Marina's outward show of friendliness. Cutter and his crew were not their friends. Magazine-cover looks did not change that fact.

THE DANGER

"Don't pretend you care about Star," Adriana told Marina bluntly. "Don't pretend you care about any of us." And she literally marched Kaz and Dante away from the Californian, past Cutter and Reardon, and over to the crackling bonfire.

"You're right, you know," Dante said to Adriana. "Star would have done the same thing."

"Star would have bitten her head off," Kaz amended with just a touch of pride. He added wistfully, "Star belongs here more than anybody. She was trying to save the captain when she got herself bent."

The three interns were saying hello to Captain Janet Torrington when they suddenly found themselves in the company of English as well.

Adriana began stammering apologies. "We're sorry, Mr. English. We know we're not invited, but we just couldn't miss this."

"I must speak with you," the big man said gravely. He pulled the three of them aside and walked them to the edge of the group.

The interns exchanged an uneasy glance.

Kaz found his courage. "We have every right to be here. The captain was our friend, too."

English nodded. "*Certainement*, you are right. I owe you this *apologie*, me. You were not to blame for Braden's death. I know this. This is fact."

Dante breathed a sigh of relief. "We thought you were going to kick us out."

"There are many people here you do not know," English told them. "Come. I will introduce."

They were surprised to find that Star was famous among the oil-rig divers. Word had spread that the Antilles platform's hospital was home to a young girl who had gotten the bends while attempting to save Captain Vanover. As Star's friends, Kaz, Adriana, and Dante were famous as well.

"The bends," groaned Henri Roux, Diver 2 on English's team. "I see too many good guys retire into the wheelchair. You make your living at nine hundred feet, sooner or later, the bends gets you, too."

Kaz whistled. "Nine hundred feet! English and I went a third that deep, and we had to carry a hundred pounds of tanks and hang off the line for two hours."

"This is different kind of diving," English explained. "Saturation diving with the hard hat — helmet. Very deep, very dangerous. No tanks. The breathing gas comes from the hose from top-

THE DANGER

side. You decompress in the bell or a chamber, sometimes for many days."

"How far down can you go?" asked Dante in awe.

English shrugged. "Me, the deepest, one thousand three hundred feet. But Tin Man, the one atmosphere suit, it goes deeper. Or the submersible — "

He fell silent. The mention of a submersible brought everyone back to the reason for this gathering.

English clapped two enormous hands together, and the assembly came to order. His voice resounded across the beach.

"We are all the friends of Braden, so you know he was a man of deeds, not words. And if you know me, you see I speak even less. So I just say *merci*.

"Maybe nobody tell you there is a hero in this sad story, a young American girl in the hospital on the main platform. She is sick because she tried to help Braden. If you work on the rig, visit her. She has much courage.

"*Merci* also for the pictures and souvenirs. They will be sent to Braden's family. Tomorrow in Florida they have the funeral. According to Braden's last wishes, it will be a burial at sea."

Kaz's head snapped to attention. "At sea?"

he blurted in dismay. "We almost got ourselves killed getting him *out* of the sea!"

English caught his pop-eyed stare. The Caribbean dive guide and the Canadian hockey player shared a moment of exquisite humor, secure in the knowledge that the man they mourned would have been laughing, too.

THE DANGER

# CHAPTER TEN

The water was cold. Star could feel it, but the wet suit kept the icy chill at bay. Besides, she was so amped about her first real scuba dive that she wouldn't have noticed a cryogenic freeze.

Her breathing was fast but controlled, the hiss of compressed air louder than she remembered from certification class. It was the Saint Lawrence River in upstate New York — cloudy as pea soup compared with the pristine turquoise of the French West Indies. But back then it was Fantasy Land, a hidden world opening up for Star Ling.

She loved everything about it, and right away. She loved feeling her disability vanish underwater. She loved that there was no law of gravity here, that with the help of her B.C., she could fly.

When the wreck came into view, an excitement took hold that electrified her entire being. She held out her glove to touch a corroded porthole, but the murk made distance difficult to judge. Kicking forward, she reached for the ship's iron skeleton, but the muddy Saint Lawrence held the image just beyond her grasp. . . .

DIVE

\* \* \*

Star shook awake, and the dream popped like a bubble. The first few seconds were like this every morning. Disorientation, followed by depressing reality.

*I can't dive. I can't even walk. . . .*

She sat up in bed, propping the pillow behind her. In the guest quarters of the humongous platform, she knew, her father was on the phone with the airlines. Ever since his arrival, Dad had been trying to convince her to return to the States for treatment.

She had resisted. "They know more about the bends here than they do at some hospital up in Boston," she had argued. But the fact was, leaving Saint-Luc felt a lot like quitting.

But quitting what? The internship? This had never been a real internship. Cutter and his team were phonies, Gallagher didn't care, and Captain Vanover was gone forever. Kaz, Adriana, and Dante had become real friends, but let's face it — they were just marking time now. It was only early August, yet the summer was over.

And anyway, Star's condition wasn't improving. If the oil-rig doctors couldn't help her, she had to give someone else a chance. Getting back on her feet again — that was the most important thing. Dad was right about that.

Last night she had given him the okay to book tickets home. It was the smart thing to do. Still . . .

The picture was always the same: a muddy shelf in the ocean's depths, the remains of an ancient vessel. And somewhere in the decayed wreckage —

*Don't think about that!* she ordered herself. *That makes you no better than Cutter!*

But it wasn't the treasure that tantalized her. It was the *challenge*. Like climbing Everest, or walking on the moon. A goal worthy enough to lend this tragic summer some meaning.

She heard footsteps and looked up to see that she was no longer alone. English stood in the doorway, his expression inscrutable.

He said, "I think maybe today you walk."

Her face flamed red. "What are you telling me? That I'm here because I'm not trying hard enough? I've hit that floor so many times even my bruises have bruises! I *want* to walk — I just can't do it!"

In answer, the huge dive guide snatched her out of bed and carried her, cradled like a baby, into the bustling hallway.

Star flailed her arms against his strength. "Are you crazy? What are you doing?"

He pulled over a rolling cart of instruments and an IV pole on wheels. Then he set her on her feet, her right hand resting on the metal tray, her left grasping the pole.

"I'm gonna *fall* — "

"Alors, fall, mademoiselle." English backed away. "Prove me *stupide*."

Her whole body was trembling. Surgical clamps rattled in the tray. A fluid bag on the pole swung like a pendulum. But Star remained upright.

All at once, her right foot lurched forward. It was only a couple of inches, but it was a step — her first since the accident. Star teetered for an instant and stabilized. Her left foot moved next, followed by the right again. The cart and pole rolled with her as she moved in a slow staccato pace down the hall.

"I'm walking!" she cried in amazement.

It all came apart in an instant. The tray overturned, sending surgical instruments flying. Overbalanced, she pulled the IV pole down on top of herself. English swooped forward and caught her a split second before she would have hit the floor.

In her astonishment, the near miss barely even registered with her.

THE DANGER

"I *walked*," she whispered in disbelief. "I'm going to walk."

When Adriana saw the message from her brother, she felt guilty immediately. How many times had she sat here in Poseidon's computer lab? Never once had she e-mailed Payton.

*Jealousy,* she admitted to herself. *He got to go with Uncle Alfie, and I didn't.*

For the past two summers, the Ballantyne kids had been working with their uncle at the British Museum. This year, Alfred Ballantyne had only been allowed one assistant on his Syrian archaeological dig. He had chosen Payton. That was what had brought Adriana to Poseidon in the first place. It was her consolation prize.

**Hi, Ade.**
**Sorry I haven't e-mailed sooner. Uncle Alfie has been keeping me pretty busy, but that's no excuse. Nobody can dig twenty-four hours a day, not even in the desert, where there's nothing else to do.**
**Two shipwrecks! And I'm stuck here, where it takes eleven hours to brush the sediment off an old jug. I'll bet you're having the time of your life. . . .**

She wondered how envious he'd be if he knew that the captain was gone, and Star might never walk again.

**Anyway, here's the thing: Uncle Alfie told me about the problem of the bone handle. Why an English artifact on a Spanish galleon? Well, I did a little Web surfing. Guess what? An entire English privateer fleet was caught in the very same hurricane that sank <u>Nuestra Señora</u>. And that's not all.**

**Check out the Internet address below. Let's see if you come to the same conclusion I did. Then I'll know I'm not crazy. . . .**

Adriana felt a twinge of annoyance. *Why does this have to be all about Payton? He's half a world away!*

But she was also intrigued. She maneuvered her mouse to the link and clicked.

The site was British, maintained by the U.K. government's Ministry of Overseas Trade and Commerce. It was a record of English shipping in 1665 — the year of the storm that had sunk *Nuestra Señora*.

According to the register, a privateer fleet had

THE DANGER

indeed sailed from the port of Liverpool in April of that year. Nine of eleven ships survived the Atlantic crossing to carry out a successful attack on the Spanish settlement of Portobelo. The storm struck in September near the infamous Hidden Shoals. There, the English flagship, a barque called the *Griffin*, was lost with all hands.

Adriana leaned back in her chair, frowning. What was Payton getting at? That the deeper shipwreck might be the *Griffin*? And the J.B. handle came from there?

But it didn't make sense. Star had found that artifact in the wreckage of *Nuestra Señora*, up on the reef.

Then it hit her.

The biggest mystery in all this wasn't the handle. It was the question of what had happened to the galleon's huge treasure. All at once, Adriana had the answer.

Privateers were sponsored by governments, but they were basically just pirates. Their mission was to raid, loot, and sink the shipping of their countries' enemies.

If the *Griffin* had met up with *Nuestra Señora de la Luz* on the high seas, it would have attacked. And if they were successful, the privateers would have stolen every single coin on board.

What, then, if the hurricane of 1665 had

destroyed both vessels? One, a Spanish galleon with an empty hold, foundered on the reef. And the other, an English barque, packed to the gunwales with plunder, sank not far away in the deeper water just off the shoal.

"Way to go, Payton!" she cheered aloud.

It was an amazing theory, a *brilliant* theory. It explained everything — why there was no treasure to be found in the *Nuestra Señora* site, and why all evidence pointed to the existence of that treasure in the second, deeper wreck.

It was perfect, Adriana reflected, but it was just a theory. There was still no proof that the other ship really was the *Griffin*, or that she had ever had any contact with *Nuestra Señora*. Adriana felt herself deflating as the elation deserted her. Payton's logic was inspired; it was probably even correct. But it was incomplete.

She was just about to close her computer's Internet browser when she saw it — a small detail on the British Web site.

According to the records, the *Griffin* had been under the command of Captain James Octavius Blade.

James Blade.

*J.B.*

THE DANGER

# CHAPTER ELEVEN

They were a strange procession down the hall of the hospital of the Antilles Oil platform. Star was at the center, taking baby steps, hanging on to the handles of a walker. Kaz, Adriana, and Dante matched her slow pace, leaning into the hushed conversation.

"Captain James Blade," whispered Star. "How cool is that? I wonder what he was like? Maybe some kindly grizzled old sailor, hobbling around on a cane with a bone handle."

"He was a privateer, Star," Adriana reminded her. "They were as bad as pirates, sometimes worse. He may have hobbled, but he wasn't kindly."

"Or he was a maniac with a whip," put in Kaz.

"The point is, he was a rich maniac," said Dante. "Or he would have been if his boat hadn't sunk. Can you imagine that feeling? All your dreams are coming true, and then — "

"I can," Star said huskily. "I'll never dive again."

Kaz didn't mean to snap, but the thought of Drew Christiansen set off an avalanche of emotion. "Don't you think that's a little nitpicky? You could be in a wheelchair right now!"

Star's eyes flashed, but she nodded sadly. "I know how lucky I am."

"When are you heading back to the States?" Adriana asked Star.

"Friday morning. Poseidon doesn't want me on the catamaran, so we have to wait for an oil company helicopter to Martinique."

"I can't believe you're leaving," said Kaz.

"My dad can't miss any more work," Star mumbled. "The choppers don't run every day. We've got to grab this one."

They nodded lamely.

"The thing is" — Star looked from face to face — "people like Cutter, treasure hunters, they spend decades searching, all for nothing. But between Dante's eyes, Adriana's smarts, and Kaz's guts, we did the impossible. I mean, we found two needles in the world's biggest haystack. If only I could dive, I'd — "

"You'd what?" challenged Dante. "Swim down to seven hundred feet and bag up a billion dollars? It can't be done."

"It can, you know," Adriana argued. "English

can do it. The oil-rig divers go that deep all the time. What did they call it?"

"Saturation diving," Kaz supplied. "But that's a big operation — a diving bell, special breathing gas, a support ship — "

"Maybe English and his friends can get the treasure for us," suggested Dante. "One-point-two billion — you can split it a lot of ways and still come out loaded."

"Are you kidding?" exclaimed Star. "English hates treasure hunters. Why do you think he's so mad at Cutter?"

"We're not treasure hunters," Dante argued. "We're just people who happen to know about some treasure. And we may as well get it, because it isn't doing anybody any good sitting around in the mud."

"And the money goes to charity, of course," Adriana added sarcastically.

"What's so bad about wanting money?" Dante shot back. "I don't see your family giving away its millions. Come on, let's just ask the guy."

"It looks like you're going to get your chance," observed Kaz.

They had reached the door of Star's hospital room. There, seated on the edge of the bed, his face unsmiling as always, sat English.

Pushing the walker, Star led the way inside. "Look how fast I'm getting. Think they've got some kind of NASCAR for these things?"

The dive guide got to his feet, towering over the interns. "*Bon.* You are all here. Now you will tell me — on *Deep Scout, exactement* what did you find?"

"Sure." Adriana explained their theory of the wrecks of *Nuestra Señora de la Luz* and the *Griffin,* and the vast treasure that lay in the ruins of the second ship. "We can't be positive, but we're ninety-nine percent sure. The J.B. handle proves it. Captain Blade must have lost his walking stick or whip during the battle over *Nuestra Señora.* That's why we found an English artifact in a Spanish galleon."

"One billion American dollars," English repeated gravely.

"One-point-two," amended Dante.

"We didn't think you wanted to know," put in Kaz. "Every time treasure came up, you got mad. What's the big interest now?"

English rested his chin on an enormous fist. "At Poseidon, I see Monsieur Cutter's name on the schedule for use Tin Man. Such equipment is not for working on the reef. I think he tries to find this treasure for himself."

THE DANGER

"But Cutter doesn't even know about the second ship," argued Kaz.

"Perhaps he knows more than you think." English paused reluctantly. "You must not jump on the conclusions. But this thing you should hear: The damage to *Deep Scout* — this was not the shark attack. It was the sabotage." He explained the tampering he'd observed on the fiberglass plates that covered the sub's temperature probe.

The interns were horrified.

"Cutter!" Adriana exclaimed. "He killed the captain!"

"He could have killed all of us," added Star. "And he nearly put me in a wheelchair."

"I always knew he was a jerk," put in Kaz. "But I never thought he was a murderer."

"I have no proof, me," English said sternly. "When I talk to him, he seems very surprised. Conviction without trial — this is not civilized."

"But how else could he know about the deeper wreck?" Dante persisted.

"We have a saying — on a small island, all the world knows your underwear size. A secret — on Saint-Luc there is no such thing. Me, I do not accuse Monsieur Cutter of murder — yet. *Alors*, however he learns of this treasure, I think he dives for it Saturday."

"We've got to stop him," Star exclaimed determinedly. "Otherwise we're letting him get rich off the captain's death."

"Stop him," repeated English. "How to do this?"

"By beating him to the treasure," Kaz reasoned. "You know saturation diving; I know where the wreck is. I'll go with you."

"*Absolument*, no."

"I made it to three hundred feet; I can do this, too."

English nodded. "You are brave, monsieur. But you are a boy, and no boy is ready for the sat dive."

Kaz stuck out his chin. "I can dive in a helmet; I can handle an air hose; I can sit in a chamber and decompress — "

"Ah, *oui*," English interrupted. "All these things you can learn. But I ask you this: You have been on my island for more than a month. How many old divers do you see? And the men who yet live, they limp, they ache from the bends, from the arthritis, from the injury. You are children from a wealthy country where danger is for the daredevils. I *must* do this job — I cannot trade the shares on Wall Street. You have the choice. Be smart."

"It's the only way to stop Cutter," argued Kaz. "And you can't do it without me."

THE DANGER

"And me," added Adriana. "This is plundered Spanish treasure in the wreckage of an English privateer! Living history! I have to be a part of it."

"Not me," said Dante. "I'll do what I can; I'll help on the boat. I swore I'd never dive again."

"Bravo," English approved. "Someone has the intelligence."

"It can work," Kaz persisted. "You know it can."

English thought it over. "We will need a ship," he said finally. "A bell. Crew who can be trusted. *Très difficile* — "

"But not impossible," Kaz finished.

The guide took a deep breath. "I will try, me."

Star sat down on the bed. "I can't believe I won't be going down there with you."

"We'll e-mail you," Adriana vowed. "You'll get every detail."

Star regarded the friends who had been closer than family for the past few weeks. "I'll miss you guys," she told them soberly. "I hope we can figure out a way to keep in touch back home."

"If this works, we'll be millionaires," Dante reminded her. "Plane tickets are chicken feed compared to the kind of money we're going to have."

Star choked on the notion that this was really good-bye. "I'd trade it all for the chance to go on one more dive with you."

THE DANGER

*08 September 1665*

*Samuel had tasted battle before, but the long slow approach to the galleon brought out in him a cold, numbing dread he would not have believed possible.*

*"Why do they not flee?" he whispered to York. "Or fire upon us? Do they not understand our intentions?"*

*"See how she lists, boy," the barber pointed out. "She's aground. A reef, mayhap. There are treacherous shoals in these seas."*

*Suddenly, smoke and flame belched from the galleon's gun ports. The roar of the volley echoed across the water. Lethal shot came screaming in on the barque. With a sickening crunch, a cannonball shattered a section in the stern, well above the waterline. The deck collapsed for a few feet around it, sending a handful of seamen sliding into the hold. But most of the projectiles sailed over the Griffin and disappeared into the water.*

*Samuel waited for the barque's guns to respond in kind. Then he noticed that all the gunners were assembled with the attack force, swords and muskets at the ready. Captain Blade had no intention of sinking this galleon, not until her treasure was safely aboard his own vessel.*

*The Griffin came alongside the Spaniard, and the grappling hooks were airborne. It seemed only a heartbeat later that scores of heavily armed privateers were scrambling up the ropes to the higher decks of the galleon. Steel-helmeted Spanish troops awaited them there. Muskets fired, and sailors with whom Samuel had broken bread for many months dropped lifeless into the sea.*

*The second wave of privateers caught the defenders reloading. The Englishmen streamed onto the deck. Swords clashed. Men fell.*

*This was a fight to the death.*

*It was well known in the New World that a Spanish galleon was an easy target for corsairs and pirates. The ships were overloaded and slow. The sailors were not trained to fight, and the soldiers were underpaid, underfed, and eager to surrender.*

*No one had shared this information with the gallant crew of a ship called Nuestra Señora de la Luz. The defenders battled like lions, sailors alongside soldiers, and even passengers. The treasure in their hold was the property of His Most Catholic Majesty King Carlos II, and no English pirate was going to get it.*

THE DANGER

Samuel had not raised his sword in Portobelo, but he fought today on the deck of this galleon. He did so to preserve his own life. Not a moment went by without razor-sharp steel slicing his way, or a musket ball whizzing past his ear. To the best of his knowledge, he harmed no one. He used his weapon only to ward off the strokes against him.

But that did not keep the blood off him. It was everywhere, spurting and spraying like water. The deck ran with gore, a flood that spilled over the gunwales until the surrounding seas were filled with sharks, driven to frenzy by the taste and smell of a fresh kill.

At the center of the carnage fought Captain James Blade, a broadsword in one hand and his bone-handled whip in the other. This was a man, Samuel knew, who gloried in battle, even enjoyed it. Yet the expression on his face as he flailed about himself was one of naked fear. The possibility of losing this encounter had occurred to him. It was not a thought that had ever crossed his arrogant mind before.

But the privateers had not traversed half a world only to fall short when their prize lay right under the deck planks beneath their feet. When the tide turned in favor of the English, it was through sheer force of stubborn will.

Seven and eighty privateers had gone into battle

*just an hour before. Fewer than half that number looked on as the Spanish commander yielded his weapon to Captain Blade, representing the surrender of* Nuestra Señora de la Luz.

*Blade accepted the sword in a sullen rage. He raised his whip and began to lash the commander, cursing him for putting up such resistance.*

*A young Spaniard, the first officer, threw himself at Blade, made furious by this dishonorable conduct. He wrested the whip from the corsair's hand and flung it contemptuously overboard.*

*Samuel never knew what gave him the courage to step forward and try to calm his captain down. "You've won, sir. The treasure is yours. You can buy a thousand whips with gems even bigger than that one."*

*The words served to placate the captain. But that did not stop him from ordering that every man, woman, and child aboard the galleon be thrown to the sharks.*

THE DANGER

# CHAPTER TWELVE

English stood in the bow of the *Antilles Adventurer*, appraising the gathering overcast.

Bad weather was coming. That wouldn't affect the divers. At seven hundred feet, the topside conditions might as well have been happening in Paris. But it would certainly be a factor for this sixty-year-old ship. Flat and bargelike, the *Adventurer* wallowed like a garbage scow even in glassy calm. Who knew how she would perform in a storm?

But the boat had two things going for her: She could handle a diving bell and she wasn't on Antilles Oil's work schedule. For an "unofficial" job like this one, English needed a craft that wouldn't be missed.

The six-foot-five figure shuddered slightly in the headwind. Nervousness was not a familiar feeling for Menasce Gérard. He was used to a masterful confidence in his ability to deal with any situation. But treasure hunting did not sit well with him. Nor did the idea of involving his Antilles colleagues in this scheme that could cost them their jobs. But mostly, taking two inexperienced teenagers to seven hundred feet seemed like madness. And yet, this was the only way. So strange, this life!

He could see them now in the late dusk, waiting on the uneven planks of the abandoned marina. Outremont harbor, on Saint-Luc's south coast, had not been used for many years. But it was the perfect place to make the pickup, far from the prying eyes of Cutter or Gallagher or anybody at Antilles Oil.

Since the harbor had not been maintained, English came for them in a dinghy.

Dante stared at the *Adventurer*. "That's the boat?"

"You were expecting the *Queen Mary*, monsieur?" English inquired sarcastically.

The young photographer couldn't take his eyes off the World War II–era ship. "Will it float?"

"Maybe you should dive with us," suggested Kaz. "Then, if it sinks, you'll have time to get out of the way."

Dante bit his lip. "I'll take my chances with the rust bucket."

Once on deck, English introduced the interns to Captain Bourassa and two other oil company

THE DANGER

seamen. A crew of three was bare minimum to run the *Adventurer*, but English didn't want to risk letting too large a group in on their plan. An oil rig was a gossip mill. People talked. News spread.

English's friend Henri Roux was also there, not to dive, but to handle diving operations from topside.

"Is that everybody?" asked Adriana.

"There is one more — " English began.

"Hi, guys."

From the main companionway, limping only slightly more than usual, emerged Star.

The three stared at her.

"You went home this morning!" exclaimed Dante.

Star grinned. "I *am* home. Wherever the action is — that's home."

"But you can't dive." Kaz turned to English. "You're not going to let her dive."

"Cool your jets, rink rat," Star soothed. "I'm not that nuts. But someone has to look after you guys from topside — make sure Henri doesn't blow the bell full of laughing gas by mistake."

"But what about your dad?" asked Adriana. "Didn't he need to get back to work?"

She shrugged. "I talked him into letting me stay. I'm all checked out of the hospital. The doctor says I'm ninety percent. The rest will come gradually."

"You're doing awesome," Kaz observed.

"But you're still limping," Dante added dubiously.

Star looked exasperated. "Bonehead, I'm still me! The bends doesn't cure cerebral palsy."

English addressed Kaz and Adriana. "It is time to press down to our work depth. This will take more than two hours, so we must begin at once."

The *Adventurer* was equipped with a decompression chamber. English, Kaz, and Adriana were locked inside, and Henri Roux manipulated the controls, gradually increasing the pressure. By the time the bell reached the wreck site at 703 feet, the three divers had to be used to the crushing weight of twenty-two atmospheres.

There was an insistent hiss as gas flooded the chamber. Adriana's ears hurt almost immediately. She squeezed her nose and blew out. There was a squeal as the pressure equalized. She would be doing this for the next two and a half hours.

*The things I put up with for archaeology!*

Star's face appeared at the chamber's window. "Ears pop yet?" she asked over the intercom.

THE DANGER

"It feels like somebody set off a cherry bomb in my skull," Adriana replied in a squeaky tone. Saturation divers breathed a mixture of helium and oxygen called heliox. It made you sound like a Munchkin.

Kaz adapted his high-pitched voice into a perfect Bart Simpson impression that had Adriana howling with laughter. Outside the chamber, Star and Dante were practically rolling on the deck.

Even English's baritone was shrill and distorted. "Monsieur Simpson, he is a diver?"

Dante was nearly hysterical. "He's a cartoon on TV!"

"Ah, yes. Your American television." English displayed no hint of a smile. "Amuse yourselves now. On the bottom, there is no laughing, only danger."

"We'll stick to you like glue," Kaz promised.

"That is no help at seven hundred feet. With the backup tank, you breathe maybe three minutes. Ascent, this means only death from the bends. *Alors*, you have one choice — the perfection."

"Aw, lighten up, Mr. English," Dante wheedled. "We're all going to be rich. What are you going to do with your share of the money?"

"I will do nothing," English replied readily.

"Come on," chided Kaz. "You could buy a nice car."

"I do not drive."

"A big house?" prompted Dante. "On the water, maybe?"

"Everything I need, I have."

"What about travel?" suggested Adriana. "Wouldn't it be great to see the world?"

English gave them a disinterested shrug. "Where do people go for vacation? The islands. Me, I am already here. But," he added, "the first money from any treasure will repay Antilles Oil for use their equipment. Another share should go to Braden's family, no?"

Star nodded. "And Iggy Ocasek. He helped us find the deeper wreck."

"I'm going to give some of my share to this guy back home," said Kaz. "A hockey player. He's got — medical bills."

"I haven't thought about what I'm going to do with my share," Adriana told them. "Donate it to charity, I guess."

Dante rolled his eyes. "Yeah, me, too. I'm donating mine to the Dante Foundation."

"For now, there is no money, only talk," English said sharply. "Remember this — gold is valuable because it is hard to get, not easy. And harder still to keep."

THE DANGER

It took two hours for the slow-moving ship to reach the coordinates of the wreck site at the edge of the Hidden Shoals. By this time, the three divers were sweltering in their watertight "dry" suits, waiting to transfer to the bell. The bell was pressurized and docked with the chamber by means of an airtight tunnel. The three crawled through into the cramped space that would be their home for the operation to come. They carried their Ratcliff diving helmets — Rat Hats.

The bell was dark and damp, and smelled like a locker room after the big game — the odor of physical labor, bodies, perspiration. The walls were curved, with view ports barely the size of CDs. There was no floor that Adriana could see. They settled themselves uncomfortably on endless piles of coiled umbilical lines. English pulled the hatch shut with a muffled thud.

According to the gauge, the pressure was already equivalent to a depth of 660 feet. *It's happening,* Adriana thought to herself. *We're really going to do this.*

Henri's voice came through the interphone box. "Can you read me in the pot?"

They could hear Dante in the background. "Hey, what does this switch do?"

A quick, sharp slap was clearly broadcast over the hookup, followed by Star's voice: "Cut it out, Dante!"

"Topside, we read you," English reported with a sigh. He added, "Please do not let that annoying child touch anything."

The *Adventurer's* powerful spotlights came on suddenly, capturing the bell like a stage performer. Inside, tubes of light leaped from the round ports. There were a few minutes of equipment checks, followed by the roar of the winch. The bell lifted shakily off the deck.

"Stand by in the pot." There was a jolt, and they were in the water, sinking through deepening shades of blue.

Adriana was amazed at how quickly the sweaty heat deserted them. She hugged her bulky dry suit. "Is anybody else freezing?"

English nodded. "This is normal. The helium — it makes you lose warmth faster than air."

As they descended quickly, English checked the umbilicals, which were really several different lines, taped together like bundles of spaghetti strands — breathing supply, phone cable, safety rope. There was also an extra hose so that hot water could be pumped through a system of tubing that crisscrossed the fabric of their dry suits.

THE DANGER

This would provide warmth against the icy chill of the deep sea.

All at once, English announced, "We are arrived."

"So fast?" blurted Adriana.

*Seven hundred feet may be an alien world,* she reminded herself. *But the actual distance to the surface is a little more than an eighth of a mile.*

English pushed aside cables, welding torches, and a few plastic sandwich bags of high-energy snacks to clear the bell's work-lock beneath their feet. He opened the double hatch to reveal water the color of intergalactic space. The blackness washed upward at first, as if it were about to flood the bell. But then the pressure equalized, halting the ocean's advance.

English helped Kaz and Adriana seal the big fiberglass helmets to their suits before donning his own. Suddenly top-heavy, Adriana overbalanced and conked her Rat Hat into the wall of the bell. "I'm okay," she muttered, recovering. The heliox tasted metallic in the close quarters of the headgear.

"Topside," English reported. "Hats on."

Adriana heard Henri's voice coming from a small speaker by her ear. "Comm. check. Everybody reads me, yes?"

"Loud and clear," she replied into the helmet's built-in microphone.

"Me, too," said Kaz. "Man, this sure beats scuba!"

The three divers stepped into flippers. "Locking out," reported English.

And they dropped into the molasses-dark.

THE DANGER

# CHAPTER THIRTEEN

The *Adventurer*'s topside dive station was an odd place for a communications center. The roar from the compressors in the gas shack made it nearly impossible to hear. But Henri, Star, and Dante bent over the console, listening to every word from seven hundred feet.

The divers had been out of the bell for an hour already, and they still hadn't been able to locate the wreck site.

"Don't you remember?" Star said urgently into the microphone. "There was junk scattered all the way down the slope, but the main shipwreck landed on kind of a shelf."

"Well, we found the slope," Adriana reported, her voice distorted by helium. "We just can't find the shelf."

"What do you mean, you can't find it?" Dante demanded. "The coordinates are right, the depth is right — "

"It's a little dark down here, Dante," Kaz squeaked, annoyed. "I can't even see Adriana and English unless there's a light shining right on them."

DIVE

"But it's there," insisted Dante. "It has to be!"

"Enough!" English's voice was stern, despite the high tone. "This is not the time for the debate. We search. And if we find nothing, we go home. *Alors*, this is all we can do."

"But Cutter's getting Tin Man tomorrow," Dante reminded them. "That's in seven hours!"

Star pulled him aside. "Let them work in peace," she said in a low voice.

"That's in seven hours!"

"They *know* that," she assured him. "But scaring them isn't going to help them find anything — "

Dante wheeled away from her and faced Henri. "I want to go down there."

The dive master frowned. "English says — "

Dante cut him off. "I see things that other people don't. I'll find that wreck site."

"No way," said Star. "You don't take a guy who isn't comfortable diving and send him to seven hundred feet."

"You do if he's the only guy who can find a billion dollars!"

"It's too late anyway," Star told him. "We've only got one bell."

Dante pointed to the lift basket that hung on the smaller winch next to the crane that controlled the bell. It was to be lowered to the wreck site to be filled with treasure. "It's going down anyway.

What's the difference if I hitch a ride on it?"

"You must descend very slow," Henri said thoughtfully. "Two hours, maybe more."

"Yeah, right," Star snorted at Dante. "You're afraid to scuba dive, but you can sit in a cage for two hours watching the water around you turn black. You won't make it, Dante. You'll freak out and do something stupid. And then you'll get yourself killed for sure."

"You think I want this?" Dante snapped. "You think I want to risk my life and spend four days decompressing? I'd be thrilled to stay topside while everybody else dives. But I'm the guy who can get it done. End of story."

Henri took Dante to get suited up while Star reported the change of plan to the divers.

"I forbid this!" exclaimed English.

The three interns told him about Dante's color blindness. "He only sees in black and white," Adriana explained, "but he can spot shadings underwater that nobody else can. If anybody can find that wreck, it's him."

English was still skeptical. "And the boy, he is not frightened?"

"He's terrified," Star admitted. "But I've never seen him so determined." She sighed. "I wish I was going down with him."

"You must be more careful what you wish for, mademoiselle," the guide told her solemnly.

Dante clung to the lift basket to keep himself from shaking. Just gearing up for this dive was enough to bring on panic. The bulky dry suit constricted him as if he had been mummified, and the Rat Hat reminded him of a medieval torture device. Dangling at the end of the umbilical, he felt like a worm on a hook.

It was not a smooth and even descent. Instead, he was being ratcheted to the depths in a series of ten-foot drops. In between, the basket would stop for ninety maddening seconds. This allowed him to adjust to the pressure, until it was time for the winch to jerk him downward once more. It was frustratingly slow, but that wasn't the worst part. Waiting for the halted basket to move again was the worst kind of mental strain.

At least he wasn't bored. Thanks to the Rat Hat's comm. system, he could listen in on the other divers as they searched. Henri gave him constant updates on his breathing mix, which changed the deeper Dante got. And Star kept him busy by asking, "How's it going down there?" with every grinding of the winch.

"Oh, great," Dante muttered, his voice

THE DANGER

Mickey Moused by heliox. "An electric eel just wrapped around my helmet, and now I'm picking up Radio Australia."

Many fathoms below, Kaz chuckled. "Good one."

"Can it, rink rat," Star grumbled. "I'm just trying to make sure the guy's okay."

"Of course I'm not okay," Dante told her. "I'm diving, aren't I?"

The blackness began around three hundred feet and, by five hundred, Dante felt as if he were suspended in ink. His hand torch provided some visibility. But the cone of light it squeezed into the void seemed to shrink the deeper he got.

*It's like being blind.* Did he really have a prayer of finding the wreck site in this nothingness?

He spotted the floodlights on the bell long before the other divers were able to see him. By this time, he had been in the lift basket so long that he wasn't sure his stiff body could even move. But it did and, at 680 feet, he allowed Kaz and English to haul him out of the tight mesh.

English carefully detached Dante from the topside hoses and tethered him to an umbilical from the bell. This would enable him to return to the surface in the pot with the other divers when the mission was over.

*Okay, time to get rich,* Dante thought.

The ship they believed to be the *Griffin* had rained debris all the way down the slant, before coming to rest on a tilted ledge at seven hundred feet.

*Find the ledge and you've found the treasure.*

He joined the search, tracking back and forth over the featureless slope. He could not have imagined such terrible visibility.

*You could swim past a five-star hotel if it wasn't right in your light.*

"What do you think?" asked Kaz. "Are you seeing any more than the rest of us?"

"Black is black," Dante replied gloomily. "In color or black and white."

In fact, he was probably seeing less than anybody. His glasses were slowly but steadily fogging inside the Rat Hat. He squinted in concentration, focusing on the dim oval his torch projected onto the muddy grade. Another hour passed. It seemed like a week.

As he panned the endless parade of sand and muck, a round object raced through his field of vision. The others might easily have missed it. But in the gray-on-gray world of Dante's color blindness, shape and texture were everything. He backtracked and picked up the circular form.

THE DANGER

It was a metal plate, pewter probably. *Definitely* very old.

Heart pounding, he shined his light to the left. There was nothing but the underwater moonscape of the seafloor.

*Huh? But where's the —*

Beginning to despair, he turned to the right.

The wreck of a seventeenth-century ship winked into ghostly existence in the murky beam.

He tried to call "Guys!" but he began to cough, choking on his own excitement.

"Dante!" cried Kaz. "You okay?"

"I found it!" Dante rasped through hacking and helium. "The shelf! The wreck!"

"Don't move," ordered English. "We come to you."

"Okay." Dante couldn't take his eyes off the remains of the old vessel. It was almost as if he expected the site to disappear the instant he looked away. Dishware, bottles, muskets, and helmets littered the angled plateau, along with larger items like anchors and cannon barrels. Ballast stones were everywhere. Half-buried timbers poked out from the bottom silt, all that was left of the spine of the wooden craft.

*Now the hard part,* he thought to himself. *Finding treasure in this mess.*

He dropped to his knees, digging an arm experimentally into the soft muck of the shelf. He cleared it away, and aimed his light into the hole. An unmistakable yellow glow shone back at him.

Dante Lewis was staring into a vast pile of gold bars.

# CHAPTER FOURTEEN

It was well after midnight, but the quiet of Côte Saint-Luc harbor was shattered by the rattle and roar of the winch of the R/V *Ponce de Léon*. The thousand-pound piece of equipment being lowered to the research deck was a sight straight out of *Star Wars*. It looked like an eight-foot-tall metal-plated robot, with side-mounted thrusters and mechanical claw hands.

It was Tin Man, Poseidon's one-atmosphere suit, capable of taking a diver to a depth of two thousand feet or more. Tad Cutter had signed it out at exactly 12:01 A.M. Saturday morning.

"I don't see why this couldn't wait until we all got some sleep," yawned Chris Reardon, guiding the huge suit into place for the ride to the wreck site. With a grunt, he added, "This thing weighs a ton."

"Half a ton," corrected Marina.

"We've only got it for a day, and I'm not taking the chance of coming up empty," Cutter explained. "The kids are onto us. English is suspicious. It's time to claim the treasure before some-

DIVE

body beats us to it." He signaled to Captain Bill Hamilton in the wheelhouse. "Ready to go!"

Thunder rumbled as the *Ponce de Léon* picked its way out of the harbor, and headed into open water. Distant lightning illuminated the overcast at the horizon.

They had not yet made it to the wreck site when Captain Hamilton cut lights and power, and called his three passengers to the bridge. "There's a ship ahead," he informed them. "Looks like an old clunker. The oil company has a few still active."

"Did they see us?" asked Marina.

"I don't think so," replied Hamilton. "I went dark as soon as they came up on radar. They wouldn't have visual contact yet."

"You did the right thing," Cutter approved. "Let's stay here and play dead until they pass by."

"They won't pass by," Hamilton told him. "They're anchored. In just about the exact coordinates we're looking for."

"No way," said Reardon in consternation. "There's no oil on this side of the island."

"English!" breathed Marina. "The kids must have told him where the treasure is. And he's put together a team of sat divers to go after it!"

THE DANGER

Cutter let fly a string of curses. "Those guys are pros! If there's anything to find, they'll find it."

"It doesn't matter," countered Marina. "If they're diving sat, they've got days of decompression ahead of them. All we have to do is go down in Tin Man and get one piece of treasure. Then the International Maritime Commission declares the wreck is ours. It won't make any difference if English and his pals pick that ship dry. They'll just be saving us the trouble."

Seven hundred feet below, the interns shrieked, sang, and sobbed out their celebration. They had been belittled, ignored, and deceived. Now, finally, they had their reward — gold, not at the end of the rainbow, but at the bottom of the sea.

Gold, gold, and more gold!

"What's going on down there?" cried Star. "Are you guys all right?"

"You — you won't believe it — " babbled Dante. "You gotta see it — "

"*Will somebody tell me what's going on?!*"

Kaz provided the answer. "Dante hit Fort Knox."

And the party spread to sea level.

For three and a half centuries, the ocean had concealed this prize from armies of treasure hunters, oceanographic experts, and professional divers. Yet four kids on a summer program had managed to unravel the puzzle — with a little help from a West Indian Frenchman named English. And Captain Vanover, of course.

The captain. It was the only melancholy note in this exultant symphony. Braden Vanover should have been here to share this triumph.

Now came the business of recovering the spectacular find. Captain Bourassa repositioned the ship so that the bell and lift basket were directly over the shelf. The divers changed from flippers to weighted boots. Swimming was no longer required. A vast fortune was buried right here. It was simply a matter of digging it up.

After eluding human hands for so long, the treasure of *Nuestra Señora de la Luz* seemed to give itself up in a single glittering moment. Kaz and Dante pulled hundreds of gold coins and ingots of all shapes and sizes out of the seabed. English yanked on what looked like a chain, only to come up with a rope of gold nine feet long. There turned out to be dozens of these. Beneath them, Adriana uncovered strings of pearls, and necklaces decorated with rubies, emeralds, and sapphires that made her mother's expensive jewelry seem like dime-store junk.

Gold and gems were easy to spot, but silver was another matter. Silver oxidizes over centuries

THE DANGER

underwater, so the valuable Spanish pieces of eight were now flat black discs. They littered the bottom like gravel.

"We need a shovel," panted Kaz. He had lost count of his armloads.

"Or a bulldozer," Dante added exultantly.

Even English had trouble keeping the smile off his normally sour face. "Monsieur Cutter, he will — how do you say — have the cow."

"I'm having one myself," put in Adriana. "And my uncle — "

"I wonder how long it'll take to get the whole one-point-two billion," mused Dante.

"Yesterday you refused to dive," put in Kaz. "Now you want to stay here forever?"

"Dante," Adriana explained patiently, "the treasure of a Spanish galleon would fill that basket fifty times."

Star cut in from topside. "I want you guys to come up as soon as you start to feel bushed. Don't try to be heroes. Remember, it only takes one piece to put a claim on the whole wreck."

It was unreal — a scene straight out of some swashbuckling adventure story. The very mud under their boots glittered from the pounds of gold dust that had been dispersed by the whirlpool of the sinking ship. It seemed as if every square foot of bottom silt held something of great value —

gemstone-encrusted medallions and crucifixes, silver cups and plates, solid-gold candlesticks, even hatbands and collars made with braided gold. Dante was disappointed when the jewelry box he pulled out of the mud turned out to be bronze. Then he opened the lid and realized that the thing was packed to the top with huge pearls.

Adriana was on her knees, gathering loose gems, when she spied a strange shape half-buried in the sand. In surprise, she realized that it was wood — blackened and made rock-hard by the centuries at depth and pressure. Intrigued, she played her light over the carved contours and curves. The artifact had been broken on one end. She frowned. Why did the jagged angles of the crack seem so familiar?

When the answer came to her, she nearly cried out in amazement. This, she realized, was the most amazing find of all. Her heavy boots sinking in the mud, she carried the piece to the lift basket and dropped it on top of the growing mountain of riches.

When she looked up again, she saw the intruder.

It was moving slowly but steadily toward them, emerging from the darkness into the cocoon of light cast by the bell. She stared at the armored contraption that was cruising in, powered

THE DANGER

by twin thrusters. For a moment, she toyed with the possibility that the depth had driven her to hallucinations. This looked like something from outer space!

And then she recognized it. Tin Man, Poseidon's one-atmosphere suit, sailing through the water like a humanoid submarine. Tad Cutter!

She tried to call out a warning to the others, but she couldn't make her mouth work. How would the treasure hunter react to the sight of the wealth of *Nuestra Señora* being loaded up by someone else? He had already committed one murder out of greed.

The aluminum-plated suit cruised past the wreck site to the lift basket, not ten feet from Adriana. A bulky arm reached into the cage, and a mechanical claw hand closed on a small gold bar.

Despite her terror, the theft puzzled Adriana. Sure, the ingot was valuable. But it was small change compared to the fortune in the basket.

Star's words came back to her: "It only takes one piece of treasure to put a claim on the whole wreck."

*We could lose it all if we don't stop him!*

Finding her helium-squeaky voice at last, she rasped a warning to the others: "Cutter!"

But Tin Man was retreating from her, gliding

steadily away from the shelf toward the cover of the ocean's cloak.

Kicking off his heavy boots for more speed, English dove for the suit like a linebacker. The comm. system clearly broadcast his "oof!" as he made contact. He hung on, struggling to lock onto the metallic shell.

"What's going on?" came Star's query from topside. "Did somebody say *Cutter?*"

Adriana didn't answer. She was already running in an awkward slow-motion gait, determined to help English, who was being tossed around like a rag doll by Tin Man's hydraulics. The six-foot-five guide looked like a child next to the half-ton suit.

"Help, you guys!" Adriana cried, launching herself into the battle. She grabbed on to the suit's huge leg and hung on for dear life.

"The bell!" English ordered in a strained voice. "Go to the bell! *Vite!*"

"No!" Adriana shrieked. But his logic was clear. If English couldn't handle this sea monster, what hope did a thirteen-year-old girl have?

*But I can't just leave him to fight alone!*

With a superhuman effort, she scrambled up the fortresslike body. Now she could see Kaz and Dante plodding across the wreck site toward them, battling against the weights on their boots.

THE DANGER

Henri was yelling in French over the comm. system, adding volume every time he got no answer.

English's grunts were directed only at the interns. "Stay away! . . . go back! . . . the bell! . . ."

Straining, Adriana pulled herself up higher, until she was looking into Tin Man's Plexiglas bubble.

A yelp of surprise escaped her.

It was not Tad Cutter in there, attempting to steal their find. The face inside the one-atmosphere suit belonged to Marina Kappas.

# CHAPTER FIFTEEN

Aboard the RV *Ponce de Léon*, Chris Reardon crouched over the communications panel, flipping switches and pressing buttons.

"Come in, Marina! Do you read me?"

Cutter sat beside him at a small fold-down table, pounding the keyboard of Marina's laptop. She had been trained on one-atmosphere suits in California. The technical manuals were saved on her computer.

"I found everything about Tin Man except where to oil the hinges," he complained, opening files at light speed. "As far as I can see, we're doing everything right."

"Then she just stopped talking," Reardon concluded. "I hope she's all right." He turned back to the microphone. "Say something, Marina. We're getting nervous here."

Lightning flashed, followed by a crash of thunder. "Weather's getting close," Cutter observed. "Maybe that's the problem."

Reardon frowned. "We won't stay hidden forever. The storm will light us up."

THE DANGER

Cutter said nothing. He was staring in wide-eyed horror at the computer screen.

Reardon glanced at him. "What?"

In answer, Cutter swiveled the laptop so that his companion could see the display. It was a schematic diagram of a deep-ocean submersible.

"That's not Tin Man," Reardon pointed out.

"It's *Deep Scout!*" Cutter exclaimed.

Reardon was confused. "Why would she need the specs of the sub? We never used it."

"The accident!" Cutter's voice was trembling. "English said it was sabotage! I thought he was crazy. But look." He paged down.

Now the screen showed a close-up of the fiberglass plates that protected the temperature probe in the belly of the sub. "Those are the exact same plates that failed on *Deep Scout.*"

"So?" Light dawned on Reardon. "You're not saying that *Marina* rigged the sub? My God, Braden Vanover *died* in that accident!"

Cutter looked pasty in the artificial light. "A submersible must have ten thousand parts. Marina has the drawing for only one of them. It can't be a coincidence!"

"Don't you understand what this means? She's a *murderer!*"

Cutter was in a full panic. "And she's down

where there could be divers in the water! Maybe *that's* why she isn't answering us. Who knows what she could be doing?"

Reardon was shaking now. "Tad, I'm just in this for the money. No one said anybody was going to get killed!"

The decision tore Tad Cutter in two. A man was dead already, and more lives could be at stake. But if he warned the oil company's ship, he would be giving up any chance whatsoever to recover the treasure of *Nuestra Señora de la Luz*, an operation he'd been planning for years.

He hesitated. A billion dollars. A life's dream.

And then he pressed the intercom to Captain Hamilton in the wheelhouse. "Bill, hail the other boat." He sighed. "And you'd better forget about buying that Ferrari."

Far below, all four hard-hat divers were clamped onto Tin Man's husk in a desperate attempt to wrest the gold bar from the iron grip of its mechanical claw.

Star's agitated voice burst into their helmets. "What's going on down there? Has it got anything to do with Marina?"

"She's got some gold!" wheezed Dante. "And she's wearing a U-boat!"

THE DANGER

"It's a one-atmosphere suit," Star said urgently. "Cutter just called to warn us. He thinks she's dangerous!"

Tin Man's flailing arm dealt a tremendous blow to Kaz's Rat Hat. The helmet protected him, but the collision with a thousand-pound piece of equipment knocked him senseless. The force of it sent him tumbling head over heels through the water, his umbilical trailing behind him. The silt cushioned his landing, but he felt nothing anyway. Everything went dark.

English pulled a long knife from a scabbard on his weight belt.

Adriana stared in disbelief. "That can't break through metal!" she gasped.

But that was not the dive guide's plan. Instead, he jammed the blade into the grip of Tin Man's mechanical claw. Using the weapon as a lever, he pried with all his might. The steel snapped, but the gold bar popped free. English dropped the hilt and snatched it up.

"Topside!" he barked. "Raise the basket!"

"Is everybody okay?" pleaded Star.

*"The basket!!"*

The cage began to rise silently, bearing its treasure trove toward the surface.

The sight of this mountain of wealth being lifted out of her grasp drove Marina to rage. Both claws swiped at English, scissoring through the water. One of the pincers caught the shoulder of his dry suit, cutting through the heavy material like it was newsprint. Frigid water flooded the dive guide's body.

"Back to the bell!" he ordered, shivering.

This time, Adriana and Dante didn't argue. They let go of Tin Man, sinking to the shelf.

Left alone against the armored suit, English was at a serious disadvantage. Marina smacked him across the chest with Tin Man's elbow joint. Then the claw reached for his Rat Hat.

Desperately, he ducked. It was the wrong thing to do. The pincers sliced through his umbilical lines, severing them all. A cascade of bubbles erupted from the heliox hose.

Knowing he only had a few lungfuls of gas left in his helmet, English exploded into action. Bracing against Tin Man's massive shoulders, he vaulted up to the suit's lighting array. He reared back the gold ingot and, one by one, smashed the three floodlights.

Marina grabbed for him again. English switched off his own light, disappearing into the dark ocean before her. She could see only the blinding illumination of the bell. More than a few feet away from that, everything faded to black.

Holding his breath as the Rat Hat filled with

THE DANGER

water, English kicked for the bell. Adriana and Dante were right below the hatch, still plodding along in their boots. He streaked past them and burst through the open work-lock. One big breath, and he was down again, pulling them inside to safety.

The broad flat deck of the *Adventurer* tossed in the worsening storm. Heavy rain pelted the comm. station and gas shack. Forks of lightning carved up the angry sky. Thunder drowned out the roar of the winch as it labored to haul the lift basket full of treasure to the surface.

Star and Henri hung on to bulkheads, still barking frantic queries down to the divers. So far, their only responses had been terrifying sounds of struggle and violence.

And then English's voice: "You are all right? You are unhurt?"

Henri let out a whoop. "They are back in the pot!" He leaned into the microphone. "This is topside. We raise the bell, yes?"

"No!" shrilled Adriana. "We're missing Kaz!"

"Missing?" Star echoed. "What do you mean, missing?"

"Marina hit him in the head!" Dante croaked. "He isn't answering us! I think he's unconscious!"

"I will find him, me," English vowed.

"We're going with you," exclaimed Adriana.

"No!" snapped the guide. "If you move from this bell, I will kill you myself! *Entendu?*"

All at once, the boiling clouds lit up like day. Lightning hit with a shattering roar, turning the *Adventurer*'s antenna into a pyrotechnics display. The thunderclap was instant, coming with a shower of sparks. The strike traveled through every electrical system on the ship, frying lights, radar, sonar, comm. panels, and appliances. Even the microphone blew up in Star's hand.

The crane that controlled the basket of treasure ground to a halt. So did the heliox compressors.

Henri was nothing short of frantic. "The backup generator!" With the compressors dead, there was no breathing gas going down to the divers.

Grabbing flashlights from a rack of emergency equipment, he and Star raced into the gas shack. The backup generator looked like an ancient car engine, about the size of a dishwasher.

Star stared at it in dismay. "Their lives depend on *that?*"

Henri pulled out the choke handle and yanked a cord similar to the starter on a lawn-

THE DANGER

mower. Like an old man with a chronic cough, the contraption sputtered twice, and then put-putted to life in a cloud of burning oil.

They held their breath. A few seconds later, the compressors clamored back into operation.

Star let out a long sigh of relief. "Now how do we get communication back?"

"With a miracle only," the dive master replied sadly. "The wires, they are — how do you say in America — toast. *Fini.*"

Star's eyes were haunted. There was no way of knowing what was going on below.

# CHAPTER SIXTEEN

"Say something, Marina. We know you can hear us!"

The weary voice of Tad Cutter echoed inside the sealed environment of the one-atmosphere suit. Marina continued to ignore him, scanning the darkness for a sign of the missing intern. What was there to talk about, after all?

She wondered how her two partners had learned that she had been behind the sabotage of *Deep Scout*. It didn't matter. They had already ratted her out to English's crew. Which meant that the partnership was at an end.

Unease began to seep into her usual confidence. This was not going the way she'd planned it. She's lost the gold bar, the proof of their find. The lift basket was out of reach, and English had destroyed Tin Man's lighting array. Now she was working blind.

"Give it up," Cutter pleaded. "You've already gotten us mixed up in one murder."

The words were out before she could hold them back. "Do you really believe I thought some-

THE DANGER

body was going to get killed? All I wanted to do was flub the dive!"

"But why?"

"Because we were *losing!*" she raged. "We're still losing! To a bunch of snot-nosed kids!"

"It's just money, Marina. It isn't worth people's lives."

"It's a billion dollars!" she shot back. "It's worth anything!"

Inside the armored suit, she stiffened like a pointer. There in the black void of the deep ocean, a faint light flickered.

The missing intern.

The plan came together in her mind. She would trade this teenager for the bar of gold English had taken from her. It wasn't too late! She could claim this treasure yet.

As her finger operated the miniature controls for Tin Man's thrusters, Tad was still raving about how it was all over, and she should give herself up.

She cut the comm. link. He had nothing to say anymore that would interest her.

Kaz came awake, shivering with cold. He remembered the altercation with Marina in Tin Man, recalled clearly the savage blow she had dealt him.

*But why am I freezing to death?*

He wriggled within his dry suit and felt no warmth from the hot-water tubes that crisscrossed the fabric. The hit he had taken must have damaged the heating hose in his umbilical.

*What about communications?*

"English?" he ventured. "Guys? Topside?"

No answer. Comms. were out, too.

With awareness, fear also returned. He could see nothing in the inky sea except for the bell, hanging in a corona of light. There was no sign of the others. Were they waiting in the pot or out looking for him? And Marina? Had she gotten away with that gold bar?

He panned the sea with his light, but the small torch barely made a dent in the blackness.

Then the glowing bell disappeared, and the huge dark shape of Tin Man loomed over him, claws reaching.

He fled right out of his weighted boots, leaving them rooted in the mud. As he swam, he realized with a sinking heart that he would never outrun Tin Man's thrusters. He needed a hiding place. But where?

He was nearing the point where the shelf ended, and the ocean floor sheered up into the slope that marked the edge of the Hidden Shoals. He was just about to douse his torch and try to

THE DANGER

lose himself in the darkness when he spotted it —
a large gash in the joint formed where the ledge
met the grade. Switching off his light, he kicked
his way inside.

The darkness was total, almost choking him.
The terror of the moment was truly paralyzing, for
he knew that he would never see Tin Man's powerful pincers. He would not realize the hunter was
near until he was already taken.

There he cowered, hugging the mud bottom
for any trace of warmth, listening to the chatter-
ing of his teeth and — another sound. Was it the
whir of Tin Man's thrusters? No, it didn't seem to
be mechanical. It was more like a low, steady
gurgling.

*What could it be? There's nothing down
here!*

After what seemed like an eternity, he worked
up his courage and switched on his torch.

What he saw turned his limbs to lead and
brought him to his knees in the sand. The opening
in the sea floor formed a large grotto with a silt
bottom and a rocky ceiling. The gurgling turned
out to be an underwater vent that sent an explosion of bubbles coursing through the cave. But it
was not this natural phenomenon that churned his
stomach to Cool Whip.

It was the sharks.

# CHAPTER SEVENTEEN

Kaz knew a lot about sharks. Their cold black eyes, torpedolike bodies, and gaping jaws full of razor-sharp teeth had haunted his dreams as far back as he could remember. His phobia had been cranked higher and tighter over the years by a personal library of books about the notorious sea predators, constantly read and reread. Kaz knew, for example, that all sharks had to swim to survive. There was only one exception to this rule: when an underwater vent created a stream of bubbles that could aerate the gills of a "sleeping" shark.

There were six animals assembled along the path of bubbles, hanging perfectly still. Five were blue sharks, ranging in length from four to seven feet. It was the remaining one, the biggest, that drew his eyes and filled him with unspeakable horror.

Clarence, the eighteen-foot tiger shark of local legend. Two tons of destructive power, with a mouth large enough to swallow a fourteen-year-old hockey player whole.

For weeks, the interns had pondered what

THE DANGER

had kept this monster in the waters around Saint-Luc while other tigers wandered the oceans. They had questioned what had lured it from the abundant food of the reef down to the empty depths. At last, the mystery was revealed — this vent, this special place.

Yet there was no moment of enlightenment, no finger-snapping understanding. Kaz realized too late that his light had been shining directly into Clarence's unhooded black eye. The crescent tail moved first — just a twitch. That muscle contraction traveled all the way along the eighteen-foot body. The head swung toward him, giving Kaz a view past the forest of serrated teeth, clear into the predator's cavernous gullet.

He felt his grip on reality starting to slip away. In that instant, he forgot Marina in the one-atmosphere suit, and a billion dollars in treasure. His universe became, quite simply, the nine feet of water separating him from his ultimate nightmare — to be ripped apart and devoured as prey.

And then the mouth opened like a garage door as the huge shark attacked.

Kaz did the only thing he could think of. He tried to insert himself into the floor of the grotto. To his immense shock and relief, there was a space for him, a fine groove in the rock beneath the silt. He wriggled into it, thinking small.

The flat snout slammed against his hip. Impact. Pain. He waited for the crushing bite, the tearing wrench of the monster's jaws.

It didn't come. The sawing teeth could not reach him! He switched off his light and huddled in the tiny niche, smothering in his own bottomless dread.

Go away. His mind could conjure up no other words. Go away, go away, go away. Shaking with hypothermia and fear, he clung to his hiding place with mindless intensity. He didn't think about the others, the bell, rescue. Here was safe; here was good. That was all that mattered.

Time passed. Seconds? Minutes? There was no clock on his terror.

It happened without warning, not a hiss, not a click. The supply of breathing gas to his Rat Hat simply stopped.

No!!!

His first notion was completely irrational — that Clarence, unable to pry him from the gash in the rock, had bitten through his umbilical in order to draw him out.

Impossible! A shark's too dumb to come up with a plan like that!

Amazingly, the crisis forced his unreasoning panic to the edges, leaving room for rational thought. This was a diving problem. He was trained for that. Kaz carried a backup tank of heliox for emergencies just like this one. But he would be unable to reach it without coming out of the crack.

With a silent prayer, he switched on his torch. The blue sharks still slumbered in the bubble stream. There was no sign of Clarence.

Water began to dribble into the Rat Hat as the gas remaining in the hose was used up.

Holding his breath, he climbed out of his hiding place and snapped the hose from the bailout bottle to the intake valve on his helmet.

The metallic tang of heliox. But for how long? At this depth and pressure, gas was gone in the blink of an eye. This tank might last an hour on the surface. But here at twenty-two atmospheres — he did the math — less than three minutes. If he couldn't get to the bell in that time, he would die.

He paddled out of the cave, legs kicking madly. He would have given anything for a pair of flippers. But there was no time to think about that now.

There it was — the bell, glowing like a distant diamond off to his left. He pointed the Rat Hat in its direction and kicked for his life. Maximum speed on minimum heliox — that's what he needed.

He was breathing too fast, he was sure.

*But I can make it!*

A dark shape moved in front of the gleaming sphere of the bell. Kaz's hope disintegrated in a puff of precious gas. Tin Man! Marina Kappas stood in the sand of the shelf between him and his goal.

It all came clear. Marina had cut his umbilical to bring him out of hiding. And now he was swimming right into the clutches of Tin Man's powerful hydraulics. It was virtual suicide. But he had no choice. He was already running low on gas. All he could do was make for the bell.

*And pray.*

Another half breath, and the tank went bone-dry. Kaz swallowed hard and stroked on.

Tin Man's armored limb swung out to meet him. The claw opened, ready to strike.

A wall of water moved, and the tiger shark was upon them, exploding out of the darkness.

Kaz went rigid, and the mechanical pincers missed him by inches. Clarence's titanic maw yawned open and snapped shut on Tin Man's aluminum plating. A single jagged tooth found a weak spot in the knee joint. It knifed between two pieces of metal, penetrating the suit's one-atmosphere seal.

There was a pop, and the weight of seven hundred feet of ocean blasted into Tin Man with the force of a battering ram. Marina never had a chance to scream. She was crushed to death in an instant.

A pectoral fin the size of a car door smacked into the empty tank on Kaz's back, sending him careening. By the time he'd recovered, his vision was darkening at the edges. He needed to breathe, needed it *now*. He could already feel himself slipping into a void far darker than the depths.

A thought came to him, one that he assumed would be his last: He had survived Tin Man, had even survived Clarence, only to suffocate just a few feet from the open hatch of the bell.

Something below him in the water was pushing him upward. With a burst of strength that was barely human, Menasce Gérard heaved him in through the work-lock. Limply, Kaz crashed to a pile of wet umbilicals on the curved floor.

Adriana and Dante yanked off his helmet.

Bobby Kaczinski took the sweetest breath he would ever remember.

*08 September 1665*

*Captain James Blade came to regret his decision to have his Spanish prisoners put to death. This was not out of any sense of compassion. Rather, he now realized that he could have used them as slave labor to move the enormous treasure from* Nuestra Señora *to the barque.*

*The treasure. For the likes of Samuel Higgins, who had never held in his threadbare pockets more than a few coppers, the galleon's hold was the king's counting house. There could not possibly be more wealth in all the world. The gleaming silver pieces of eight made a mountain thrice the height of the tallest man aboard the* Griffin. *There were enough gold bricks to build a palace. Pearls and gemstones spilled out of huge chests. Just the loose objects on the deck planking, lying where they had fallen like so much garbage, would have bought and sold empires.*

*The gold bricks were the heaviest. Each one seemed to weigh four times what it should have, and even the smallest armload was almost too much for*

THE DANGER

*the exhausted and wounded privateers. Only forty men remained. Of their number, five were too grievously injured to work. One thing was certain, though. There would be no amputations now. York the barber had fallen in the battle for* Nuestra Señora, *a musket ball having pierced his heart.*

*Samuel thanked God that the bone-handled whip had been flung into the sea, for surely they all would have tasted it at some point during their labors. The work was slow, and the captain was not a patient man.*

*As the sun rose high over the yardarm and then began to set, Blade stood by the makeshift gangway that connected the* Griffin *to the much higher deck of the galleon. From that vantage point, he took stock of every coin and candlestick, cursing and berating the seamen who bore the burden of his newfound riches.*

*"Stir your stumps, you lice-ridden scum! I intend to be many days from here when the Spanish fleet comes looking for this rubbish barge!"*

*The captain would not even take the time to move the treasure below to the barque's hold, so anxious was he to be away. With the wealth of the East and the New World piled about the deck among coiled lines and water barrels, he gave the order to set fire to* Nuestra Señora de la Luz.

*Dusk was falling as the* Griffin *pulled away from*

the blazing galleon. James Blade straddled his deck, chortling with triumph.

"Aye, Lucky is the name for you, boy. Fortune smiled upon me the day you came aboard this vessel."

A figure suddenly appeared amid the smoke of the burning ship. The Spaniard was not much older than Samuel, a cabin boy who had hidden himself deep in the galleon's many lower decks.

With a howl of defiance, the boy twirled a smoking ceramic firepot in a sling over his head. And then the flaming weapon was flung into the air, a streak of orange in the darkening sky. Every soul aboard the Griffin saw it, and yet it could not be stopped. It struck the deck not ten feet from Captain Blade and Samuel. As the earthenware pot shattered, the burning matchsticks ignited the packed gunpowder at its core.

There was a sharp report as the device exploded, spraying hot pitch in all directions. Cries of pain went up among the crew as the searing brimstone splashed onto exposed flesh. Samuel felt a hot stab on his beardless cheek. The captain bellowed in agonized fury.

As the embers flew, a single fleck of fiery sulfur found the collapsed area of deck in the barque's stern. Directly below were stored the ship's powder kegs.

THE DANGER

*No attacking navy could have had the effect of that single speck of flame as it settled upon the volatile barrel stacked among two and twenty others.*

*The* Griffin *blew herself to pieces. In a matter of seconds, Samuel found himself in the water. It was that sudden.*

*Like most of the crew, he could not swim. He floundered in the waves, splashing wildly for just a few seconds before dipping beneath them.*

This is it, then, *he thought.* What a strange place for an English climbing boy to end his life.

*That life had not been a happy one. Yet as he sank deeper into the blackness, he realized wistfully how very much he wanted to live.*

*Suddenly, he was struck in the chest by a hard object rising from below. Instinctively, he clasped his arms around it, and it bore him upward. He broke to the surface, gasping and choking, and stared at the object that was keeping him afloat. It was a piece of the ship's carved figurehead, broken off in the explosion.*

*"Boy — Samuel! Over here!"*

*A short distance away, the captain flailed at the water in some semblance of swimming.*

*Samuel stared. There were no other cries for help, no struggling sailors. Of forty men, he and Blade were the only two left alive.*

*"Samuel — hold on, lad, and kick your way over to me!"*

In this most dire of circumstances, Samuel thought of the murdered Spanish prisoners, the victims in Portobelo, the abused crew of the Griffin, and of Evans the sail maker, who had died at this cruel man's hands.

*"Hurry, boy! Your captain needs you!"*

Without hesitation, Samuel began to paddle in the opposite direction. He paid no attention to the volley of threats and oaths that were hurled after him. And when the tirade stopped, Samuel looked back and noted that James Blade had disappeared into the sea.

THE DANGER

# CHAPTER EIGHTEEN

Dawn was breaking through the overcast as the storm moved off to Martinique and points east. Captain Bourassa and the skeleton crew aboard the *Adventurer* set about repairing the ship's fried electrical systems.

Star paced the deck like a caged tiger, her limp barely noticeable because of her speed and grim tension. It had been four hours since they had last been able to speak to the bell. And then the divers had been involved in a life-and-death struggle against an adversary in a half-ton suit.

"How soon till we get comms. back up?" she asked for the fifth time that hour.

Henri had the console open and was soldering burned wire. "No sooner for the asking so much," he replied, and added kindly, "English, he is the best. If anyone can bring home your friends — "

*That was the problem,* Star thought. *English was a great diver, but he wasn't all-powerful.*

*If anything's happened to them, I'll never forgive myself for surviving!*

DIVE

What a weird twist — that getting bent might have saved her life.

She bit back her impatience, and frowned as the *Ponce de Léon* approached out of the morning mist, and began to draw alongside. Through the haze, she could make out both Cutter and Reardon on deck.

A deep resentment welled up inside Star. Cutter had been the enemy from the beginning. Why trust him now? True, he had warned them about Marina. But what if that was a trick? A lift basket stuffed with a fortune hung dead in the water, somewhere below the *Adventurer*, waiting for power to be restored to the winch. Any piece of that load could be used as evidence in court for a treasure hunter to claim the wreck as his own.

At that moment, Star didn't know what ordeal her friends might have been through, or even if they were alive or dead. But she could be certain of this: They would never forgive her if she allowed their find to fall into the greedy hands of Tad Cutter.

She squinted at the winch, trying to size up the amount of cable wound around the wheel. Surely the basket wasn't too far beneath the surface now.

As she climbed the metal ladder down to the

THE DANGER

dive platform, the words of her doctor resounded in her ears: "You must never dive again. Another case of the bends, and you will surely be in a wheelchair for life."

*Sorry, Doc, but this one's a must.*

And she jumped into the sea.

Her fears disappeared the instant the water closed over her. How could anything that felt so right do her harm? She held her breath, descending effortlessly along the winch cable. She kept her eyes open, almost enjoying the stinging salt. The ocean was clear and quite bright despite the fact that the sun had not yet burned off the morning mist.

At last, the basket came into view, hanging at about forty feet. Her heart nearly stopped at the sight of it.

*Oh, my God! I knew they found treasure, but this is the mother lode!*

Silver turned black; pearls and gems faded. But gold was always gold. It was spectacular — something out of a fairy tale.

She grabbed a solid-gold candlestick and reached for a rope of pearls to wrap around her neck.

Her hand froze. *No. Just proof. Nothing more.* She kicked for the surface.

When she climbed back aboard, her exhilaration was total. No pain, no stiffness. Star Ling was a diver again.

She was sitting on the platform, catching her breath, when the lift bag broke the waves right where she had been swimming seconds earlier. Shouting for Henri, she took a boat hook from the rack and fished the bobbing float out of the water.

She gawked. Fastened by waterproof tape was a simple sandwich bag. Inside the clear plastic was a torn piece of paper bearing the message: TEAM OK. RAISE BELL.

Her heart soared. They were alive! Only —

*How are we supposed to raise the pot without out electricity?*

And then Cutter appeared out of the haze, piloting a Zodiac inflatable over to the *Adventurer*.

He called, "What can we do to help?"

When the diving bell finally broke the surface, English and the three interns were astonished to find themselves deposited not onto their own ship, but to the deck of the *Ponce de Léon*.

What was going on here? They had narrowly escaped Marina only to be delivered right into the hands of Cutter and Reardon.

Luckily, Star was there to explain the situation through the intercom. "I think Cutter's our friend

THE DANGER

now, believe it or not. He's a treasure hunter and a reef wrecker, but he didn't know what Marina was doing. And when he found out, he warned us right away."

"Marina didn't make it," Kaz said soberly. He offered no details. It would be a while before he would be ready to discuss this particular adventure.

"Anyway, Cutter's giving us a ride over to the oil rig," Star concluded. "Captain Bourassa will meet us there. He's got to go slow over the reef because there's about a zillion dollars hanging under the *Adventurer*."

English glared at her through the small view port. "I hope you know this by *inference* only, mademoiselle with the wet hair, and not because you are foolish enough to dive there."

They were about halfway to the Antilles platform when the helicopters began to arrive, filling the sky with their machine-gun rhythms.

Dante peered out at them. "Big doings at the oil rig."

English laughed mirthlessly. "One billion dollars. Many zeroes attract many friends."

Adriana gaped at the aircraft that filled the skies over Saint-Luc like circling hawks. "You mean all this is for *us*?"

"I believe you Americans have a saying about — hitting the fan?"

The decompression from seven hundred feet took four long days. By the time the divers stepped out of the chamber, the contents of the lift basket and even Star's gold candlestick sat in the hold of a French warship that patrolled the waters over the wreck site at the edge of the Hidden Shoals.

Court claims on the treasure of *Nuestra Señora de la Luz* had been filed by Poseidon Oceanographic Institute, Antilles Oil, and three countries — France, England, and Spain.

Centuries after the days of the great treasure fleets, the same three governments were still bickering over Caribbean gold.

The claim filed on behalf of the four teenage interns, who had discovered not one but two seventeenth-century shipwrecks, was rejected by the International Maritime Commission.

Tad Cutter and Chris Reardon made no claim at all.

THE DANGER

# CHAPTER NINETEEN

Kaz knocked on the door of the small cottage in the center of the village of Côte Saint-Luc.

English greeted the four interns and ushered them inside. "You leave tomorrow. This is what I hear, yes?"

Star grinned. "Poseidon has officially invited us to go home. Gallagher finally turned his back on the camera long enough to kick us out."

"Yeah," Dante said bitterly. "So he can hire lawyers to go after our billion dollars."

"Ah, the money." English dismissed this with a contemptuous shrug. "You are better off without it. It brings only complications."

"And private jets," Dante added feelingly.

"Two lives are lost," English reminded him. "No treasure is worth that."

"He knows," Kaz said gently. "He just wants to sulk. It's like therapy."

"We brought you a going-away present," Adriana announced.

English cast a disapproving glance at the enormous shopping bag that was being carried between Adriana and Star. "Then give it to someone who is going away. Me, I stay here."

"This one you're going to like," Adriana promised. She tore the bag away, revealing the wooden object she had found buried with the treasure at the wreck site. "It was the only thing the government didn't impound. They prefer gold, I guess."

English examined it with mild interest. "It is a carving," he observed. "Like the one I already have." He picked up the figure and turned it over in his arms. "The body and hindquarters of an animal. The head is missing."

"No, it isn't." Adriana was almost dancing with excitement. She crossed the small parlor and lifted the other piece from the fishnet hanging in the window. "The head is right here."

The dive guide frowned. "But this is impossible. The head is a bird. The body is some kind of beast."

"There's a mythological animal with the head and wings of an eagle and the body of a lion," Adriana explained. "It's a griffin. This artifact comes from the wreck of a ship called the *Griffin*."

Holding the eagle out in front of her, she walked up to English and lowered it on top of the carving in his arms. The jagged ends fit together like two puzzle pieces. One half was bleached by sun, the other blackened by centuries underwater. But there was no question that this had once been a single sculpture. Now it was whole again after more than three hundred years.

She stepped back and admired the effect. "This is the figurehead from the bow of the *Griffin*. If your ancestor floated ashore on part of it, then he was from that ship." She looked at him long and hard. "The *Griffin* was English, which means you are, too. Your family legend — it's all true."

Menasce Gérard was not often overwhelmed, but this was one of those times. At last, he managed, "You American teenagers — "

"I'm Canadian," Kaz reminded him.

"You bring me my history," the guide persisted. "I — I have no way to repay you."

Star regarded him solemnly. "I think saving our lives a thousand times probably counts."

English gazed at their faces as if committing each one to memory. "I will never forget you." The giant stood there for a moment awkwardly, and then opened his arms.

There was room for all four of them.

*09 September 1665*

*Samuel came awake with the piece of the wooden figurehead still clutched in his arms, and the gritty taste of sand in his mouth. He shook himself and sat up, spitting and choking.*

Alive! *he thought. He had not expected to be so.*

*He took in his surroundings — a beach, palm trees, a pleasant floral scent on a tropical breeze.*

*An island.*

Captain Blade was right about one thing, *he thought.* I am lucky.

*He stood up, shaking with hunger and thirst, and spied a village just in from the beach. He could smell food cooking. Children played among the huts.*

*Now several people were heading his way. They resembled the natives Samuel had seen along the coastline around Portobelo. They reached him, exclaimed over him, brought him water.*

*"I'm English,"* he tried to explain, pointing to himself. "English."

*They did not understand, nor could he make sense of their strange words. But the message of welcome was clear. The feeling that welled up inside him was something close to joy.*

*Samuel Higgins had never belonged anywhere. But this was a place where a young man could make a life for himself. Start a family.*

*Leave a legacy.*

# EPILOGUE

The X-ray machine at Martinique airport picked up the strange object in Star's duffel bag. Security officers swarmed from all directions. Star and her three traveling companions were pulled aside into the restricted area, and a search of the luggage began.

The agent in charge rummaged around the bag and pulled out the carved whalebone handle that had once belonged to Captain James Blade of His Majesty's privateer fleet.

"I totally forgot about that thing!" Star exclaimed.

And then the huge stone inset above the initials *J.B.* caught the light and flashed deep green fire at them. The interns stared at it, mouths agape. This was the first time they had seen it free of its encrustation of coral. It was magnificent.

A junior agent pointed urgently at the brilliant display. "Monsieur — *regardez!* The gem!"

With disinterested eyes, the inspector looked from the four teens in shorts to this huge garish stone.

THE DANGER

"Do not be ridiculous," he chided his subordinate. "It cannot be real. An emerald that size would be worth two million dollars!"

With a snort of disgust, he tossed the artifact back into Star's duffel, and passed the interns through.

"Souvenir tourist junk!"

# ABOUT THE AUTHOR

GORDON KORMAN is the author of more than forty books for children and young adults, including the Island series and the Everest series, as well as *The Chicken Doesn't Skate*, the Slapshots series, and *Liar, Liar, Pants on Fire*. He lives on Long Island with his wife and children.